D0952510

THE
WAKING
FOREST

ALYSSA WEES

DELACORTE PRESS

Text copyright © 2019 by Alyssa Wees
Jacket art copyright © 2019 by Leo Nickolls

All rights reserved. Published in the United States by Delacorte Press, an imprint of Random House Children's Books, a division of Penguin Random House LLC, New York.

Delacorte Press is a registered trademark and the colophon is a trademark of Penguin Random House LLC.

Visit us on the Web! GetUnderlined.com

Educators and librarians, for a variety of teaching tools, visit us at RHTeachersLibrarians.com

Library of Congress Cataloging-in-Publication Data
Names: Wees, Alyssa, author.
Title: The waking forest / Alyssa Wees.
Description: First edition. | New York : Delacorte Press, [2019] | Summary: "When the lives of a girl, who has terrifying visions, and a witch, who grants wishes to children in the woods, collide in the most unexpected of ways, a dark, magical truth threatens to doom them both"—Provided by publisher.
Identifiers: LCCN 2018022935 (print) | LCCN 2018029205 (ebook) | ISBN 978-0-525-58118-5 (el) | ISBN 978-0-525-58116-1 (hc)
Subjects: | CYAC: Magic—Fiction. | Witches—Fiction. | Wishes—Fiction. | Sisters—Fiction. | Foxes—Fiction.
Classification: LCC PZ7.1.W4288 (ebook) | LCC PZ7.1.W4288 Wak 2019 (print) | DDC [Fic]—dc23

The text of this book is set in 11.8-point Sabon MT Pro.
Interior design by Jaclyn Whalen

Printed in the United States of America
10 9 8 7 6 5 4 3 2 1
First Edition

For Mama, a good witch

Part One

Chapter 1

IN THE WOODS

L et's start with the Witch in the Woods.

    Only children could find her, the Witch, led by foxes faintly glowing in the darkness between sleeping and waking. Together they traveled through dreamland until they came to an archway like an eye half open, big enough only to crawl through.

Beneath the stars, the moon a bouquet of blue-violet bruises, the Witch lived in a castle with turrets of unnaturally thick tree trunks and broad walls of entwined branches and leaves, the battlements formed by the oversize molars of some unfathomable animal. The crisscrossed bones of the portcullis gleamed in the milky midnight light as the drawbridge of melded cloven hooves lowered over a rushing red river.

At the end of a winding hallway illuminated by row upon row of skeleton-hand sconces, each holding a steady flame that burned without the aid of wick or wax or wood, the Witch sat in a seat carved from a canine tooth nearly twice her height, situated at the very center of the castle in a wide, round room with no ceiling, the walls stretching up, up, up and curving inward, just slightly. The foxes could see her, every facet and feature, all at once, a full picture. They grinned and curled up beside her bare feet, licking their paws and waiting and watching.

A single fox with orange fur so dark it was almost red perched on the arm of her throne, watching now as a troop of bright-eyed foxes, trailed by a girl and a boy with their arms intertwined, eagerly approached the inimitable Witch.

The children could focus only on one small piece of her at a time: lips glossed in silver starlight, onyx eyes lined with gold glitter, curling black hair threaded with pearls. Kneecaps hard as diamonds, just visible beneath the hem of her scarlet dress; thin hands and long fingers, nails short and bitten. Smooth skin stretched taut over the sticks and bulbs of her bones, slick and shining with an eternal, unbreakable fever.

As the pair came closer, the Witch saw that these were not quite her usual visitors. The girl was not a child. She had seen sixteen summers, or perhaps seventeen, nearly the same number as the Witch herself. The girl had long, light hair, and blue eyes with lashes so fair, they could hardly be seen. She was a spill of sunshine in the shape of a girl, golden and firm, and she walked as if afraid she might fall right through the floor, every step delicate, tentative.

The boy was even older than the girl and was surely her brother, for though they looked nothing alike, there seemed to be a kind of magnetic trust that kept them tethered side by side. He had an angular face with lips red as wine, hair black as soot, flesh paler than a ghost moon at high noon. There were gashes on the backs of his hands, old ones and new ones, crossing in all directions, shallow ones over deep gouges, scabbed over and reopened.

The Witch curled her fingers against the arms of her throne, not quite fists—but almost. She scratched the slick ivory surface, the skirl of nail against tooth echoing around the chamber. The red-furred fox at her side lifted its head and growled. She had never growled at any of the children before.

When the Witch spoke, her voice was cream burnt at the edges, unspooling from her long dark throat like twisted obsidian silk.

"I am the Witch of Wishes," she said. "What would you ask of me?"

The children knew exactly what to ask for, always, and that was why only they could find her. But these two were much older than those little ones, and so not content to merely receive their wish and be on their way.

"What are you?" breathed the girl, staring squarely at the Witch while her brother beside her smiled, lips pressed together as if he already knew the answer. But the longer he stood there gazing at the Witch's castle, the more his smile hardened into a grimace. He looked at the snapping foxes and the lopsided stars and the brambly walls, and finally back at the Witch.

"What is this place?" he asked. "Where *are* we?"

The Witch smiled, her maw growing wider, so no one would ever guess how her atoms were held together by an unheard howl. Her world, her castle—it had not wanted to be created. It had been pulled out of her sleeping heart, and it had *hurt*. The pain had never faded, a perpetual poison with no known antidote. But she could not, would not collapse; her world must go on.

And even as she grinned, she did not stop scraping her throne, peeling enamel instead of her own skin, the itch inflaming her backward-beating heart.

"What would you ask of me?" she said again.

The girl grabbed her wrinkled skirt and curtsied, a movement quick and clean, her cream-curls bouncing around her shoulders.

"I wish to stay here with you," said the girl in a rush. "I want to grant wishes to those who need them most. I want always to live in a dream."

The Witch hesitated; no visitor had ever asked something like this of her before. It was the one wish she knew she should not grant—this world was her own, and she must live here alone. For the girl this was only a resting place, a sighing place, its gate open to her once and then never again. To stay would be to sleep, neither dead nor alive, on and on until the end of time.

No, the Witch decided, she would not grant the girl's wish.

But the girl did not have to know that.

Nestled in the crimson soil of the Witch's heart bloomed an amaranthine rose with petals of velvety blood and a stem of sturdy bone spotted with thorns of pointed incisors, shivering in time with her pulse. Knowing another would burgeon in its place, she reached inside, tearing through skin and muscle and bone, and plucked a pointed petal, the same as she did for every child who came and told her their wishes. For each petal was the same in size and shape, but their flavors were unique, endless essences for endless wishes: bubble gum for a baby brother, lavender and honey to never go hungry, a cinnamon stick to make a new friend, spiced apple for a pet dragon invisible to all but the wisher, a sour smear of bile for revenge on the schoolyard bully, mint chocolate chip for a sick grandmother to get better.

But the Witch knew that this particular petal would only dissolve into periwinkle dust that tasted of salt and blood and rust—an empty promise, a placeholder. With callused fingertips, the Witch brushed the girl's soft palm as she presented the petal. She and the boy both watched as the girl placed it on her tongue and swallowed.

"Now, come closer, wishful one," said the Witch when the petal was gone. "What do you offer me in return?"

The girl checked her pockets, but they were empty. For a moment she looked up at the Witch, panicked, but it was not in coins that the Witch traded favors. What use had she for money? No, the Witch dealt in a different kind of currency: footprints and freckles and blisters about to burst; contusions and scrapes, scratches and slashes and faded bronze scars; warts and welts and wisdom teeth still submerged in pliant pink gums; spider bites and sheets of gooseflesh and drops of hot blood pricked fresh from quivering fingertips; loose eyelashes and curled toenails and even entire shadows. The children gave what they could. And the Witch accepted all of it, dispossessing them of the things they thought they would not miss. She heaped their pain upon her altar in the courtyard of her tooth-and-tree castle, a clean stone slab in a shaded glade. Someday, surely, their amassed agonies would outmatch her own.

"A lock of your hair will do just fine," said the Witch, before uttering a short spell and producing a knife out of the air. She gave it to the girl, who paused only a second before taking the glimmering blade and shearing a long strand from the back of her head. The dagger melted away to nothing in the girl's hand as she passed the curl to the Witch.

Without moving her head, the Witch turned her eyes sideways to the boy. Above the chamber, clouds like broken bones jutting through flesh scraped their way across the sky. She waited.

"What do *you* wish?" he said at last.

The Witch frowned. That was the third question the boy had asked. No child had ever asked a question. "I am the Witch of Wishes and have everything," she replied. "I want for nothing."

"Do you?" he said, stepping closer to her. "Do you truly have everything?"

The red-furred fox at her side grumbled again.

The Witch placed her hands on her knees and said, "I will not ask a third time."

"There must be something you want," the boy insisted. "There must be something missing."

But no, but no, the boy was wrong. The castle, the foxes, the altar, the gifts—*this* was her wish. Everything, all hers.

Even the cool diamond rain that now began to fall through the open roof of the castle belonged to her and only her, the clench-jawed, wet-haired Witch of Wishes in the Woods.

"You have wasted your wish," she said, stamping her foot and sending a tremor through the ground.

With a withering look at her brother, the girl reached a hand out to steady herself on his shoulder. The Witch's fingernails sparkled like cut crystal in a sudden lunge of lightning anointing the sky as she leaned forward and tapped each child on the temple. Once. Twice. "Wake *up*."

And they were gone.

Left alone on her throne, the Witch stitched her sternum back together with a needle fashioned from a long, sharp fang, each loop pricking her skin. When she was finished, she bent her bare knees to her chin, pressing her thighs to the red ribbon threaded through the stale skin of her chest. The foxes snorted and shuffled, but the Witch ignored them, closing her eyes and trying to force the boy's voice, his question, out of her heart and out of her mind.

But it was stuck fast, sinuous and deep, repeating like a song, like a prayer, like a plea.

What do you wish?
What do you wish?
What do you *wish?*

Chapter 2

IN THE DARK

Alternatives to screaming: Hold your breath. Chew the inside of your cheek. Push your face into your pillow. Stuff the hem of your T-shirt far into your mouth. Wrap your arms around your ribs so tightly that you fear your bones will break and your lungs collapse. Pretend you don't have a mouth or a chest or a throat with which to produce such a sound. Close your eyes and smile.

Smile, and maybe even laugh, just a little, however much laughter you can manage, even if it's only a squeak, when all you really want to do is yell and thrash and cry, cry, cry and never ever cease.

Do whatever you have to, because screaming startles people. Especially people who are your parents. At two o'clock in the morning. And you are eighteen years old. Too old to have your neck wrung by nightmares. Nightmares, which are only in your head and cannot hurt you.

But.

My nightmares have never been *only* in my head.

It's the scent that rouses me. The air is thick with seething saliva and torn fingernails and burning bile. Standing in the doorway of the attic, I look down and see my own corpse sprawled like a doll on the floor: nothing but bones stuck with flaps and flakes of skin, a rotting skeleton, the wood beneath bloodstained and wet. I know it's me only because of the hair: still thick and black and shining on what's left of my scalp.

I stare for half a second, and then I scream.

It takes only a few seconds, a few beats of my rattling heart, before my sister Rose comes running out of our bedroom one floor below and races up the stairs.

"What's happening?" she cries, reaching for my hand.

My only response is to scream again, this time with less conviction behind it, a question rather than an exclamation. Two more pairs of footsteps pound through the house, and our parents stumble up behind us. Dad lunges past me and pulls the chain to snap on the light in the stairwell: from black to bright white in a sliver of a second. At once the shimmery grime of sweat and blood and shadow where my body lay seems to sink into the floor like water draining through a sieve.

"Rhea, what happened?" Dad asks, leaning against the attic wall as my two youngest sisters, Renata and Raisa, come to stand behind Mom a few steps down, their hair stringy and askew. They are used to this, my visions, but still they are there in the doorway, gawking as I make a spectacle of myself for the second time this *week*.

"Why are you up here?" Dad prods.

I take a deep breath, Rose's hand cold in mine. So cold—corpse cold—it makes me shiver.

"I was having the dream again," I say as calmly as I can, and behind me Raisa tips her head back and groans, not wanting to hear about this for the millionth time. "You know—the one with the door at the top of a spiral staircase? I climbed it like I normally do, climbing for what seemed like forever, and when I reached the top—*I opened the door.*"

Here I pause, my stomach clenching, because I've never actually opened the door in the dream before. Usually I wake up as soon as I touch the handle, startled but not surprised to find myself in the same spot I did tonight, in front of the attic door. Then, after taking a few moments to steady my quivering heart, I hurry back downstairs and into bed. No visions, no screaming, no impromptu family gathering in the narrow stairwell.

But tonight everything changed.

"When I opened the door in the dream," I explain, "I opened the *attic* door here. And when I looked down, I saw a—um, a body. Dead."

I don't tell them the body was mine. To have grisly visions is one thing, but seeing myself dead is something wholly new and far more frightening. And when I glance at Rose, she shudders as if she knows.

"You mean you were sleepwalking?" Mom says, her curly

black hair flattened on one side of her head. "But that's odd—you've never sleepwalked before."

"Oh." I tug my hand out of Rose's gentle grip and rub the corner of my eyes so I won't have to look at Mom or Dad or anyone. "Right, yeah. Weird, isn't it?"

My parents know about the recurring dream, but I've never said anything about the sleepwalking, which has only started in the last few months. I keep hoping it will stop. It isn't like I'm stumbling around the house breaking things or hurting myself.

But it hasn't stopped, and now I've been caught.

Mom and Dad look at each other, and I can see the worry in their frowns.

"It was all just a dream, love," Dad says at last, turning to me. "It can't hurt you."

"Breathe," Mom adds. "Relax."

A pair of green eyes glows in the dark from the far side of the attic, which might alarm me if I didn't know for sure it was only Gabrielle, my pet fox. She's been my constant companion since the day she found me, and hasn't left my side despite my parents' initial reservations. Gabrielle and I have a special connection that I know I'm not imagining: Even from several feet away I feel her little heart beating as if it were my own, our pulses tangled up together. Now she sniffs around as if to make sure there are absolutely no dead bodies hidden in the room. Finding none, she slinks out of the shadows and follows us as we all shuffle down the stairs. Yawning, Renata and Raisa drag their feet back to their own room, while Mom and Dad follow Rose and me into ours.

"You have an overactive imagination, Rhea," Mom says as

I slide into bed, Gabrielle jumping up and curling at my feet. "But it's not real, remember? It's only in your head."

"I'm not overactively imagining anything," I reply stubbornly. "I'm *cursed*."

The visions have been appearing for as long as I can remember. When I was little, most of them were simple, no more than a flicker, there and gone: the ceiling of my bedroom crumbling to ash as I lay in bed awake. The sky cracking like dry skin, the stars crawling across the universe like mites. Thorny brambles sprouting from the wood floors of our house and twisting up the walls like vines.

But as I grew older, the visions matured, so when I'm on a crowded street or in the grocery store, people start to look different too: some have wet, green-blue hair, salt water dripping from their fingertips; others have eyes that flash, lightning-fast; and a few have horns and moss between their teeth; still others are rendered nothing more than deep, dense shadows slinking across the floor. Once, a large metal mailbox outside the post office transformed into an enormous animal with the body of a lion and the head of a human, blinking at me and letting loose a storm-snagging roar.

And then there is the wood, clustering thick behind our house. Where normally there is open space, a tall dark forest rises, an endless swarm of close-together trees with leaves the color of bone, and gleaming spiderwebs stretched like strings of saliva between the trunks. The forest goes on and on and on, no end in sight, and every time I've tried to enter—it vanishes. Just like that.

But I've never had a vision like *this,* like my own dead body before me. It's getting worse. *I'm* getting worse—and I don't know why.

I'm not even sure that the therapist my parents sent me to, when I was seven and just old enough to find the right words to explain what was happening to me, would know what this was. She said I had severe anxiety, and she taught me breathing techniques to help me calm down when I started to panic. Techniques that would probably be helpful if I could actually remember what they were when the visions come. Mostly I just forget how to breathe altogether. Or worse, like tonight, I scream.

"I know it *feels* like a curse, Ree," Dad says, "but it's not. Anxiety affects a lot of people, and that's okay. You're not alone, and you will get better. Always remember that."

I nod and settle back into bed. Mom and Dad shuffle out and flick off the light, but as soon as I hear their door click closed, I run to the bathroom and brush my teeth—cinnamon toothpaste to cancel out the flavor of moldering meat in my mouth, the only thing left of the vision. I keep my gaze on my own eyes in the mirror, daring my face to deteriorate, to display my demise again.

But when my reflection doesn't change, doesn't crumble or corrode, I say, all in one breath, *"I am not afraid, I am not afraid, I am not afraid."*

If you say a thing often enough, it's bound to come true.

A ghost appears in the mirror. She wears my bony body and my features: the same olive skin and thick black hair, brown eyes and long fingers and pink pearl earrings. But where my lips are tight and white, hers are forged into the sharp scythe of a smile. And when I see her, I smile too.

She says, *Listen, you. Fear itself doesn't hurt.*

She says, *You could be pierced from stomach to spine with an iron blade, and though your body would bleed, still your soul would remain untouched.*

She says, *Go back to bed.*

I stare.

"Okay," I say, even if it is only to feel my own lips move and not the ghost's.

I go to bed but not to sleep. Rose's little night-light is hard at work on her side of our bedroom, while five feet away I lie in near-complete darkness.

From across the space between us, the faintest of murmurs reaches my ears.

"Am I going to die?" Rose whispers, and I don't answer right away, confused. "Is what you saw a premonition of the future?"

It takes me another moment to realize: She thinks the body I saw was *hers*. She misinterpreted the glance I gave her. Right then I make a decision. Though I know it's cruel, I won't correct her. It makes me feel like we're in this together.

"No," I say flatly, willing for that to be true. "It was a bad dream."

"Are you sure?"

"Yes," I lie.

"Would you tell me if I was going to die?"

"Yes, I would," I lie again.

"What do you think happens when you die?" she asks, shifting her weight toward me.

For a moment, I consider this. Not *what* I want to say but how I want to say it. Since I started having visions, I often think about the afterlife while I lie awake at night. I don't think of it in logical terms—for all we know, the afterlife is just an endless nothingness—but rather, I think about what I want it to be. What if, after we die, we live in a dream of our own making all the time, without ever having to wake up? If I think of it like that, then it doesn't seem so terrifying.

So now I ask myself: What would Rose's dream be like?

"I think you become the wind, and you can go anywhere in the world you want to go. You can go to the stars, if you want, and even the brightest ones won't burn you."

After a pause she says, "That doesn't sound so bad."

"No, it doesn't," I agree.

"Good night, Ree," she says, and her breath scintillates in the space above our heads, sticking to the ceiling like static on a television screen, eerie and bright. Mesmeric.

I blink once, twice, and it's gone.

"Night," I say. Sometimes I wish I could tell her everything, everything that keeps me awake at night. But telling her or anyone else would only make it more real.

Because there's more. In the vision, and for a few moments after I shook myself awake, behind the attic door that I'd opened, I heard someone breathing. A long and loud and ragged inhale.

The kind of breath someone would take if they were about to scream.

The minute the first morning light appears, I get up and wash my face, no bony ghost saying hello. Last night's vision was the first time I've ever been able to get past the stairwell door, and I don't want to forget a single detail. Hurrying back to my room, I see that Rose's bed is now empty too. I rummage around in my nightstand until I find a journal with a plain black cover, every page blank. The one Mom gave us a long time ago, back when she first started homeschooling us and told us our dreams were important to remember and to write down. Mine were always the same: the darkness, the staircase, the door. I didn't bother opening the book. Now I can't waste a minute. Stealing a pen off Rose's nightstand, I sit on my bed, one leg dangling over the edge, and I write.

When I'm done, I chew on the end of the plastic pen and look the words over, my handwriting slanted and loose: *A door at the top of a tall spiral staircase. A prickling in the backs of my knees that warns me to turn back and to run as fast and as far from the door as I possibly can. I never open it. I must not open it—there are secrets behind it and to know them would be to live forever after with a terrible burden, to swallow those indigestible secrets and feel them always inside me, gnashing in my stomach, chewing through my veins.*

But I'm done not knowing, so I reached out and gripped the knob, and I turned it.

Here is usually where I wake up.

But last night, I did not.

The coolness of the metal knob in my palm, the sickly

screech of the hinges, a decayed carcass on the floor. A breath hanging in the air belonging to something or someone else. And a scream.

I've always wondered what was behind that door, and now I know.

Or do I? Because the more I think about it, the more I'm certain it's not my dead body. That's what I saw when I opened my eyes, sure, but I don't think my body is there in the dream. Because I heard breathing behind the door. And if I am dead, then who is breathing?

With a groan, I throw the journal and pen down onto the bed. Gabrielle raises her head, questioning.

"I'm hungry," I tell her, standing up, refusing to think about this any further until I've had some breakfast. "Let's go."

I find Renata in the kitchen, eating alone at the table. The sun shines warm and bright through the open window to her right, illuminating one side of her face and casting the other in shadow. She smiles when I come in.

"Shay wants me to tell you that she forgives you," Renata says with no prelude, her hair in a high ponytail slumping to one side of her head. She tears off a corner of her buttered toast and drops it onto the ground for Gabrielle.

I'm not sure which part of this statement to address first. I walk over to the pantry and pull out a box of chocolaty cereal, pour myself a bowl.

"Forgives me for what?" I ask finally, sitting down across from her. We're the only two at the table—Rose no doubt already at her ballet class, Raisa probably still sleeping, and I can see Mom and Dad working in the garden.

"For running away!" she says, flicking her milk-shiny spoon for emphasis, as if she can't even believe I asked something so obvious. Her dream journal is open on the table beside her cereal bowl, pen resting in the center crease. "She says you don't have to be scared to come back, because she forgives you, and a lot of other people do too. What's done is done, and now she just wants you to be safe."

"Ah," I say, nodding. "Okay."

And I should just leave it at that. But because I'm curious, and because I only ever have one dream while Renata has so many, and *mostly* because my heart knocked on my ribs at the words *scared* and *forgives,* knocked hard and fast like a rock tossed at a window, like someone saying, *Let me in, let me in, let me in*—which doesn't make sense anyway, because my heart is already *in,* isn't it?—I say something I regret as soon as it uncurls from my lips: "Okay, but who is Shay?"

Renata drops her spoon into the still-full ceramic bowl with a clatter and a splash. She stands, arms long and palms pressed flat on the table as she stares across at me. "Shay, Shay!" she cries, stamping her foot twice. "She eats men and she's your friend and she loves you!"

"Oh, oh, of course," I backtrack. "I just—"

Renata turns and runs from the room.

I finish my breakfast before following her, allowing some time for the silt of her despair to settle. Her journal still lies open on the table, and though it's tempting, I don't lean over to read it. My sisters haven't been as ambivalent about their dream-keeping as I've been over the years, but Renata is the most prolific of us by far. She even talks about the people in her dreams as if they were old friends, as if we know them too, and when we tell her that it's not real, she becomes confused, upset.

And then she hides.

Usually we know right where to find her; over the years, we've gotten to know all her favorite spots, become familiar with her proclivity for seeking the spaces where no one else would think to go. The seashore is one—specifically, she prefers to wedge herself between two boulders near the local lighthouse a mile down the coast. Another hiding space is a particularly deep dip in the sidewalk outside the local cemetery. She likes to stand there after a storm, up to her calves in rainwater, staring at the graves beyond the black iron fence.

And her easiest-to-access slip-away spot: the corner of the closet she shares with Raisa, tucked far to the side of the double folding doors.

It is there that I find her, in the closet, her knees pulled tight to her chest. When I open the sliding doors, she tips her head back against the wall, the tube of her trachea protruding from her pale throat, embellished with a trident of tender veins. I lower myself to the floor and crawl inside, crouching beneath the clothes hanging above our heads. Together we close the doors; now we're entirely in the dark except for a thin line where the doors don't quite touch.

"I just want to find the place where I begin," she says. "That's what it's all about. The place where I begin. Because I don't think it's here, Ree. I don't think it's here."

I match her position, folding my knees to my heart. "I don't think it's in this closet either."

"You know what I mean."

And I sort of *do* know what she means, sitting here in the semi-dark and the semi-silence. I have a scratchy, restless feeling, as if my soul were grinding against my skin, my bones, not necessarily wanting to get out but urging my body to go to impossible places, convinced I can touch the stars and not burn.

At least, I think that's what she means.

"So," I say, "tell me more about this Shay of yours."

She lifts her head from the wall. "Who?"

Renata's dreams are ocean waves, rushing in and rushing out. Floating on the surface for a while before sinking and drowning, all the way down.

I sigh. "Never mind."

We continue to sit in the closet in silence, the closeness of the walls and the thickness of the shadows reminding me of the attic. Will I sleepwalk again tonight? And if I do, will I have the vision again? Or will it be a different vision this time? Now that I've thought it over, I truly don't think the vision of my corpse is a premonition, despite Rose's fears. None of my other visions have ever come true. Possibly it was a latent fear manifesting itself, a constant worry that something bad might happen, to me or to my family. I want us all to be safe and together and happy, always.

But if my dead body isn't really what's behind the door in my dream—then what or who is?

"Wait," I say aloud, an idea blooming. Beside me Renata startles, having been lost for a moment in a private reverie. "The attic! What if I slept in the attic? Then I wouldn't sleepwalk, because I'd have nowhere to go."

I could still sleepwalk to another part of the house, but why would I? In the dream I'm always climbing up the stairs, and if I'm already as high in my house as I can go, it stands to reason that I'll simply stay put. And that I might then dream of whatever or whoever is really behind the door.

"It's so dark and cold up there," Renata says as I jump to my feet and push through the closet doors, this time leaving them open. "Won't you be scared?"

But I'm already rushing through the house, too frenzied by my idea to respond.

"Rhea, what is it?" Mom asks when I come bursting into the garden, out of breath. She's wearing a floppy sun hat, a smudge of mud on her chin. "What's wrong?"

I tell them my idea.

Dad nods, gazing past me as he thinks about it. His hair is thick and black, but the stubble all over his jaw and his chin is a stark silver, gleaming in the sunshine. After a minute, he smiles. "I think something can be arranged."

For the next six hours, there's a chorus of scraping and banging and even a bit of swearing as we clear out the attic, transporting sunken cardboard boxes to the basement and a clunky, dusty old stereo straight to the trash. There are clothes Mom and I sort for donation, along with other odd trinkets and useless treasures my sisters snatch right up: a jewelry box that must have been fatally submerged in water at some point, with a headless ballerina that twirls to a discordant, drowning dirge; a hot-pink lava lamp that emits a dull glow after being plugged in; a crushed bouquet of fake flowers; and a deck of cards missing every single queen. Only a few pieces of furniture that no one wants to get rid of are left alone. Dad carries up a spare bed from the basement, with me following, lugging a fan in case it gets too hot.

After a final skirmish with several long-legged spiders and a thorough dusting, my new room is finished. All I need to do is wait for night, when the dream will come again.

Gabrielle paces on the bath mat in front of the shower while I get ready for bed. For a minute I simply stand in front of the mirror, waiting for my ghost self—or whatever she was—to appear in the glass, smiling and shining and saying wise, aching things that maybe only sound wise and aching in the dead of night. When it finally seems like she's not coming, I reach for my toothbrush, and suddenly I can see straight through my sternum to my heart, like my skin was a window all this time that was just waiting and waiting for me to notice and look inside. My heart, right there, red and jarring and wrong, wrong, wrong—*hearts are meant to be heard, not seen*—and it's not beating so much as it's opening and closing, opening and closing, very, very fast. Almost like a mouth, gasping, or a fist, unfolding.

Slowly, as if I might scare off a fly, I bring my fingertips to my chest—but all I feel is warm, smooth skin. Exhaling, I drop my hand, and the illusion is gone, just as if it never happened.

None of this is real.
I am not afraid.

There's a knock on the bathroom door as I pick my tooth-brush up and put it into my mouth.

"Yes?" I don't say it so much as croak it, my mouth full of bristle. A grimy croak, scratching and scrambling its way past my teeth. I choke, spitting into the sink.

"Are you okay?" Rose says through the door, and it's nearly the thousandth time she's asked me that since I woke up this morning. I don't answer, swirling water in my mouth instead.

When I open the door a second later, she comes in and immediately presses the back of her always-icy hand to my always-hot forehead. I'm tall but she's taller, and she stoops her wiry frame down a little to level her eyes with mine. Her long golden hair is still pinned in a high bun from her ballet class, her bare shoulders spotted with pale freckles, her blue eyes blinking too fast, too frequently. It's strange, how we can look nothing alike and still be related, sisters only a year and a half apart. In almost every way, even below the surface, she is morning and I am midnight.

Her skin grows warmer as she lends me her chill. "I don't think you should go to the attic," she says quietly, peering into my face. "I think you should stay with me."

"I'm sure Ren would be happy to sleep in my bed to keep you company," I say. "Or Raisa, if you ask very, very sweetly."

"It's not the same, though." She sighs, sucking in one cheek and chewing on it. "How long will you be up there?"

I breathe, in and in and in, stalling. There are a thousand true answers to that question, but none of them will make her feel better.

I do not say, *I don't know.*

I do not say, *Indefinitely.*

I do not say, *Forever.*

"You could come with me," I say instead, even though I know it's an empty offer. I mean, this is *Rose* I'm talking to. Rose, who would follow me anywhere in the world I wanted to wander—except at night. Rose, who keeps fresh batteries near her bed for when her night-light burns out. Rose, who often sleeps with her eyes half-open and the curtains fully drawn because even the insides of her own eyelids are too dark.

She removes her hand from my head, and already I feel too hot without it there.

"You know how colors aren't really *there* in the dark?" she says, reaching up to unwind her bun, pulling pin after pin out of her hair to make a haphazard pile next to the sink. "I think it's that way with beauty too. That's why monsters dwell in darkness—because ugliness doesn't need light to exist."

My heart squeezes hard as I parse her words like a riddle.

Just yesterday, my sisters and I decided to spend the entire day together at the beach. When we ran out the front door on our way to the shore, I spotted something in the street: a butterfly, a huge one, tipped on its side, its black and blue and violet wings fluttering uselessly, its little legs scrabbling to right itself. In our sleepy town, there wasn't much traffic in the late morning, and I crossed the road to where the butterfly wriggled on the edge of the hot pavement. I crouched down to assess it, to ascertain whether its struggle was real and not conjured by my volatile imagination. Renata ran right past, smiling at the sky, unaware of anything below the soft shelf of clouds high above our heads and the warm wind skimming her cheeks, the siren song of the waves smacking the sand like the ocean licking its lips with a watery tongue.

"Don't touch that thing with your bare hands!" Raisa called as she sprinted by me. She flipped around to skip backward as she spoke. "Germs, disease, death!" Then she laughed and turned back around, to run after Renata.

The butterfly was real, then, and I made a scoop with my hands, unsure how to proceed, worrying that picking it up would only cause more damage. I couldn't quite tell what was wrong with it, other than that its wings, flapping madly, didn't seem to catch the air, to lift it off the ground. I vacillated, its antennae twitching. Should I shovel it up, or—

A shoe slammed down onto the bug, a flip-flop squish. I teetered backward, catching myself with my hands in a crab-crawl position. Looking up, I blinked at Rose, who dragged the bottom of her shoe along the pavement, wiping off the varicolored viscera of the smashed butterfly.

I stared and stared at her, unmoving, even as the smooth pavement scorched my palms, even as the sunlight knifed into my eyes, the world becoming blurred and metallic around the edges.

"I ended its suffering," she said in an exuberant hush, her yellow hair shining, her bathing suit as red as the flush in her cheeks. She tilted her head to the side, as if she couldn't comprehend why I might be upset, why I didn't understand.

"I was going to move it out of the way, Rose," I said finally, pushing myself to my feet. My knees cracked as I straightened them. I wrapped my fingers around her wrist. I wanted to make her feel the hurt, just a little, and my hands were still smarting from the heat of the road. "I was going to save it."

"I ended its suffering," she said again, not shaking off my hand as I thought she might. Her breath came very fast, and her fingers flexed and curled, flexed and curled. Her eyes never left mine. "It wasn't beautiful anymore."

"It was always going to be beautiful," I replied coolly, "no matter what."

Rose shook her head.

It wasn't beautiful anymore. Her words echo inside me, joining with the present.

Ugliness doesn't need light to exist.

That is why Rose despairs of the dark: she would rather look her monsters full in the face, would rather know their exact size and shape, than to acquiesce to the wildness of her imagination, caught in that shadow-swathed place where her mind can conjure the very worst things, where her fear can fester and distort.

"Well, I think it's the opposite, actually," I say, folding my arms and leaning on the bathroom sink. "I think there's beauty in the things we can't see but that we still know are there. Like wind, or music."

She says nothing, dislodging the last of the thousand yellow bobby pins that were holding her bun in place, and letting her hair fall around her shoulders. Her fingers curl around the edge of the counter as she stares at her reflection in the mirror, barely blinking. Then, after a long moment, she turns to me and smiles. Like a winter sun, bright and cold at once.

"Go," she says gently. "You look like you haven't slept for a week."

"Wow, thanks," I say with a little laugh, pushing off the ceramic and stepping into the hallway. "Sweet dreams. I love you infinitely."

She smiles brighter. "Infinitely."

As I'm walking toward the attic, Mom and Dad come upstairs and give me hugs like I'm suddenly moving far, far away.

"I love *you*," Dad says to me, before turning to blow a kiss to each of my sisters, Rose in the bathroom and Renata and Raisa in the room they share. "And *you* and *you* and *you*."

"I love you too," I say, before quickly slipping into my room. With a glance at Gabrielle, who pointedly looks away like she knows I want privacy, I change into a pair of sleep shorts and a soft old T-shirt, listening as Renata says her usual prayers in her room next to mine—*loudly*, in her high-tide voice, churning and exultant, because she believes this is the only way her prayers will be heard.

"Dear water, wind, and stars! Dear fire, frost, and stone!" she says now as I tug my shirt down and grab my pillow. "Send us your crash and your splash and your whoosh and your bang! Send us your flash and your snap and your shake! Please watch over us and keep us safe! It's the darkest night yet, and I never want to sleep again. Amen, amen, amen."

"If you don't go to sleep, I'll prick your finger until you do," Raisa grumbles, her words reaching me through their half-open door.

"That won't work on me," Renata says, her voice back to low tide. "I am not the princess in this story."

"Well, *obviously*. But the spindle doesn't have to be magical, my dear," Raisa says, mock-sweetly. "Blood loss will work just as well."

Renata laughs, a quick, cracking sound, and there's a soft smack as Raisa launches a pillow at her. I step quietly from my room, wishing that falling asleep were that easy, like a spell: a prick and a sigh and then nothing but dreams.

My sisters finally settle into silence as I hold my pillow to my chest and head to the narrow staircase at the end of the hall, past the bathroom and my parents' bedroom. Gabrielle is at my side, as always, and not for the first time, I wish I could tell her how grateful I am for her constant company and how her growls echo in my chest, the way the pain in my palms matches the prickle in her paws when she steps on something thorny. Our odd connection makes me feel less alone.

It's been eight years since Gabrielle trotted out from the woods behind our house and came right up to the back door as if she belonged inside with the rest of us. Her very sudden and very confident arrival was strange, to be sure, and was made even stranger by the fact that there are no woods behind our house except for the ones I see in my vision. I thought Gabrielle would disappear when the woods did—but somehow, miraculously, she didn't, and I'm glad she's here with me tonight.

We climb together, up and up and up, up to the attic, to the room that will relieve me of my dream—and hopefully my visions too.

My foot finds the top step, and I clutch the pillow more

closely, my elbows clasped tightly to my body, fitting into the curve of my waist. Even with the door here wide open, I don't think I can extend my arms straight out to the sides without my fingertips jamming into the narrow walls. The light from the hallway below barely reaches us, but I know what is here. There's a bed near the door, and across the small space is a dresser with three crooked drawers, a floor lamp, and a nightstand heaped with books whose spines are cracked, mostly biographies of royalty throughout history: the Romanovs, Nefertiti, Empress Dowager Cixi, the House of Medici. I'm coming here to sleep, not to read, but it makes me feel better to have them close. Comfort books, like comfort food.

But the best thing about the room is that there are no windows.

Gabrielle trots farther inside, and I shut the door. Its hinges give a rusted rasp, and the room collapses into total darkness, the space swollen with an unbroken shadow. For several seconds I blink, shivering, but not because it's cold. I think, *If beauty is banished from darkness, then I am the ugliest thing here.*

I fall backward onto the bed, and the springs gasp, then sigh. I want to fall directly asleep, to skip the restless period of waiting for sleep to come. Gabrielle leaps onto the bed, and, like a thrown stone bouncing over a lake, I feel her relief rebounding across my ribs, relief that the sheets are soft and that there is nothing to frighten us here.

Or maybe that's my own relief. We have held each other up for so long that sometimes I can't discern the difference between us.

I lie on my side, and Gabrielle curls into the crook of my knees.

It is so, so dark.

And still I can't sleep.

Gabrielle can't either, so she stands and slinks up to my pillow. I reach out and pet the coarse fur on the back of her neck as she lies down beside my head, keeping my thoughts warm.

I try to swallow but my mouth is dry, and my fingers are scrunched in Gabrielle's fur. Her unease collides with my own, two storm fronts crashing, and I'm alone even though she's here, because she's *part* of me and doesn't count.

This room doesn't feel safe the way I thought it would. I can't see the walls, and if I can't see them, how do I even know they're there? I feel as though I'm spinning in space, unmoored. Dizzy. Lost.

I can't sleep.

I can't sleep.

I can't sleep.

In the peculiar quiet of the absolute dark, I sit up in bed, cross-legged, wondering if it was a mistake to come here. Wondering if, maybe, even this darkness cannot help me escape myself.

I'm so deep in these thoughts that it takes me a few minutes to notice it: the darkness, breathing. The darkness itself is breathing.

Or.

Someone is breathing in the darkness.

I don't know which frightens me more.

It's exactly like in my dream, except now I'm awake. Holding my own breath, and silently urging Gabrielle to do the same, I hear it: long drag in, short whoosh out.

Again . . .

And again . . .

And again.

Gabrielle snarls once, then goes silent.

For an absurd second, I think the breath belongs to a small bird. Trapped in the top of our house, frantic for escape—the whisper of wings, the flutter of feathers, tiny eyes squinted, the click of a closing beak.

But no, this is not a bird. Maybe it's the house, then, the walls and the roof and the floorboards settling, trying to get comfortable. Like me, maybe the house is restless, blue lips and sleeplessness, plagued with nightmares of wind and fire, of gutted rooms and windows cracking like bones.

But it is not that either.

I stare into the unwavering dim. I want to say something, to give the dark a name so that it won't be so monstrous, so grim and devouring. But I can't think what.

Maybe, though—maybe it's just my sister, come to beg me to return to our room because she misses me. Because she can't sleep without me near. And maybe, maybe I need her too.

"Rose?" I whisper at last. Even my heart is quiet, listening.

"No," a voice says, cutting through the darkness. A voice not my own, and certainly not my sister's. A voice like a syringe stabbing my skin, quick and clean and deep. The voice of a boy. "Not Rose," he says.

A scream implodes in my throat, choking me as I swallow it back down. Sinuous terror spills through my veins, electric. I am up and off the bed, stumbling, clambering for the switch on the lamp, when a hand—a human hand—touches my wrist, gently. Hot fingertips graze my wild pulse.

"Wait," says the voice, the boy, the darkness. "Please."

I wrench my wrist away from his cautious grasp, my heart pounding as I stand still, so close I feel his breath trail across my skin. Gabrielle curls herself around my leg and growls, snapping her jaw in warning. I hear the click of her teeth and know that if the boy does not back away, Gabrielle will bite him until he does.

"I really must beg that you stay," he says quietly, and his breath skims my cheek from above. I step back, away from what must be the lamp before me, even though I can't see it. After a moment he sighs with relief, and I back up until my spine presses against the door to the stairs, my hand clenching the knob behind my back. Even if we were at opposite ends of the small room, though, we would still be close.

"Please, my sky," he says more urgently now.

"What do you want?" I hiss. "Who are you?"

"Who am I?" The intruder speaks slowly, evenly. "Oh, I think you know, Rhea Ravenna."

He casts my name like a spell, like a curse. I let go of my lungs, exhaling. "Do I know you?"

"Oh yes." He pauses. "And no. Yes and no."

"Well," I say, and Gabrielle growls. "Which is it?"

He laughs: rabid, enraptured, a sound somewhere between

an elegy and an alleluia. "We have met a thousand times before, you and I. But I don't think you remember."

"Of *course* I don't remember," I cry. "You're not—"

Real. I was going to say *real.*

Because this is a dream—it has to be. *He* is the one who was breathing behind the door. But—

But his hot hand on my wrist. His needle-prick voice. His scent, faint but there, clinging quietly to the stiff, still air: a plump fresh apple plucked high from a tree.

"How did you get in here?" I grip the doorknob, ready to flee at any moment.

"Have you considered," the boy says, "that I was already in the room when you entered?"

I shake my head, remembering too late that he can't see me. "The room was empty."

"Was it?"

"No one was here," I say, although my breath catches on the last word. Another gruff rumble tumbles from the back of Gabrielle's throat.

"Are you sure? Were you looking for anyone?"

I press one palm to my face, my flushed cheek. I could flee; I could run. Would he grab me, follow me?

"Well, of course I wasn't looking for you," I say after several seconds. "I don't even *know* you."

"You did, once," he says. "But not now."

"Where are you?" I blink, fast, but still it's so, so dark, just the way I wanted it. "What are you doing?"

"I'm sitting atop the dresser, if you must know. Legs

crossed, elbows resting on my knees. My chin lifted at about, oh, a fifteen-degree angle—"

"Stop. Just stop talking, please."

He obliges. But the silence seems to smirk. I can feel the bite of it, like steel teeth scything into the skin of my heart.

The Darkness. That's how I'm coming to think of him. A gutted shadow supported by a black glass skeleton with a taunting crystalline grin.

"Are you a ghost?" I ask the smiling Darkness.

"No," he says. "I am not a ghost."

"What, then?"

His smile glints and grows—I *feel* it rather than see it. "I think you know, Rhea Ravenna."

"How did you come to know my name?" I demand. "And what is yours?"

"Your bones quivered and sighed my name last night, when you finally opened the attic door." He speaks quietly now, so that I have to lean in to hear. "Listen to them. Tell your heart to hush. Silence your breath. Just for a few seconds. Just so you can hear. Your bones know even if your brain does not."

"You know what?" I say, twisting the knob, "I'm just going to open this door and let in a little light to confirm that I'm not talking to a ghost."

"No!" I hear his soles hit the ground as he jerks to his feet. Then, more softly: "If you do that, you'll never see me again. I swear to you, you will *never* see me again."

"Maybe I don't *want* to see you again." I smile, triumphant in gaining the upper hand. I square my shoulders, even if he can't see me. Though I'm fairly certain he can sense my movements the way I sense him. "Maybe once will be enough."

"*Please.*"

I hesitate, even though I know, I *know* I shouldn't. I pause, and I do not open the door after all. The boy, this Darkness, an inoculation, my veins frothing with fright, foaming with fascination. Gabrielle rubs her face against my shin, wanting to leave, to run, to hide.

"If you don't mind," I say, in what I hope is an imperious but dispassionate tone, "I'd like to go to sleep now."

"By all means," says the Darkness, the tension in his voice relaxing. "I don't mind at all."

"I *mean*, I want you to leave. Now, please. Or I *am* going to open this door, and you can't stop me."

The air quivers. The silence slurps us whole, then spits us back out.

"All right," he says at last. "Besides, shadows don't sleep, as it happens." Much quieter, though, he adds, "And dreams, well—they're always asleep, aren't they?"

There is a sigh, the release of a long breath. A sticky breeze brushes my cheeks, my hair. The boy somehow, supposedly, leaves the room. I wait, unmoving.

Is he *really* gone?

No. I bury my fingernails into the perspiring flesh of my palms.

I can still hear him, smell him, feel him. The Darkness.

Smiling.

Breathing.

Slowly.

I gather my pillow and my fox and abruptly tug the door wide open, and still it is so, so dark. With Gabrielle clinging to my calf, I run down the stairs into a wan tangle of light in the hallway. Suddenly I can't stand the thought of sleeping in this house at all, so I clutch my pillow tighter and creep along the corridor to the main stairs, and then down to the first floor, where I snatch an old sleeping bag out of the coat closet. On tiptoe, I sneak through the foyer and out the front door, race across the street on bare feet. Away, away, away from the house and the room inhabited, infected, infested by the Darkness, far enough down the beach that it—*he*—can't crawl out and get me. At least, this is what I tell myself. I am safe here, outside.

For a long time I lie on my stomach in the sleeping bag on a soft swatch of sand, my elbows spread out over the pillow and my chin in my hands. Gabrielle nestles into my neck, our faces close together looking back at the windowless attic. Both of us watching, waiting, hunting the hunter.

A car trundles down the road, its headlights fanning in front of it, but their spectral fluorescence doesn't quite reach us. I stare at the house, a lone three-storied white box with green shutters and blood spots of geraniums in flowerpots on the porch, a crooked mailbox with a broken red flag that swings toward the ground. For a moment, between one blink and the next, its walls appear as torn strips of skin, rippling in the warm summer wind like clothes on a laundry line.

After a minute, an hour, a lifetime or ten, I roll onto my back. Except for the few popped pustules of stars and the waning wart of the moon, the sky is dark. But this darkness is ordinary, and it does not speak. It does not breathe.

My only wish now is for sleep. Or maybe not sleep exactly, but waking—the natural reset after a solid night's rest, fresh sunlight and soft cotton pajamas and a hot breakfast. If I can only fall asleep, I think everything might be okay. The Darkness—maybe he will have left. Maybe I will wake and laugh at this nightmare.

Maybe.

I close my eyes and repeat a prayer, a plea: *I am not afraid. I am not afraid.*

I am not afraid.

Chapter 3

IN THE WOODS

She said, "Wake up."

She said, "Follow me."

She said, "Come and play."

The Witch smiled, shaking off thoughts of the strange visitors from the day before. She scratched behind the foxes' ears before galvanizing them from their rest, singing softly as she nudged their ribs with her toes, her exultant hum setting the leaves to vibrating and the wind to whirling. The foxes needed nothing from the Witch of Wishes, and for that she was grateful. They slept in clusters all around the base of her throne, forming a ring of fine auburn fur trimming the dais, but when she called to them, they stirred and stretched their legs. They followed her to the glade, where from the heap of offerings on her altar she selected a child's detached shadow and twisted it tightly in her hands, ridding it of its accumulated darkness. When the dust had been thoroughly drained, she compressed the light that was left into an orb and tossed it into the air, so high that it stuck to the sky. The foxes yawned, snapped their jaws, winking in the dull, dripping light of the shadow-wrung sun. They tilted their heads as the Witch of Wishes pirouetted around the glade, before they joined the wild waltz.

The foxes had not learned this yet, but it was something the stars knew well, and the Witch knew it too: The burning scream inside you hurts less when you keep moving, keep going, keep reaching, in whatever way you can.

This was the Witch's way, and had been every day— dancing under the warm shimmer of the transient sun. Until the morning when the Witch looked out at the foxes gathered around the glade and noticed a stranger among them.

At first she ignored him, this intruder with sleek black fur who smelled of apples and cinnamon and secrets. She did not like that he appeared the day after the curious pair of older children, and neither did the other foxes, who kept their distance; only the red-furred fox approached him and snarled. The Witch called her guardian back, inciting the foxes to join in her midday revels as if nothing were amiss. Falling into a fast-footed rhythm, the Witch leaped and laughed, the sunlight silvering her dark hair. She glanced over her shoulder to see her foxes galloping dutifully after her.

Every fox but one.

At once the Witch halted, and several foxes crashed into her calves, their wet noses swiping the backs of her knees. She swiveled toward the stranger and marched over to him, hands on her hips.

She said, "Dance."

She said, "Now."

She said, "I will use your bones to drum the beat of our song, if you will not join along."

But the strange fox only lifted his head, and smiled.

Chapter 4

IN THE DARK

A colony of sleepless seagulls squawks as they fly past where I lie in my sleeping bag, their white feathers ultra bright in the sun's glare seeming to shine from everywhere— from above, from below, from the pockmarked pavement of the street, from the undulant skin of the sea.

Was he real, the Darkness? If I were to go back to the attic, would I still find him there?

Gabrielle rises to her feet, arches her spine, before lying back down on my pillow. I turn my head to the side and nearly cry out when I see another blanket-wrapped body beside me on the sand. Face angled away, a fan of yellow hair spread across a pink pillow, and a grainy netting of sand stuck to her cheek and the tip of her nose.

Rose.

I exhale, relieved. I lift my hand to shield my eyes, and a woman jogging down the edge of the street mistakes the gesture for a wave. She raises her hand to me in greeting as she passes; her long brown ponytail swishes back and forth with each step, headphones looping to connect her ears to a device strapped to her arm. The wind seems to rip the plait right out of her scalp, and for a moment she's bald, her scalp glowing like a second sun.

I kick out of my sleeping bag and lean back on my hands as Gabrielle raises her head, the fur on her chin matted flat. When she looks at me, I see that her pupils have shrunken, shriveled.

She feels it first, a thousandth of a second before I do: a wisp of cool air. It skitters across my shoulder blades, the nape of my neck. Not a breeze—a breath.

He's here, I think.

No, he can't be.

But he must be. Somewhere, somewhere on the other side of all that light. Pick the sun off the sky like a scab, and there he would be. The Darkness, the night.

"Ree?" Rose twitches, then sits up, the blankets pooling around her waist, revealing her creased red T-shirt, the hem stretched out of shape around her neck. After a long, languorous yawn, reaching her arms up, she smiles at me. "Good morning. How did you sleep?"

I shrug. "No worse than usual."

"Really?" she says, knocking her shoulder against mine. "You didn't just have the *best* rest of your life out here, beside the sea and beneath the stars?"

I pretend to look all around, searching. "What stars?" I point to the sun. "Oh, wait, I found one!"

She laughs, and I give her a wink. "I guess we're too close to the city to see much at night. But the sea—the sea is nice."

Rose scratches Gabrielle behind the ears, and my fox closes her eyes in contentment. We sit in silence for a moment, comfortable. After a while, though, I look at Rose and ask, "So how did you know I was here?"

"I heard you run down from the attic. You didn't come to bed, and you weren't on the couch." Tugging an elastic off her wrist, she bends her neck and braids her hair. "I started to panic, but then I saw that the closet was open and the sleeping bag was gone. I thought about Renata and her hiding places and then found you here." She looks up—not at me, but toward the sea. "I didn't want you to be alone."

Gabrielle sits up now, fully alert, and I feel again the ribbon flush of fear that clenched tightly around her spine and mine when we first realized that the darkness in the attic was breathing, alive.

"You know when you told me," I say, piecing my words together carefully, "about how beauty needs light to exist but ugliness doesn't? Like colors, kind of?"

She nods, scratching at the corner of her eye.

"Well." I look down at my torn fingernails that no polish can save. After a few seconds I say it, fast: "What if I told you that there's a boy in the attic? And he seems to know me even though I don't know him? And I don't know where he came from or how he got there?"

What I want is for her to tell me that there is no such thing as ugliness, as monsters. That they exist only in metaphor and human minds. And even in dreams they are out of touch, out of reach, out of sight. Intangible.

But.

She says nothing.

She says nothing, and the breath I'm holding won't last.

I poke her cheek with my finger, and her colorless skin is cold. "What would you say to that? If I meant what I just said?"

"*I'd* say that sounds super sketchy."

We both turn at the sound of Raisa, who approached so quietly, neither of us noticed. She wears shorts and a blue bikini top to match her silvery blue-dyed hair pulled into pigtails. Squinting behind hot-pink sunglasses, she drops down beside me and stretches her legs out long in front of her.

Renata skips up just a few seconds behind, dressed similarly but in a belted yellow one-piece and a sun hat with a wide droopy brim over her loose brown curls. She grins, flopping belly-down onto the sand.

"Um, how much of that did you hear?" I ask them, my face flushing as I realize they must have heard at least *some* of what I've just told Rose.

"Oh, every word," Renata says cheerfully as she etches her initials into the sand with her fingertip, completely oblivious to my embarrassment. "Your voice carried clear across the beach."

"I can't believe you guys slept out here," Raisa says, opening her eyes wide and flexing her bare feet. "You should've at least left a note. Mom and Dad were seriously freaking out until they saw you through the window. I mean, do you even *know* what grave misfortunes can befall a young woman on her own, unaccompanied? Thieves, cutthroats, bird droppings, men's rights activists—"

Just then five teenage boys in board shorts pedal by on their bikes. I recognize them from the neighborhood down the street.

The boy at the front with long brown hair under a baseball cap stops, and the rest follow suit, staring at us. "Hey, look, guys. It's the Raving Ravennas! How you ladies doing today? Is there enough room at the table for us to join your mad tea party?"

Raisa huffs and holds up her middle finger at them, then turns to us, as if to say, *See? Grave misfortunes.*

I have a reputation among my peers for being a bit of an oddball. Because of shrieking while running from mailboxes, and gawking at people when my visions make it look like they have a bird's beak instead of a mouth. Not to mention keeping a fox as a pet. My sisters defend me when they can, but all the kids around town tease us. They think we have secrets, and maybe we do. Secrets we don't even know ourselves, locked away in the restless, breathless blooms of our hearts, coiled in the roots of our souls. Juicy secrets. That's the word people use—*juicy*.

But I think, especially after my encounter with the Darkness, that if we have secrets, they aren't juicy at all. I think, more likely, our secrets are *bloody*.

The other boys snicker at Raisa, while the one in front waves his hand. "Aw, you know I'm only kidding."

"Kindly shut *up*, Brett," Raisa says. "This party is extremely exclusive. Witches only."

"Come on, guys," another says, and shrugs. "Let's get out of here before they summon a demon or something to eat us."

"Who said anything about summoning a demon?" I yell before Raisa can retort. "We're perfectly capable of eating you *our*selves."

Brett laughs, tipping his head back, and the muscles of his tan stomach clench. He sets his feet back on the bike pedals. "Hey, have a good day. And see you around."

"Yeah, have fun with your séance, or whatever it is you're doing," another one adds. "Tell the ghosts I said hi."

Immediately I think, *We are the ghosts.*

And I don't know what I mean by that, exactly. But I think it's true.

Still sniggering, the boys push forward on their bikes and ride away. It's quiet again, or as quiet as it can be, with the repetitive smack of the sea on the shore and the warm scuttle of the wind.

Raisa chews on the shiny ends of her pigtails, watching the boys' retreating backs.

"Anyway," she says to me eventually, "you were saying something? About a boy in the attic? And I *know* it couldn't have been one of those idiots. They're too stupid to figure out how to pick up a girl, let alone pick a lock."

Everything feels so dry all of a sudden: my mouth, my skin, my eyes. The sand, the breeze, the sky. I didn't expect an interrogation when I mentioned the Darkness—I only wanted Rose to say that he wasn't real, that I fell asleep without realizing it, and then that would be that. I could also dismiss him, forget him, and be done. But she didn't, and now my internal scales tip over completely.

"I don't know *what* he was," I say.

"Was he cute, at least?"

I scoop a handful of sand and sprinkle it over my knees, my thighs, the beginning of burying myself alive. "I didn't see his face."

Renata grabs some sand too, and drops it over my calves, absentmindedly helping me. "Oh, he's probably come to kiss you."

"Well, *obviously,*" Raisa says, tilting her head so Renata can't see her roll her eyes. "Rose? What do you think?"

The faintest blush spills down my cheeks at the mention of kissing—and of kissing *him*, specifically. Would it be like kissing a ghost, a shadow? Would our lips even touch?

But then I remember his hand, his very warm, and very real *hand*.

I concentrate on Rose, funneling sand through my fingers. She brings her thumb to her lips, gnaws at the thin skin around her nail. She stays quiet.

"No, Ren—it was just really dark and he wouldn't let me turn on the light." I plunge both of my hands deep into the hot sand, trying to stop their shaking. "It—he—was actually really terrifying. Terrifying and—I mean, he said he *knows* me. He says we've met before."

Raisa stretches her arms up over her head. "Well, why don't we just go look?" She shrugs as if it's that easy and hops to her feet, skipping toward the street, not bothering to look back and see if we follow.

Gabrielle startles to her feet as I stand, as I trip and scramble to grip my sleeping bag, my pillow.

"No!" I call, careening after Raisa in what feels like slow motion, the sand searing my heels and toes. Out of the corner of my eye, I see Rose snatch up her blankets and start after me, Renata trailing behind. Raisa pauses at the side of the road, waiting for me to catch up.

"What if he's dangerous?" I say, panting as I come to a stop beside her. "What if—"

"Dreams can't hurt you, Ree." Raisa shakes her head and reaches to pick up the pillow that's tumbled out of my overstuffed arms. "Dreams aren't dangerous. And I'm sure that's all this faceless boy was. A very silly dream."

This is exactly what I wanted Rose to say.

But.

I don't feel any better about it, and I can't put my finger on why.

Clutching my unrolled sleeping bag to my chest, I swallow and shift my feet, feeling sand everywhere. I think she's wrong, actually—some dreams *are* dangerous, the ones you try the hardest to forget. Because then they grow gaunt and bladed, and will come back clawing up your throat.

"I still want to check it out," Raisa says as the others approach. "Let's go, okay?"

"*Wait—*"

And again she bounds away and is already halfway toward the house before I can finish my protest. Renata shrugs with a vague sort of smile, and Rose says nothing. *Why won't she say* something? We tiptoe-run across the blistering asphalt, and then the dewy grass of the front lawn squelches beneath our grimy feet. Off to one side, Mom's garden flourishes, an eclectic collection of early summer blooms: bright hydrangeas like puckered pink moons; sun-melt peonies; evanescent irises with gaping periwinkle tongues; and gawking marigolds, fire-cream orange.

I try not to notice how the walls of the house pimple like cold skin as we step onto the porch and let ourselves inside. I hold the door open for Gabrielle, and then dump my sleeping bag onto the couch before hurrying after Raisa.

"Girls, I made waffles!" Mom calls as we pass the kitchen. She stands proudly in front of the waffle iron on the island, spatula in hand. A mostly empty bowl of batter rests next to a bottle of maple syrup and a plate stacked with golden waffles. Another platter lies next to it with a much squatter pile of blackened bacon strips. The scents of sugar and char tangle together in the air. "There's fresh strawberries for you, Rose, in the fridge. Bacon's crispy too, Ree, the way you like it."

"By *crispy,*" adds Dad, who's seated at the kitchen table with a crossword and a coffee mug in front of him, "she actually means *burnt.*"

"No," says Mom. "I mean *crispy.* Super extra crispy."

"So, in other words, burnt," Dad says, and Mom pantomimes whacking the back of his head with the spatula.

"Oh," I say, stopped in the archway beside Rose, "that sounds gr—"

"We'll be right back!" Raisa interrupts, waiting for us by

the bottom of the stairs, unseen by Mom or Dad from their vantage in the kitchen. "We're on a very important mission, not to be delayed or deterred."

"Well, all righty, then," Mom says, just as Dad twists suddenly in his chair and hits his pen against the spatula. She laughs, shifting and attempting another smack, this time trying to get in a real blow. But Dad blocks her, swiping up a stray spoon from the table and holding it in his other hand, rising to his feet with his knees bent. I want to keep going, but I'm torn, and Renata is too. She claps, bouncing on her toes as she watches them, an eager spectator. Mom talks as they spar, circling around the kitchen. "Just heat the waffles up a little in the microwave when you've completed your mission, okay? Your father and I are going to run errands soon."

"Sure," Rose murmurs, but I don't think they hear. She tugs at my wrist, and we leave Mom and Dad to their happy duel.

"What are they doing?" Raisa says, eyebrows arched and one leg lingering on the third step.

"Sword fighting," I say.

"They're so weird."

Renata giggles. "It's cute."

We file down the second floor hallway, all of us quiet until Raisa suddenly stops.

"And here we are!" she says in a beatific tour-guide voice, pausing with a foot on the first step. "The Shadowland of Boys Unseen! Now, ladies and gentlewomen, please keep your arms and legs at your sides at all times. These undomesticated boys are vicious and known to devour anything fleshy and female in sight. Ready?" She smiles, and we nod. "Follow me!"

Rose hooks her hands over my shoulders as we begin the short ascent, like children making a train so we won't lose each other. Her hands are cold, as always. I try to place my hands on Raisa's shoulders, but she scowls and shakes me off. Renata comes last, and I don't look back to see if she's holding on to Rose the way Rose is clinging to me.

I hold my breath. Hold it until it hurts. Until it burns. I don't let it out until the very last second, a mere moment before I faint dead away.

And then we're in the attic, only a little light drifting in from the bottom of the stairs. Raisa slides her feet over the creaky wood, fumbling for the lamp.

"Hello?" she calls, then swears as she hits her toe on what must be the bedpost. With not much in here to stub a toe on, she really lucked out. "We come in peace, okay? We want to know why you're hanging out in our musty old"—the lamp suddenly clicks on, light swarming the small room—"attic."

We blink, looking around. There is no one here but us.

Renata crouches down to peek under the bed. Finding nothing, she straightens and shrugs. "Well, that's really the only hiding place here."

"You have to turn off the light," I say, and Gabrielle sidles up to my leg, her fur scratching my calf. "It has to be completely dark."

Raisa tilts her head, closing one eye to peer at me, as if she'll understand me better from a slightly different angle, a crooked perspective. "Then how will we see him, genius?"

"We won't," Rose whispers, her soft breath blooming over my back.

"He doesn't *want* to be seen," I say. "I don't think—I mean, I don't think he *exists* in the light. It sounds crazy, but that's where he is. *What* he is," I correct myself quickly.

"Okay, sure," Raisa says, and though she scrunches her lips, dubious, she obliges and switches off the light. Rose releases my shoulders, and I bend my elbows to clasp her hands behind my back. Our fingers entwine, and I feel the pulse on the side of her knuckle. It's a sloppy pulse, surging fast at first and then a little more slowly, shallow and strong and shallow and strong again. And almost perfectly in sync with my own.

We wait.

Four girls and a fox, standing in the dark.

I think I feel a prickle on the side of my scalp as if a hair has been plucked, but gradually the feeling blossoms into a more tender tug. The sensation reminds me of if someone were to twist a lock of my hair around their finger, spooling it like thread on a bobbin, around and around and around.

Slowly.

Gently.

In the dark.

"Rose?" I whisper. "Are—you—"

But her hands are still linked with mine, and as far as I know, Raisa and Renata are still on the other side of the room near the lamp, the bed between us.

"I—have to—go." I spin around, smashing into Rose, who stumbles backward but does not fall. Somehow, despite our sightlessness in the dark, she reaches out and grabs my wrist, pulls me down the stairs after her. Gabrielle's toenails scrabble on the wood floor as she chases after us. Renata is next and Raisa last, stomping down the steps, panting. When we are all in the hallway, we stare at each other with wide, wide eyes.

"Yeah, okay," Raisa says, hunched over with her hands on her knees, her pigtails falling forward. "What exactly were you *so* freaked out about? There was nothing there!"

"You—you freaked out too!" I say. Rose's clammy hand is still clamped around my wrist.

"Only because you freaked out first! *You* scared me more than anything." She straightens. "What do you think, Rosie?"

Rose says nothing, stares at nothing but at a point just over my left shoulder. Back toward the attic. My scalp tingles. Exactly *there*, above my right ear, and nowhere else.

"Rose?" I prompt, and her eyes swivel between the two of us. Finally she shrugs, before turning and walking quickly into our room.

"*I* didn't freak out," Renata murmurs, her eyes glazed over. "But there was definitely something there."

I don't quite know what to make of this; I look at Raisa, and she smirks. Torn between asking Renata to elaborate and finding out why Rose walked away, I eventually shrug and follow Rose into our room. I find her perched on the edge of my bed, her head bowed. For a long moment she doesn't move at all, and I'm just about to make sure she's still breathing, when she looks up. She smiles, and it is like she has never been afraid of anything, ever, in her whole life, and certainly wasn't terrified of anything in the blotting blackness of the attic only seconds ago.

"Rhea," she says with purpose. "Don't worry."

And then her crisp golden exterior starts to undulate, her immaculate facade a mere mirage, and I see her as something else, something spectral and soft, terrible and tear-able: her skin melts to molten silver and sloughs from her skeleton like drops of starlight.

It's over in a blink, the most elegant entropy I have ever seen.

Unaware of my vision, she walks over to me. Hugs me, her arms sliding under mine, wrapping around my ribs. Her hands join in a fist and squeeze my spine.

"Beauty is poison to monsters," she says, still holding on to me. I lay my head on her shoulder. "They love beauty, covet it, but they can't have it. So you see, you're safe from any danger. You're *safe*, Rhea. You are."

She releases me and steps back. I try to smile, but it sits on my face all wrong, slanted and stiff. My scalp begins to burn, like a thousand tiny teeth gnawing through to my skull.

But despite my unease, I decide she's right. The Darkness *had* to be a dream. No, more than that—a *nightmare*. Because I can think of nothing more terrifying than a dream like this, which is only in your heart and cannot hurt you, until it suddenly reaches out and touches you.

Chapter 5

IN THE WOODS

The Witch approached the black-furred fox, holding a freshly plucked petal from her heart in her glittering palms. No fox had ever eaten of her heart before, and even the Witch did not know what would happen when this one did.

The ageless, endless queen of the tooth-and-tree castle had grown tired of the mysterious fox repeatedly refusing to dance, night after night disregarding the Witch's orders and commands. No manner of slyly threaded threat or spun-silk words of coercion could convince him to obey. Now the disobedient fox sat in the center of the clearing, and the Witch dropped the petal in front of him. It fluttered to the ground, sparkling in the sunlight.

"Eat," she said. "Eat."

For a moment, just a second, the fox hesitated and did not move. Then he bowed his head and scooped up the petal with his tongue. The Witch waited while he chewed, a dribble of blood leaking between his lips as he swallowed.

"Now dance," she said. "Dance."

The fox blinked once, twice, three times. Then he danced, prancing on his thorn-pricked paws. He twisted and writhed, lurched and sighed as his fox form fell away in clotted clumps of dark fur and wilted whiskers and muddy claws—all of it dropping to the rough ground of the glade.

Where once there had been a fox, there now lay a boy in tattered clothes.

And not just any boy, but a familiar one, with powder-pale skin and hair so thick and dark it shamed the space between stars, lips to rival the reddest apple, and scrapes on the backs of his hands.

"You are no fox," she hissed. "And you have already been here once. What evil magic have you used to trick me?"

The boy lying on his back—breathing too fast, blinking too much—looked up at the Witch. Her cheeks flushed when she noticed his chin and his jaw, shimmering wet with the ichor of the petal from her heart, now in his burbling human belly. So terribly intimate, the vestiges of a hallowed meal smeared across his skin and teeth. He had deceived her, stolen from her. She crouched over him, one hand clenched in the dirt at her feet.

"No magic," he gasped. "I simply transformed, and I was allowed through your gates."

The Witch glared at him, tightening her fist in the dirt, aggravated further by her own oversight. "You are no fox," she repeated, "and you are not a child. You have no purpose here. Leave."

"You are right," he gasped. "I am neither of those things.

But I *do* have a purpose. You are the Witch of Wishes, we both know. Yet who will grant your wish? Who else but I, I who have managed to enter the Woods over and over and over again, as none but the foxes have done?"

"I need no wishes." The Witch shook her head and straightened her long legs, the wind ruffling her skirts, her hair. She stood over the Fox Who Is No Fox and said, "I have everything, and you—you are nothing. A trickster, a lie, a dry kiss on closed lips. You are not welcome here."

"You dismiss me so easily?" he said, and winced. The Witch knew he was in pain—it hurt to be born, and to be born again, even if the rebirth was simply a regeneration of one's own, true skin. "I can help you leave this place, this dream, this long-suffering sleep. I can wake you up."

The Witch licked her lips and glanced at the foxes gathered at the edge of the glade, hardly moving, barely breathing.

"There is a way," he added. "And I know it."

"You *lie*," said the Witch. "And I do not care, for you are wrong. I wish for nothing."

"At least let me tell you a story. A story of the outside. Wouldn't you like to hear of the country beyond your Woods, the lives of the children when they are not asleep? Haven't you ever wondered what the world is like?"

The Witch raised her eyes to the sky, and the stars lifted their light as a human might lift her chin, and pretended that they were not listening in, not waiting to hear what the Witch of Wishes would say to this Fox Who Is No Fox. The real foxes blinked, and the trees shrugged their wooden shoulders as the wind scarpered across the clearing, sifting through the

Witch's long hair, setting her scalp to tingling. For one second precisely our Witch's heart skidded to a stop, one lost pulsation in a procession of a thousand, thousand contractions of muscle and blood. She rested a hand on her chest, her fingers tracing the scarred skin where she had stitched herself back together, again and again and again.

"All right," she said at last, and led him into the castle. "You may tell me about the outside. But—" She held up a hand as he started to smile in triumph. "If I decide I do not want to hear any more—do you promise you will stop?"

At once he nodded.

"I promise," he said, pressing both of his hands to his heart. "Now let's begin."

The Fox Who Is No Fox sat before the dais while the Witch of Wishes on her throne listened to his descriptions of the World Beyond the Wood. Though there were many worlds, he explained, he knew of only one, the world where he was from, a world powered by magic. He was from the country with the crystal kingdom, and it was of this tiny piece of that tiny world out of a thousand, thousand, *thousand* tiny worlds that he told her, beginning with the small but important things: seasons and city lights and steaming cups of cinnamon tea, pine nuts roasted in phoenix flames and sour blackberries plucked from the thorniest bushes. A popular game called Crone, in which all the players either won or lost together. A night sky that, in the northernmost places, was so saturated with silken stars that even at midnight the world would appear as bright as at noon. There were academies of higher learning, and anyone who wished to could study at these schools—except the maculae.

"Who are the maculae?" the Witch asked in a whisper, the strange word squirming up her throat and searing her lips. The Fox Who Is No Fox leaned forward, eager to explain, but then the Witch's throat burned, and she did not dare say the word again. Did not even think it. "Never mind. Speak of something else."

He looked at her for a long moment, and she could not quite meet his gaze. Finally he nodded, and described instead the phenomena of sparkling tornadoes and glitter-rain hurricanes, winds ripping roots and tearing trees out of the ground like hair from a scalp. He warned her of Star Fire, flames so potent, they could burn through steel, it being magic in its purest and most solid form.

"That comes from a star? How?" the Witch asked. "Even with magic, it seems very hard."

"It is. First you command the star to fall," the Fox Who Is No Fox said. "Then you catch it in your hands, and kill it."

"You would have to be very powerful even to *touch* a star," the Witch said, glancing up at her own. "To touch it and not burn."

"Yes," he said, and then moved on to disaster, to dread. He told her of war. People in chains. Hard balls of magic fired like gunshots, punching through bone, through brains, the impact like being jolted awake from a dream but in reverse. Ghosts, with empty eye sockets and sore throats.

And just before the blue-violet glaze of dusk, before the

Witch cupped her hands to catch the spun-shadow sun as it fell, deflated, from the sky, the Fox Who Is No Fox leaned forward and said, "Do you wish me to stay?"

"No," said the Witch of Wishes.

"Do you wish for me to come back?"

After the briefest of pauses, the Witch said, "Yes."

"Until tomorrow, then."

Chapter 6

IN THE DARK

With full, syrupy stomachs we sit at the round table on the back patio by the garden. Thanks to the sugar, my nerves haven't calmed down a bit since our visit upstairs, and I'm glad that, even though it's summer, Mom likes to keep teaching us, keep our minds pliant. Sadly, though, today none of us is fully concentrating. I'm between Mom and Renata, with Rose and Raisa across from me, and Gabrielle curled in my lap, asleep. I deliberately picked this seat, the one that faces the yard, so that my back is to the house.

To the attic.

"It's too hot out here," Raisa says, letting her body go limp in her chair, sliding down as if she's going to slip right under the table and disappear. She tosses her arm over her eyes, shielding them even though the umbrella in the center of the table adequately casts us all in shade. "I can't think properly in these conditions."

"We could go inside," Renata suggests, sipping her glass of lemonade.

"It's hot in there too! It's inescapable."

"It's really not that hot," I say, and it isn't: seventy-five degrees at most, clouds like skulls rolling across the sky, wispy ghost-bones to block the sunlight. The scent of lilacs is sticky in the air, and the sea gently hits the sand like hands clasping in prayer.

"Listen, girls. We're learning about something fun today," Mom says, flipping through a thick textbook.

"What subject?" Rose asks, idly fiddling with her hairpins, pulling them out of her bun and sliding them back in. She doesn't even have ballet today, but still she likes to wear her hair up.

"History," Mom says.

"It better be the history of torture methods or I don't care," Raisa declares. "Starting with *this,* being forced to do schoolwork in the summer."

"Do you really have something better to do?" I say. A flash of orange through the rosebushes just beyond the cement of the patio catches my attention, but it's gone before I can even blink twice. "What else would you be doing today?"

She lifts her arm from her eyes. "Why, cleaning my room, of course. Just like Mom asked me to."

Renata snorts, but she quickly flips to a scowl as Raisa grabs her lemonade glass and places it far out of reach, making her get up from the table to retrieve it.

"Okay, here it is." Mom props the book on the table so we

can all see. She points to a full-page photograph of a long, three-storied, mint-green castle with dozens of white columns and gold accents. "Beautiful, isn't it?"

Like always, there is no warning. One second I'm staring at the picture, and the next my gaze lifts, past the book and over Mom's shoulder, catching sight of the woods.

The woods.

The woods that do not exist.

Gabrielle's head jerks up in response to my sudden stillness, every muscle locked in place, every muscle except my heart, firing over and over like a gun, beating bullets of blood, twice as lethal and just as loud.

A cool wind drags across my cheeks and my throat like fresh-cut fingernails, and I shiver. Every time I see the trees, they seem to have grown, taller and thicker and darker, the spaces between them as black as beauty turned inside out. Every time, they seem to have crawled a tiny bit closer, just enough for me to notice.

You are not there, I think. *You are no forest at all.*

Mom's voice comes to me like an echo, like a dead star's light taking centuries to travel and only now just reaching me. "Who lives there?"

"A princess," Renata says.

I twist my fingers into the fur at Gabrielle's neck, holding on tight.

"An heiress," Raisa counters.

I remind myself to blink so my eyes don't start to sting, to breathe so my lungs don't start to squeeze.

"A witch," Rose whispers, and my heart stops, an empty cartridge. Gabrielle groans, and I stare and stare and stare at Rose.

Because she's not looking at the photograph in Mom's book.

She's looking at the woods.

Or, rather, where the woods would be if she knew they were really there.

Which they aren't, except for me.

She only says it once: *A witch,* and then silence. But the words get stuck in my head like a stilted song, and when my heart starts again, my pulse repeats them too.

A witch, a witch, a witch in the woods.

And suddenly I *feel* the witch, there at the center of the woods, just as I feel the boy in the darkness. She's a shadow falling across my heart, a rose blooming in the total dark.

And she's screaming.

The yells reverberate in my head, like my own thoughts but louder, and her screams are unlike anything else, exactly the sound the moon must make at its fullest, a crackle to frenzy the wolves.

No, not the wolves—*foxes*. And lots of them.

"Rhea?"

"What?" I shake myself, but the woods don't disappear and the scream doesn't stop. "I mean, yes?"

"Who lived here?" Mom says patiently, tapping the picture. "Do you know what this is?"

"Um, yes," I say, trying to shut out the cacophony within me. "It's the Winter Palace in St. Petersburg. The home of the imperial family until they were killed about a hundred years ago."

"I was right! A princess *did* live there." Renata beams, and it seems all wrong to me, how she can smile when someone is screaming. But of course, she doesn't hear it. I eye Rose, eager to know if she hears it too. "Anastasia Romanov! She's the famous princess, the one who escaped. She's still out there somewhere, safe and sound."

"She'd be a *very* old woman by now, but yes," Mom says, lowering the book. "There is a rumor she escaped the soldiers who came for the rest of her family."

"It's not true, though. She didn't escape." I pull my eyes away from the woods, focusing on my sisters. Remembering to breathe. "What happened was, the royal family was on house arrest when they were awakened by their guards one night and told to get dressed. The girls—um, let's see, there were four of them: Anastasia, Maria, Olga, and—and Tatiana, I think. The girls and their brother, Alexei, along with their parents, the czar and czarina, were brought to the basement and told to wait. Then guards entered the room and opened fire. But the girls had jewels sewn into their dresses that they kept from greedy nonfamily members, and the jewels were what saved them, at first, acting like a shield, the bullets bouncing right off. Anastasia and Maria managed to escape out the door, and they ran into the woods. That's how the rumor started— people claimed Anastasia and Maria got away. But they didn't. They were hunted down." I pause. "That's just one version of the story, though. However it happened, all the royal family's bodies were accounted for, in the end."

"How do you even *know* all this?" Raisa demands.

"Anastasia's ghost told me," I say, glancing again at the trees, and then quickly away. *Don't look, don't listen.* "No, dummy—I *read* about it."

Mom huffs at this. "Girls, can we please—"

"Well, *I* heard it happened like this," Renata says, rising out of her seat in sudden excitement, her cheeks flushing. "The princess had magic and the others didn't—that's why they were afraid of her and wanted to kill her. Her mother had magic too, and she was the first to die, and the princess was so upset that she ran into the woods with the soldiers chasing after her. But then she escaped by falling into a sleeping spell. *The end,*" she finishes. "Except that's not really the end because she's still there, waiting to wake up." She turns to me. "So you see, Ree, you're wrong. The princess *is* still out there. She's just dreaming."

"You know what? You're right," says Raisa, tipping her chair back on two legs, her hand gripping the table to keep her from toppling over completely. "That's a way better story, Ren. I pick that one."

"It's not about which one you like better." My heart twists, and I'm not sure why. "It's about the facts."

Raisa lets her chair slam down to its normal position. "What is a myth to one person may be a memory to another."

"Okay, okay," Mom interjects, taking control of the conversation again. "We are way off topic. Ren, that was an, um, *interesting* story, but I'm afraid Rhea is right. None of the princesses survived."

The screaming builds and builds, so lurid and grating, it

could shatter me like a mirror at any moment. I can't ignore it any longer. *She needs help,* I think. *I need to help.*

Gabrielle leaps off my lap as I stand. They're all looking at me, Mom and my sisters, and though I can barely hear myself speak, I say, "I'll be right back."

And then I run.

I run, off the patio, through the garden, and into the not-woods, with no real plan beyond *Make it stop, make it stop, make it stop.* Bare feet on dry grass, a dragonfly flitting past my face, buzzing as it twists to get out of my way, a sudden burst of sunlight as if through an empty eye socket in the clouds. Sunlight that does not touch the woods, no matter how bright.

I enter the blackness between the trees, and the forest does not vanish.

No—it *collapses.*

The branches curl in on themselves like fingers into a fist and the leaves drop all at once, a scratchy swirl of anemic green. The trunk nearest me begins to tip, and I jump out of the way into the path of another falling trunk, and another and another, until I'm forced to dart backward out of the woods. I stumble on a raised root and tumble to the lawn, the brief spark of sunlight from before now gone. I watch as the trees twist and tilt and crumble in a great plume of dust. Broken branches, cracked trunks, shriveled leaves—when the dust clears, floating up and up and up, all of it is gone.

It happens in perfect silence, and I have no idea when the screaming stopped.

"Rhea?" Mom calls, but I don't move. "Was there a bug on you or something?"

"Not a bug." Raisa snickers. "A *boy*. A shadow boy, chasing her."

I look at Gabrielle, panting next to me. Would it have hurt, I wonder, if the not-real woods had crushed us? Does something both imaginary and not have the ability to cause harm?

Would it be like embracing a ghost?

It was just a dream, love, my dad said the other day. *It can't hurt you.*

When I finally stand and turn around, it's not because I'm sure. I am breathless and mud-stained, my heart beating faster than ever, and my whole family is watching me. I know I need to pretend I'm okay, with them trying to figure out what the hell just happened and what they should do about it.

"I need to lie down." I walk toward the patio. "You're right, Ray—it's too hot."

I don't even wait for a response—I continue right past them, into the house and up the stairs, and throw myself face-first onto my bed, quivering.

Mom comes in to check on me a minute later. "Need anything?" she asks, rubbing my back.

"No, I'm feeling better already," I say, even though I'm not. "Don't worry; it will pass." And I hope beyond hope that it does.

I don't get up for an hour, and even then I stay in the room, avoiding the window and working through a book of brain teasers and riddles to distract myself from thoughts of the woods, of the witch, and of the Darkness especially, thoughts I'd really rather not have just now or ever, really.

What waits for a kiss that does not come?

What dreams and dreams until it comes undone?

I think and think but come up blank. After a while, I close the book. It's the first puzzle I haven't been able to answer.

I wait until I hear Raisa and Renata bundle themselves off to the beach and Mom leave for her gardening group meeting. Then, with a blanket draped over my shoulders like a cape and a pillow clutched to my chest like a shield, I climb down the stairs, slowly, quietly, wondering if this is how it will be from now on, me tiptoeing around my own home as if there might be a phantom lurking in every corner—and if sometimes, just sometimes, the phantom might be me.

I find Rose alone in the kitchen, rummaging through the fridge.

"Did you see them?" I say, a little too loudly in the hushed ambience of the half-empty house. "Did you see the woods?"

"What woods?" she says, without turning around. She doesn't startle as I would have if someone had crept up on me. Rose never startles at anything, as long as there is daylight.

"The ones in the backyard."

She straightens but still doesn't turn. "Are you feeling okay?"

"Rose!" I rush to her side, push the fridge door closed. She finally looks at me. "Why did you guess a witch lived in the palace? Does that really look to you like a place a witch would live?"

With a yogurt in one hand, she walks over to the counter and pulls a spoon from the utensils drawer. Her calmness is maddening. "I feel like a witch would live anywhere she wants."

I hug the pillow closer to my heart. "Well, mostly they live in the woods!"

"Says who?"

"Says stories! Myths and fairy tales and stuff."

She shrugs. "Maybe she lives in a palace *in* the woods."

"Maybe," I reply, turning the thought over in my head.

"Anyway, I have no idea," she says, her teeth clanging against the spoon as she takes a bite of yogurt. "*I'm* not a witch."

I slump against the refrigerator, disappointed. Even though I knew, I *knew,* that of course she didn't see the woods. No one else ever sees the things I see.

I let my head fall back, my eyes on the ceiling.

Except—well, there may be one person who does.

"Want to go to the beach?" Rose says, pulling my attention back to her. "We could have a sand castle–building contest. We could build a whole kingdom. And I'll even let you destroy it when we're done. I know that's your favorite part."

Relaxing my grip on my pillow-shield, I smile. Rose never lets me stomp on our creations when we're done, even though the wind and water will wash them away anyway.

"Yes," I say, and Rose bounces on the tips of her toes, pleased. "Challenge accepted."

I turn, and she follows me up the stairs. But my initial elation at Rose's offer seems to bleed right out of me by the time we reach our room.

A witch, she said.

A witch.

Chapter 7

IN THE WOODS

All night the Witch plucked petals from her heart, bequeathing wishes of every form and flavor to the children who sought her in their dreams, but every minute she awaited the return of the Fox Who Is No Fox, longed to hear his voice sculpting things she would never see, places she would never be, people she would never meet. Her loyal foxes paced at her feet.

The children—they wished. And the Witch—she waited.

And waited.

And waited.

Finally he entered the castle, shrugging off his fox-flesh and transforming back into a boy.

"Come." The Witch beckoned him closer. "Now."

"As you wish," he said, and bowed.

He sat before her with his head tilted back, the better to look at her, his throat long and pale.

He spoke.

And spoke, until his voice was razed to a rasp, and then he

began a history lesson, the intricate past of the World Beyond the Wood: revered reigns of kings and queens, conquests and revolutions, bloody battles and insufferable sieges. Even the stiff whiskers of the foxes stopped twitching to hear.

After a while, the Fox Who Is No Fox moved on to mythologies: monsters and maidens, heroes and villains; he stared at the sky and expounded on gods, vast and varied. Angels and devils, saviors and crusaders, religions and worship.

And when he started to tell a fairy tale, a fantasy of cruelty and courage and beauty and despair, of curses and kisses and curiosity that kills—of this the Witch wanted no part.

"Speak of something else," she said.

He sighed, and told her instead of an ancient pirate's daughter who was known for her finely crafted poisons, a girl with glass behind her eyes and skin perfumed in the cloud-scent of death. She let the Fox Who Is No Fox sit upon the dais with his back to her. As he spoke, she tangled fresh flowers in his hair, blue and yellow and riotous violet, petals shining like bruises. The Witch asked for more, more stories of heroines exactly like that pirate's daughter, and he obliged. He had stories like stones in his hands, so many, and she wanted to hear them all.

Well.

Not quite all.

"Once there was a girl," he said, while the Witch wove him a crown of roses, "a girl whose name is—"

The Witch curled her hands into his hair and tightened her grip, fingernails to scalp. He winced and arched his neck against her bare knees.

"This sounds like a fairy story," the Witch warned.

"I assure you, it is not."

She relaxed her grasp, just a little. "What, then?"

He lifted his chin, twisting at the waist to look up at her. "It is more of a . . . a secret history, if you will."

The Witch didn't respond. Instead she released him, his head fell forward, and she pushed herself up and out of her throne, to step widely around him.

"Go home," she said at last, her head bowed and her back to him, arms crossed tight over her heart.

"But—"

"That is enough."

"But I—"

"You promised!"

The Fox Who Is No Fox stood, and the flowers fell from his hair. He walked quietly around her, but she did not look up again until he was gone, did not let her arms or her heart relax.

Quietly, to no one but herself, she said, "That is enough for now."

Chapter 8

IN THE DARK

Rose lies on her back with her right arm hooked over her head and one leg dangling off the edge of the bed, unconsciously offering her foot as food for the kind of monsters that crunch cubes of ice between their molars, impervious to the cold and the frostbitten beauty of snowdrift souls.

I wait until I'm certain she's asleep before I rise and inch backward, toes on the carpet, creeping, sliding, ready to slip back under the sheets at the slightest sign of her stirring.

"Stay here," I whisper to Gabrielle as she stands to follow. "I won't be long."

I had plenty of chances to go back to the attic during the daylight today, even after hanging with Rose. Plenty of chances to return without my sisters, but I squandered every single one of them.

Later, later, later, I told myself. Then: *Never, never, never.* But *later* and *never* have converged, canceling each other out.

Now, now, now.

The smart thing would be to stay away, to forget, to pretend it never happened.

But.

Two nights ago I opened the forbidden door in my dream for the very first time, after years of reaching and grasping and waking with the taste of disappointment mixed with relief rusting in my mouth. And last night, I found a boy in the attic who claims to know me, and it can't be a coincidence, can it? And though it seems impossible, I can't help but wonder: In opening the door, did I somehow release him? Release him into my life, or worse, into the waking world?

I've always been sure there were secrets behind that door, and maybe now I can get some answers. Answers about the visions I'm cursed with, about the creatures I see, and how I can sometimes see my heart through my ribs. About the woods, and the witch.

And about the boy himself.

Gabrielle follows me anyway as I skulk out of our bedroom and into the empty hallway. We walk together up the stairs, but when I open the attic door, I step inside and close it quickly, shutting her out. She paws at the wood, scratching and whimpering, but I ignore her and walk farther in.

The room could be as small as a teacup or as vast as a universe, ever expanding. The door, the bed, the floor directly beneath—these are the only real, solid things in the absolute darkness. The heat spreads through the room like a rash, and already I am starting to sweat. I reach the bed, bend, and crawl backward, until I hit the wall. Eyes closed, eyes open—it makes no difference. But I keep them open anyway.

Even though I'm determined not to let him catch me off guard this time, his voice floats and twists like steam so that I don't know where it's coming from. When he speaks, I press my spine against the wall so hard, it hurts.

"Rhea Ravenna, you have returned."

Again he uses my name like a spell, an incantation somewhere between sinister and sacred, demonic and divine.

"Who are you? *What* are you?" I lift my chin and take a long, steady inhale. "Why couldn't we see you, when my sisters and I came earlier? Was it you, tugging on my hair?"

"You can tell yourself it wasn't me, if it comforts you to do so. Pretend it was one of your sisters," he says, and I feel the blade of his grin. I want him to answer my other questions, but he says nothing more.

"Where are you?" I say, disoriented.

"On the dresser," he says. "Don't worry. There are whole worlds between us."

I can't even begin to guess what he means by that, so I file it away for now. "You know," I say, "I don't think it's fair that you know my name but I don't know yours. I don't even know anything about you."

He sighs. "Oh, my sky, your name has been stuck in my throat for so long. You are an itch in my heart, an itch I have never been able to scratch."

As he speaks, I feel it too. *An itch.* Not an ordinary twinge, not a sting of discomfort wriggling on dry skin. This itch has teeth, and it started as a seed I did not know was planted. A seed that is now, as his words water it, a sprout. A biting bud of tiny canines, crooked and corroded.

I put a hand to my chest and scratch my nails across my sternum, even though it doesn't help. "An itch you couldn't scratch—until now?"

"No. I can never scratch it, Rhea Ravenna, and that is the point."

"*Stop.*" I drop my hands. "Stop saying my name like that."

A pause. "Like what?"

"Like—like you know something I don't."

He grins. "But I *do* know something you don't. Haven't you been listening?"

"Yes, and you haven't said even one thing that makes any *sense.*"

"You want to know my name?"

I nod, eager, even though he can't see.

He says, "I propose that we play a game, you and I."

"A game." I exhale. "What kind of game?"

"A guessing game, of course." A pause. "You like games, don't you? Puzzles and riddles and rhymes."

My heart itches, twitches, beats even faster. "What are the rules?"

The dresser creaks. Sways, as if a weight has been lifted. The Darkness stands, only a foot away. I know, because the space before me, around me, feels steadily warmer. And when he speaks, his voice is louder, nearer.

He says, "I will give you three tries to guess my name."

"What?" I almost laugh out loud. "What are you, Rumpelstiltskin?"

He isn't the least amused. "Rumpel—what? I don't know what this means."

"You've never heard of Rumpelstiltskin? Where are you even from?"

"The same place as you."

"And what place would that be? Wonderland?"

"I suppose there's wonder, and there's land," he says wryly. "But I would not call it *wonderland*, no."

"That's not what I— Never mind." I chew my cheek, thinking. Is he actually serious about this? He wants me to guess his *name*? I mean, that doesn't seem *so* unreasonable—for a fairy tale, for a dream.

"Only three guesses?" I ask. "What happens if all my guesses are wrong?"

"Then we both lose." His voice is hard now, and I hear him grinding his jaw. "We both lose, and the game is over."

I know I should keep to the questions I came here to ask, but I'm not quite sure how to steer the conversation back around. And maybe playing his stupid game is the only way I'll get answers anyway. "Will you give me any clues?"

"Yes. In fact, I'll tell you a story."

"A story?" I say, and Renata's voice, breathless, crawls like a spider through the back of my brain: *The princess had magic and the others didn't. . . . But then she escaped by falling into a sleeping spell. The end.*

Now that I think about it, the way she said it was strange. Did Renata mean that the princess escaped, and that was the end of the story? Or did Ren mean that falling into a sleeping spell was how the princess escaped the *end*—the end of her life, the end of the world, the end of the story itself? But how is it possible to avoid your own end?

I shake my head. "I don't want to hear a story."

"Oh, I wouldn't be so quick to refuse if I were you. It might be the only thing to help you remember."

It's so, so hot in this tiny room that he suddenly feels so, so close. Leaning over me.

I am not afraid, I am not afraid, I am not, not, not.

"All right, and if I guess correctly?" I raise my chin, staring at the Darkness, staring at nothing. "If I win? Will you show me your face?"

"If you win, I will give you a gift." He whispers now, and it is I who lean closer this time. So close I can feel the heat leave his lips. "If you win, I will *take your curse away*."

I let out a breath, a breath sharp and fast, somewhere between a stuttering sigh and a fracturing cry. And for a second the unnatural darkness surrounding him disperses, just enough that I can see the figure of a tall, thin boy—barely more than a silhouette. Jarred, my gaze falls down to the scream of blue veins beneath the blanched skin of his forearms, then up to the line of his jaw tensing as he jerks away from me, stepping backward to the center of the room. He knows I can see him—not well, not well at all, but I'm not supposed to see. I'm not allowed a glimpse, not yet.

Then the darkness swoops back in and congeals, glomming together around him, thicker and blacker than ever. Both of us are silent for a long while, trying to recapture what we let loose. What just happened? I don't think either of us knows; he seems as surprised as I am.

"So you know? You know about my curse?" I say, half eager, half terrified. "You know about my visions?"

The darkness undulates, dips and eddies, but does not disband. Not again. The boy's guard is up, and I will not breach it a second time. Not tonight, anyway. "Are you willing to play?" he asks.

I wrap my arms around my waist, trembling. "What do you know about my visions? Do you know what they mean? Do you know why I see things that aren't there?"

"You will only know that, my sky, when you know my name."

"Why do you call me that? *Sky?* And how do I know you're even real?" I'm almost shouting now, but I don't care. I stand, scrambling toward the door. "How do I know you can do what you say?"

"*Will you play?*" he hisses. "Yes, or no, Rhea Ravenna? *Yes. Or. No?*"

"*Yes,*" I snap, in a voice that could crack the sunlit sky in half, a straight clean break bleeding black and clotting with tiny tinsel stars. "Yes, I'll play. I'll play and I'll win, and then— then I will know who and what you are."

I find the doorknob with my fingers, and as I do, the nameless boy veiled in shadow whispers: "Ah, but you are wrong. You are wrong, Rhea Ravenna. By the end, when you win, you will know who and what *you* are."

I wrench the door open and descend, hands on the wall to steady myself. Clawing, clambering. At the bottom, I trip to my knees. It doesn't hurt, not as much as the malevolent itch still raging in my heart. I shudder, and shield my eyes with the backs of my hands in the sudden sphere of pale light, crushing after the density of the darkness.

Gabrielle is there, waiting for me, her eyes bright with anger. She wanted to come with me, to protect me. She'll forgive me soon enough, I know, but now she bites at my legs. Hard enough to hurt but not to break the skin. She nips once at my knee and then starts toward the bedroom. She stops in the doorway. *Come on.*

I stand and follow. As I grasp for sleep, curled in bed with my back to Rose, Gabrielle beside me, a song skitters through my mind, over and over and over. Slow at first—and then fast, faster, fastest.

It goes like this:

> *I will take your curse away.*
> *Away, away, away.*
> *Your curse, my sky, my sky, my sky.*
> *Your curse is mine, is mine, is mine.*
> *Yours to give and mine to take.*
> *I will take your curse away.*
> *And all you have to do, my sky,*
> *Is say my name, my name, my name.*

Chapter 9

IN THE WOODS

The crescent moon snuck away to nap behind a cloud, and its snores were like milk splashing in a cup, and the Fox Who Is No Fox did not come. The Witch walked back and forth across the glade, silent, her heart stiff inside her. Her feet ached, her knees popped, but the Witch of Wishes did not stop pacing.

The foxes' howls wilted to a whisper and then to a rasp and then to nothing. But still the Witch did not stop pacing.

Only when he glided into the glade, his lips so red that it hurt to look at them, did the Witch stop.

She faced him, and held out her hand, hoping he would not notice how her fingers trembled with relief. She had been afraid he would not come back again, after she'd sent him away.

"Dance with me," she said.

He said nothing.

"Please?" she asked more sweetly.

"I do not know how," he said.

"Then I will show you," she said.

The Fox Who Is No Fox stepped toward her, edging almost sideways, as if approaching a spooked animal. The Witch waited.

Finally they joined hands, and their fingers fit together, bone wrapped around bone, skin touching skin. He could feel her pulse, but it was much too slow for someone who had spent so much time pacing. The pulse of someone a breath away from death.

"I can still give you what you wish for," he said. "I can—"

"I wish for nothing," she said, quiet and fierce. "Nothing but that you dance with me. Will you or won't you?"

"I will," he said, and they began.

Their steps made the music and their respirations set the rhythm, accelerating, accompanied by the creamy clatter of the moon's sleep-snuffles as the shadow sun simmered, and the faint, hoarse crying of the foxes, the patter of the foxes' paws as they circled. Sometimes when the Witch danced, she was sinuous, delicate, merely skimming the earth as though intent to fly away.

But this was different. Feet stamping, smacking the ground, arms swooping, reaching, their hands breaking apart and coming together again. Whirling, knees bent, head back, spine twisted. Flushed cheeks and runaway breath, pulverizing their fears beneath their cramped, cut-up feet.

The Fox Who Is No Fox had said he did not know how to dance, but that didn't matter. His body knew; his legs and hips and shoulders knew. His heart knew. At first he followed the Witch's movements, but when he finally forgot that he did not know how to dance, he harmonized his steps with hers, moving around her and with her: he was the punctuation in her sentences, the knot at the end of her thread, the clasp on the chain of her necklace. She could exist without him, dance on her own, quite well, in fact—but it was he who brought her back around to herself, somehow. Transformed her line into a circle.

Only when the sun sagged sideways, yawning yellow light, did the Fox Who Is No Fox retract his hands. "It is time for me to go," he said.

The Witch stopped. It was so, so silent in the Woods, and it hurt. It hurt to be so still. The world ached, and she did too. The foxes were asleep now.

The Witch stared at the Fox Who Is No Fox, her lips parted and her eyes stretched wide. Her hair was a perfect mess. "What is the story about?" she said.

He bit the inside of his cheek. Three times, hard. She saw his skin pucker. He was so pale, he was almost transparent, unreal. Fading.

"What?" he said.

"The fairy story that is no fairy story." Her voice was overbright and dizzy, a destructive dizziness not unlike a child's desire to demolish a castle they've just built in the sand, before someone else comes along and smashes it. Nothing lasts. The Witch knew that—but sometimes we can have a say in the way we fall apart. She said, "What is it about?"

Slowly he smiled. "Do you wish me to—"

"Just follow me." The Witch turned and walked into her castle, suppressing the urge to skip. Her stomach wriggled with the slightest hint of hunger, but there was nothing for her to eat. Tonight she would feast on a story, and nothing more than that.

Chapter 10

IN THE DARK

I wake up with a song in my head, a tune but no lyrics. Something about a sky, and a name.

Then, all at once, I remember.

The Darkness, grinning. And a game. A game to guess his name.

But before I have too much time to think about it, I hear a low muttering coming from my closet on the far side of the room. My heart clenches.

Is it him?

I rise, slowly, glancing at the empty bed next to mine and wondering how long I've slept. Gabrielle tries to grab my shirt between her teeth, to stop me. I shush her, tiptoeing across the room as the noise grows louder. Placing my palm on the knob, I throw the door open.

I'm so relieved, I laugh. But the sound withers and comes out as a cry instead. Renata is crouched in the corner, teetering on her toes, thighs to chest, pricking her fingertip with a sewing needle. Blood on the carpet, three drops. And from her throbbing throat, a cold whisper that burgeons and steams into a hot, searing screech, "Wake *up*, wake *up*. Wake up wake up wakeupwakeupwakeupwakeup *wake up*!"

"Ren? What are you—"

When she looks up and sees me, she lunges. It happens so fast: the scrabble of skin and nails, tumbling backward, my tailbone banging the floor, my tiny sister on top of me. A nightmare mess of limbs and the quiet of concentration as we tussle and I try and fail to flip her off me. I gasp at the sudden jab of the needle in my chest, not too deep but deep enough to pierce the skin, the horizontal drag of its tip across my sternum.

"*Wake up,*" she says, thick sticky tears in her wide-open eyes. She has the fever-sweat sheen of someone set on stopping the shoreward shove of the sea, once and for all and forever.

And then it's finished; she scrambles sideways, crab-crawling away. She stands, staring down at me, and I blink up at her, wheezing. I touch the line she's carved into my chest. There's barely any blood, but it still stings.

"I dreamed I was dreaming," she says, the needle nested in her fist, the porcelain parts of her eyes cracked with dead-end veins. "And I finally woke up. I woke up in the dream, from the dream, just for a second. And it felt like rust on the rim of my heart. Creeping over my skin. Like blisters, and it hurt. It hurt a lot, actually."

She makes a sound as she leaves the room, somewhere between a cough and a cackle. I stay there on the floor, stunned. I'm not sure how long I lie there. Long enough that my heart sags against my ribs and the cut scabs over. Long enough that Rose comes into the room and says, "Have you seen Ren? It's been a while since anyone saw her. And we found her phone stuffed under her mattress, as usual. We tried Cadence's house to see if she was there, but I guess those two haven't been friends for a while now. Did you know—"

Too quickly, I jerk upward, and the blood drains from my head. For a moment my vision is completely obscured by popping speckles of black and gray.

"What happened to your chest?" Rose kneels before me, inspecting.

"I was attacked." I press the heels of my hands to my temples, steadying myself as the world wobbles. "At least, I think. I'm not really sure, actually."

Without another word, she leaves me and goes to the bathroom, then brings back a half-empty tube of antibiotic ointment. She squeezes some onto her finger and dabs at the thread-thin slash.

"Start from the beginning," she says, and I recount everything that has happened since I woke up.

Raisa appears in the doorway just as I finish. "Hey! What did you do to Ren?"

"Nothing!"

"You upset her!"

"No, she attacked me unprovoked." I point at my chest. "Look at what *she* did to *me*."

"Well, *you* better find *her*," Raisa says, eyeing the scratch over my heart. "Anyone check her hiding places?"

"Not yet."

"Let's look," Rose says before Raisa can launch more accusations at me. Rose's cheeks are colorless and slightly shiny, appearing almost icy. "Mom is starting to panic."

For now, it seems that figuring out the boy's name is going to have to wait. I get dressed quickly before meeting the rest of my family downstairs, where we silently slip into our shoes, grab our purses and keys, and swirl out the door like water down a drain.

The entire afternoon is spent searching the shoreline, Rose and I each traversing in opposite directions while Raisa rides her bike to the lighthouse, and Mom and Dad drive downtown to circle the streets, to check outside the cemetery. Gabrielle follows me, and I taste the caustic cream of anticipation foaming at the tip of her tongue just as surely as she feels the tangling of my veins into a bloody bouquet. Before long, she's panting from the heat and I'm exhausted. I meet the others back at the house.

"We'll find her," Dad says, kissing Mom on the cheek as she bustles around the kitchen where we stand, preparing sandwiches for dinner before we start back out again. "We always do."

Together, we eat quickly, quietly. Right now food is fuel and nothing more. We are not allowed to enjoy it without Renata here too.

As we get ready to leave again, Rose hangs back.

"I think I'll stay here," she says. "Someone has to be here in case she comes back, right?"

"Good idea," Dad says, and I volunteer to take the beach again, this time on my own.

Closing the door, I look both ways before crossing the sand-brushed street, then kick my flip-flops off as I finally reach the open beach. Then I sprint, as fast as I can, my hair bouncing, snarling and sticking to my neck, Gabrielle huffing after me. It's dark down by the water, but the darkness is uncontained, billowing from here to infinity. Ordinary.

The wind flips up the hem of my dress as I run, soft fabric flapping around my hips. But I don't care at all. Who is here to see me? Only a few stray stars, pale and burning. With only open space and open sky and open sea everywhere around me, I feel like I'm the only person in all of existence.

As I run, trembling in this unobstructed stretch of space, I pretend that I am magic. I pretend I can conjure storm clouds with my hands and summon fires that don't scorch my skin as I balance the flames on my palms. I pretend I can whisper words that will make the listener fall in love with me, only for a few minutes, only long enough for a slow dance and a quick kiss, a wistful sigh and a flushed goodbye.

I pretend I can locate Renata with ease, calling on the wind to look for her and report back to me. That way, she would never be lost. She could wander anywhere, and we'd always know exactly where to find her.

The sea races in. I stop so abruptly as it rushes to meet me that I slip on the soggy sand and fall backward. I scramble back on my hands and push myself to standing, cold water gushing around my feet, my knees, wetting my dress. Gabrielle stands a few yards back, well away from the waves. I start to call Renata's name, quietly at first and then more loudly.

When I turn back to look toward my house, I see trees

instead, rising taller than they should, like a thousand giant bones stuck straight up in the ground.

The woods are back.

There's no screaming this time. At least, not yet.

I sprint—back up the beach, across the road, and behind the house. Gabrielle bites at my ankles, begging me to turn around, but I can't. I *can't*—or anyway I don't want to, and right now that's basically the same thing. I stop a dozen feet from the neat line of impossible trees, completely out of breath. I take a tiny step forward, and another and another.

But.

The trees don't vanish. And they don't collapse.

Just when I'm close enough to touch them, afraid to go any farther, someone comes up next to me, so softly that I don't hear her until she's right there at my side. I turn, only slightly, absorbing her in pieces: sand like sugar crystals stuck to her knees, her shorts and shirt completely sodden, drops from her hair sliding down her arms. I'm afraid that if I stare directly at her, she'll disappear.

"Sorry I stabbed you," Renata says. "I would say I didn't mean to, but that would be a lie." She presses her index finger lightly against my temple. *Wake up, wake up, wake* up. "I did mean to. I'm just sorry it hurt you. These things do, though. They hurt."

"That's okay." I wait for her to explain, reaching for my phone in my pocket to text the others that she's okay, before I remember that my dress doesn't have pockets and my phone is sitting somewhere inside the house behind us. Suddenly I'm anxious to get back, to get away from the woods that might disappear or crumble at any moment, before the screaming starts and doesn't stop—but I'm also afraid that if I try to haul Renata home before she's ready, she'll resist and run away again.

"Have you ever heard of calenture?" she says, lowering herself to sit cross-legged in the dewy grass. "Do you know what that is?"

"No." I drop down beside her and let my head fall forward onto the shivering steeple of my knees, the woods so close, so close that they could almost take her. "Where have you been? Everyone is freaking out."

"It's an old-fashioned word for heatstroke," she says, ignoring me. "It used to refer to sailors and the delirium that would sometimes sneak up on them. It made them see a green field of grass where the waves rolled endlessly in all directions. Confused, they'd fling themselves overboard and drown."

"That's really sad."

"The sun and the sea don't care who lives and who dies."

"What does this have to do with anything?"

"Isn't it obvious?" Renata blinks, laying her head on my shoulder. "It's the same in the dark, most likely. Complete darkness, I mean, a form of calenture. If you stay in it too long, you become delirious, and start seeing a meadow where there is only water. A forest where there is only flat land. It's almost like dreaming."

My heart starts to beat so fast, I feel it pulsing everywhere: in my stomach, my neck, my temples. "Wait, Renata, what do you mean? Have you seen a forest where there isn't one?"

She slowly shakes her head, and doesn't speak.

"Why are you doing this?" I roll my shoulder, shaking her off. Something is really, really wrong, but I don't know what it is. The air is warm, but the wind blowing in from the woods is cold, and her voice—it's somewhere in between, with a rhythm like the sweep of retreating waves, like foam and forgetting. "What's gotten into you?"

For a moment, she is silent. Then: "She's not there, you know."

I finally turn to look at her, straight on. She's just a darker shadow in the dark, a perfect silhouette. "What?"

"The witch." Impossibly, Renata nods toward the trees. "You're always looking for her. But she's not there. Not anymore."

Everything in me goes quiet at this. "How do you know about that?" I whisper. "I thought I dreamed her."

She smiles. Her teeth shine. "You did."

When I look to the forest, it's gone.

"You have to come find me, okay? I can't stay here anymore, but I'll be waiting for you. We all are." Renata leans closer, and her sigh streams across my cheek. "Good night, Rhea. Good night."

"What do you mean, good—" I jump to my feet, intending to follow her, not keen to let her get away again. But she's not there. Not beside me or behind me or anywhere else in the field. Gone, as quickly and completely as the woods.

"Renata?" I call, spinning in circles, searching. "Where are you? Where'd you go?"

The soft scrape left by her breath is fading fast from my skin, and when I stop and look down at the squishy grass, thinking to simply follow her path, there are no footprints. There is nothing, no imprint to indicate she'd ever been here at all. I should have snatched her and dragged her home while I had the chance.

When I turn to the house, Dad's car is in the driveway, and just seeing it parked there impels me up the back steps and through the door. I traverse those few yards more quickly than any other distance I've covered all day. Gabrielle follows, her tail bristled. I swing the door open with too much force; it glides on its hinges and hits the wall. I come around the corner into the kitchen. My family is gathered around the island— Mom and Dad, Rose and Raisa.

No Renata.

Dad says something, and they laugh. Mom and Raisa for real, but Rose—she tries. I can tell it's only an attempt, because her mouth stretches and her lips part in imitation of a laugh, but she brings her hand up to swipe at her nose, like she's trying to cover the false sound that's slipped out, just a scratchy scuff of air. Her laugh, her true laugh, is like a bold step onto a fresh sheet of morning snow, the crack of its frozen crust beneath your boots. Short and sharp and revelatory, and so satisfying that you will want to hear it again and again and again.

"Hello?" I say, unmoving in the archway separating the foyer from the kitchen. It seems like every single light in the room is on. Overbright and blinding.

My sisters are facing me, on the other side of the island, but Mom and Dad twist around to look at me. Both of them smile, and that's when I notice the ice cream in their hands, vanilla soft serve in waffle cones. Rose has mint chip in a cup with a plastic spoon, and Raisa holds the bent straw of a shake to the corner of her mouth.

"We brought your favorite," Mom says, and she pushes a paper cup across the countertop: chocolate, two scoops with star-shaped sprinkles. I take it slowly, still a little uneasy. I don't see Renata, but she must be here. If she were still missing, they wouldn't have stopped for ice cream.

"We're telling the story of how we met," Dad says as I come up beside him.

"*Again,*" says Raisa, chewing on the end of her straw to hide her smile. If Raisa is smiling, then they *must* have found Renata. Maybe she's in the bathroom. I force myself to relax and listen.

"I was just getting to the part where your mother becomes obsessed with my constellation tattoo," Dad says, grinning. "My favorite part."

This tattoo is only one of several: an upside-down crown on the left side of his upper ribs; a pair of eyes on his left forearm, both of them wide open; and finally the one on his back that's a series of small black dots, connected by a thin, faint line.

He says the dots represent stars and the line forms the contours of a constellation. But it is no constellation that exists in our charted sky, and that is exactly what had my mother so captivated: an imaginary arrangement of stars.

"He told me he'd made it up, but I still swear I've seen it before," Mom tells us, and I glance down the hallway, wondering when Renata is coming back. "It seems so *familiar.*

But I looked in every book in the library, and I never found a match."

Laughing, Dad hooks his arm around Mom's neck, where her sole tattoo, a rose in full bloom, is inked at the nape. His elbow at her ear, he pulls her in close and kisses her forehead.

"PDA!" Raisa shrieks, setting down her shake and slapping her hands over her eyes. "Make it stop!"

But it does not stop; Mom hides her face in his neck, leaning in, and even her long black fishtail braid sways to the side to be closer to him.

I stick my spoon into the ice cream so that it stands straight up. Dad continues, Mom wryly interrupts, and Raisa laughs and squeals. Only Rose says nothing, does nothing, stares at her ice cream as it slowly melts. She's still wearing her black leotard and pale pink tights from ballet earlier. Something shifts, and I remember she told me, once, that the only time she feels truly awake is when she dances.

It's not that I forgot it, exactly, but staring at her now in the kitchen with Renata gone, it hits me. Not alive—*awake.*

Wake.

Wake up.

Wake up, wake up, wake up.

A stitch of pain snakes through the slit over my heart, and I bring my hand to my chest. Everyone is so cheerful that it's easy to believe they found Renata. Where *is* she, though? If not in the bathroom, did she go straight upstairs to bed? She must be here somewhere, or else they wouldn't be so calm.

Without warning Gabrielle opens her mouth and sticks her teeth into my shin, fangs pinching skin. Not hard enough to bring blood to the surface, just a reviving little nip. I understand her meaning at once: *Say something.*

"Your mom, being the woman I love," Dad goes on, "went and—"

"So you found her, then?" I interrupt. "I mean, she's home. Right?"

Dad pauses. "Who? What?"

"Renata," I say. "Is she upstairs, or gone at a friend's?"

Mom lifts her head from Dad's shoulder. "Ren . . . Who?"

"Your youngest daughter. Renata. Fourteen years old. My s-sister," I say, choking on my own breath. I wrench my gaze away from their alarmed looks, their spines straightening, heads shaking. I look to Raisa, who shrugs, then to Rose. She stares at me, head tilted to the side. "*Our* sister. Renata. She was missing and you went to find her. And now you're back with ice cream, so I just thought—I assumed she had just come back. Because otherwise you wouldn't be so, so— *happy.*" I pause, but no one says anything. "Is this a *joke?*"

"It wouldn't be a very funny one if it were," Raisa says. She's not smiling anymore. No one is.

"But—" I falter, and Gabrielle bites my leg again, harder this time. "Ow, Gabby, *stop.* Ray, you share a bedroom with her."

"What, that cupboard up there? There's barely enough room for me and a few spiders, let alone me and another person."

I shiver, a tidal tremble beginning at the tip-top of my spine and spiraling down my shoulders and ribs, waist and hips and thighs, careening all the way to my knees.

"Are you okay, Rhea?" Mom drops Dad's arm and starts to drift toward the cabinet where she keeps the homemade remedies and medicines made from the things she grows in her garden. I know which one she's thinking of as she reaches for the knob, the one made from various nectars and essences specifically for lessening panic and terror.

"Yes, I'm—" is all I can manage.

"Are you having a vision?" Dad says, wrapping a hand around my elbow, squeezing for reassurance. "What do you see?"

"The usual," I whisper, and it's not a lie, not exactly; as soon as I say it, as soon as I think it, I look around at my family, and the skin of their chests bubbles and boils, dribbles off the slatted bones of their ribs, leaving gaps through which I can see each of their velvety hearts. "I dreamed I was dreaming and—"

You're always looking for her, but she's not there.

Not anymore.

"Mom, I'm okay," I say as she stands on tiptoe, fingers reaching toward the highest shelf. "I'm just going to go to bed now. I'm tired, that's all."

They stare as I bolt out of the room, Gabrielle pattering after me, up the stairs and to the room Raisa shares—has *always* shared—with Renata.

I survey the room, not quite daring to step inside. I can see all I need to from here, and what I see is this: nothing. Nothing at all.

I mean, there are *some* things in the room. Raisa's things—her twin bed, pushed into the far corner, the pink-and-orange tie-dyed comforter kicked into a mound at the foot, revealing electric-blue bedsheets stretched over the mattress. Shoes and bras and underwear scattered on the carpet, erupting from the open closet doors, clean clothes indistinguishable from the dirty; a tall dresser topped with the tarnished jewelry box from the attic; the window on the far wall open only an inch, admitting a shy breeze that tousles the pink curtains. Vintage movie posters tacked to the walls, and a desk with coffee cup stains on its wooden surface where another bed should be. Renata's bed.

Her bed, which was stacked with half a dozen fleece blankets because she was always cold, and lots of pillows because she liked to build a fort around herself at night. Her collection of scallops and whelks, corals and conches, mussels and mollusks arranged like a mural on top of her nightstand, a cut crystal bowl brimming with misshapen pinkish pearls.

Her bed, her belongings—all of it is gone.

I turn and run to my own room, just across the hall. I fumble for my phone on the nightstand. I hold it in both hands, clumsily swiping, jabbing the screen, but there's not a single photograph with Renata in it, where once there were dozens, pictures of the entire family and some of just the two of us, her holding the camera while I grinned a grin that somehow, always, managed to look more like a grimace.

I slump down on my bed, letting the phone slip out of my sweating palms. I'm shaking so hard, I couldn't scream even if I wanted to.

What are the chances that I would make a deal with the Darkness *and* Renata would vanish the very next day? What are the chances that I would feel an itch in my heart, and the next morning she would stab me in that exact *same* spot?

I will take your curse away, he said, not *I will take your family away.* But he shouldn't be taking *anything* away yet because I haven't even won the game. Is this some kind of punishment for letting an entire day go by without making a guess? What else does he have up his sleeve?

And what if I guess and never get it right? What then?

We both lose, and the game is over.

I realize now I stand more to lose than just a game.

"I am not afraid," I whisper, alone in my room. "I am not. I am not, I am—"

I am, though. I am afraid.

Renata is gone, and no one remembers her.

And I'm pretty sure this is my fault.

Chapter 11

IN THE WOODS

The Witch and the Fox Who Is No Fox sat side by side on the dais, leaning against the base of her throne, a careful inch between them. The children were still hours away from arriving, and the first stars were just yawning awake, shaking themselves from dreams of glitter and dancing and dizziness. The Witch tucked her hands under her knees and did not look at her companion. He smiled at her anyway, and in a quiet, steady voice, he began his story.

Once there was a girl, a girl whose name is forbidden now, and all her life she lived in a crystal castle overlooking the Second Sea to the north and the city to the west, where iron was built into the facades of the buildings and enchanted train tracks circled around them. It was from the ashes of an old stone castle that

*this new fortified city had been built, so that those
who lived to the south in Graiae Forest, a thousand-
acre wood, would not dare to visit, for it was said that
the city's iron weakened the forest dwellers' magical
abilities, keeping them at bay. And likewise, none from
the city were allowed into the forest, for the danger
posed by the sylphs and gray gorgons, the sprites and
sphinxes and manticores, who lived inside.*

*You see, her world was one in which magic
rushed through the clay veins of the earth and some
humans were born with two hearts, one inside the
other, the smaller of them pulsing with magic. Their
human hearts longed for the city, but their magical
hearts yearned for the forest, and so this community
belonged everywhere and nowhere at once. They were
called the maculae.*

*Though in the minority, these maculae were feared
and revered in equal measure. By royal decree, they
were given a choice: have their wrists bound in chains
made of iron, the bane of all magic, so that their
abilities were kept contained until the king of the
realm called upon them to use their powers; or remain
independent but rendered magicless by the removal
of their second heart, before being banished to the
Heartless Hollow deep in the forest. In exchange
for the former, they were given riches and honored
in festivals. Titles were bestowed upon them—the
more extraordinary the ability, the higher the ranking.*

*They lived full and opulent lives, or so it seemed—as,
remember, they just couldn't use their magic as they
pleased.*

Immaculae, *the king called his servants.* Spotless,
pure.

They are dangerous, yes, *he told his people,* but
that is what the chains are for. This way, everyone is
safe.

*Our girl was a macula—but she did not wear
chains, for she kept her powers a secret. Her
grandfather was the king, and that made her a
princess, the only child born to her father, the crown
prince. Her mother, the future queen consort, had
magic too—magic she also kept secret from everyone
but the princess. If it were known they were maculate,
each would have to make the choice, just like all the
other maculae caught using their magic freely: accept
the chains and lose their liberty, or keep their freedom
but without magic. Rules were rules, and it did not
matter that they were royalty.*

*But the princess did not want to hide away in her
castle, gazing every day out her window at the woods
where she knew, just* knew, *she belonged.*

It isn't safe there, *her mother warned her, seeing
that sneaking gleam in the princess's eyes, the
restlessness and the yearning for freedom.*

*For a long time, the princess refrained from leaving,
but eventually her longing for the woods grew stronger
than her fear. And so she cast a glamour over herself*

and snuck out of the castle at night, fleeing to the forest where the monsters lived. Where she could be a monster too.

On that first venture inside, when she was barely nine years old, she came face to face with a manticore not twenty feet into the shadows. The beast paced in front of a tree, glancing at the princess with each quick pivot of her paws. Her claws were long and glowed in the dark.

Hello, little one, and where are you going? Alone, I see, but unfamiliar with the ways of the wood.

Her breath smelled like blood blisters and worms and burnt flesh.

How do you know I'm unfamiliar? *the princess said, doing her very best impression of bravery.* I belong here, same as you.

The manticore raised her gold-gray eyebrows. Is that so?

I have magic.

Ah. That would be why you have brought no weapon. You think your magic is enough.

It can be if I need it to be. *The princess eyed her.* Will you eat me, manticore?

No, my sweet. *The manticore stopped pacing and smiled at her with each of her three rows of teeth.* We only eat the ones who think they can get away.

Oh, I see. You won't eat me because I *know* I can get away.

The manticore threw back her head and laughed.

105

A manticore's laugh is not at all like their slippery, sliding voice. Their laugh is hard and abrupt, like stone clacking against stone, a tumble of pebbles into a stream. The princess loved it, immediately and immensely.

Come with me, my dear macula, and I will introduce you to the trees.

The trees?

You must make friends with them first. If you make a foe of the trees, you will never be allowed to come back.

The manticore introduced her to the trees and to everyone worth knowing in the woods, to the satyrs and sylphs and the sphinxes, to the shape-shifters and heart-wrenchers. Among them, two girls—one a gray gorgon, a girl with silver moonlight for hair. Any human who chanced to gaze into her amethyst eyes was instantly turned into shadow. The other girl was a nymph who made her home in the Grimly River that circled the darkest part of the forest. Here with them the macula was not royalty but just another bright creature trying to hide in a dark world, where their light made them suspect and easy to find.

The princess grew from a child to a young woman, and each night she went to the forest to see her friends and to practice her magic, to scream the words to make clouds gather and grate, make thunder without rain, make lightning without pain, conjured for no other reason than that she was alive and had magic inside her. The darkness concealed her as she slipped from the castle, swallowing her sighs and the patter of her slippered feet. She was far more afraid of her grandfather and his soldiers and what they would do to her if she were discovered than she was of any of the creatures living in the forest, but she sought solace in the fact that were her magic known, she would be the very thing they *feared the most.*

Often the princess ventured all the way to the dark center of the woods to visit a small group of orphaned maculae known as the Forest Forgotten, the older ones looking after the littlest among them. She brought food and water and other supplies, and helped to build and repair their modest wooden shelters. After the work was done, they played hiding and finding games, laughing as they weaved between the trees, hopping over logs and jumping in the leaves. When at last the children grew sleepy, the princess told them stories.

Someday, *she promised with a wide, trembling smile,* every one of you will live in the palace with me, where we will play all day and dance all night.

This was her life: Princess by day and macula at night.

It was exhausting, being two girls, living two lives. Her little moon heart began to swell, distending with secrets and raw with rage. She wanted to be a princess and she wanted to be free, and what was so wrong with that?

Her life might have gone on like this forever, half of her hidden, but one day a young Immacula with shining black hair and chains around his wrists approached her in the castle hallway alone.

Your Highness? *he said, and her eyes were already drifting away, tracing a mental path to the nearest exit.* My name is—

Excuse me, *she said quickly, picking up her skirts and giving a shallow curtsy. She did not talk to the Immaculae if she could help it, for fear that they would divine her secret if they came too close.* I have to—

Please, I need to talk to you, just for a moment.

She pivoted and made to leave, but then, just loud enough for her to hear, he said, Your Highness, I know you have magic.

At this she stopped. Slowly she turned back around. Obviously this changed things. She stared at him, her mouth, her throat, her heart going dry. He stared back, but she saw no maliciousness in his dark eyes, only an eager desperation, his brows drawn together. He bit his lip as he waited for her answer.

Come with me, *she said, breaking the silence.* Follow at a distance, so that no one sees us leaving together.

Discreetly trailing behind, he followed her out of the hallway and through the castle, all the way to the north wing. It was old and crumbling, the only part of the castle still made of stone. The king had told her never to go there, but she often did anyway, drawn to the dark and the damp. Only once they were alone did the princess stop and look at the boy.

How do you know my secret? *she demanded at once, and he visibly shivered in the chill air of the stone hallway. He glanced around, as if he'd had no idea this part of the castle was there.* Who have you told and what do you want from me?

I have told no one, *he rushed to assure her, rubbing unconsciously at the iron cuffs around his wrists.* I have this ability—I can see a macula's magic through their skin, the slither and the hiss of it. Yours glimmers gold all around you like a halo—the brightest aura I've ever seen.

The princess eyed him for a long moment, thinking of her similar ability to feel a macula's magic through their skin if she touches them. Then she leaned against the wall, exhaling. If you have known since the first time you saw me, why approach me now?

I've tried many times to reach you, *he replied with a small smile,* but you're always running to your room when you see me coming.

Abashed, she began to return his smile, before she remembered herself and forced her expression to remain neutral. Well, so what do you want with me?

She listened, then, as he told her his story, a morose tale of his parents, whose macula hearts had been cut out of their chests, and his undetected maculate sister hidden away in the Hollow, stuck in an attic lest anyone discover her magic.

I am sorry, *she said when he had finished, lowering her eyes and fiddling with the fingertips of her silken gloves.* For you and for them.

Then help me, *he said, taking a small step toward her.* Help my family, and bring down the king.

I've tried again and again to convince him that the maculae are not dangerous, *she said quietly,* but he refuses to believe me. What more can I do without violence? There are curses for those who would harm their kin.

That may be true, *he said, with such sorrowful understanding that her gaze snapped up in surprise.* But the king is not your kin. We, the maculae, are your kin. *I* am your kin. I have two beating hearts, same as you. You are not alone.

She shook her head. When I am queen, I will change things. When I am queen, people will *listen.*

Your Highness, we cannot wait that long.

When next the princess spoke, it was in a whisper. What if my light is not bright enough to sever this darkness? You may think me the sky, but I am only one small star.

The Immacula bowed his head, and lowered to one knee before her. I know you are powerful—I sense it. Together we can change things. *Now,* not later.

Slowly, her breath tangling in her throat, she peeled off her gloves and pressed her hands to his cheeks. At once she felt his magic, sparking, golden and sure, warming her palms and sending a gentle tingle up her arms. She hardly knew him, and yet she found she did not want to let go. No one had ever asked for her help—or offered theirs in return.

You are not alone, *she said to herself, and the words felt false in her mouth, like smoke, like ash, like things long dead. But then she thought again of the manticore, the gray gorgon, and the nymph, who were her friends. She thought of her mother, and of this boy's sister, and she thought of the world she ached to see, all of them free.*

She had no plan, no strategy, and she was not prepared to seal a promise she was not sure she could keep. But maybe, maybe this was a beginning.

I will, *she said to the boy at last.* But not quite yet. Your Highness—

Please. I need just a little more time. I must make preparations and consult with the others of the forest who would fight for our cause. We will fight this war only when we *know* we can win. *She dropped her hands, and already missed his warmth.* It is best if we do not speak again. Not until I call on you. Not until I am ready.

The princess led the Immacula out of the old part of the palace, making him vow he would not return there again, not without her. She hardly knew him, and didn't know if she could trust him—but his vow would have to be enough for now.

He knows my secret, *she thought, and there was something thrilling in this, even as it frightened her that he had the power to reveal her truth to the king. She went back to her room, already thinking of when she would call on the black-haired Immacula again.*

Only, the next day, the princess found her mother in the rooftop temple, laid out on the altar with her throat torn open, the violet wound gleaming like a rain cloud obscuring the moon. Her body exsanguinated, drained of both blood and magic.

The princess screamed, loud, louder, loudest—and once she had started, she could not stop.

Murder, murder, murder.

The king searched in vain for the assassin. Rumors rippled through the city; the princess heard whisperings that the woodland creatures had conspired to kill the future queen, to instigate a war.

The princess heard these rumors but did not know what to think. They would not kill their own. In her grief, she could hardly think straight at all. For days she spoke to no one.

And then, in a trance, the princess confused misted sunlight for bright starlight and a corpulent cloud for a full ivory moon, and she stumbled to the forest not at nightfall but at noon. She pressed her forehead to a tree and scratched at the bark. A wild thing, lost.

That's when she was caught.

It was the eighth day she had lived without her mother. The guards noted her strange behavior, the sparkles on the ground marking her footsteps. The guards fetched the king, and the king then went with his soldiers and the crown prince to the forest, where the soldiers seized her as she slumped against a tree. Their armor glinted in the dull sunlight threading through the clouds, and she knew, though she wore only a simple summer dress of deepest scarlet, that her armor was stronger than theirs.

What is this? *yelled her grandfather.* What is this all about?

The girl raised her palms in the air. Rain fell, swift and silent, tiny cold drops that stuck to her chin and her hands and her neck and her hair, glittering like diamonds on her skin. She opened her mouth, and laughed.

What devilry is this? *Her grandfather slapped her, wiping the sparkly drops from her cheek.* Stop this at once.

She stopped, but only so that she might see his face better, a short white beard and withered blue eyelids, quivering. And his soldiers, unmoving—they didn't scare her. Not anymore. The thing she had dreaded her whole life had finally come to pass, and there was relief in that.

Like all captured maculae, she now had a choice. Except this time, her grandfather made the choice for her. Her father begged the king to reconsider, but his pleas went unacknowledged. Two soldiers held the prince back while another stepped forward with a fire-hot iron and branded the backs of her hands with the mark of the Immaculae: on the right an eye wide open, and on the left an eye shut tight. She screamed as the blistering heat seared through her.

The king said, You are hereby accused of maculacy, which you have hidden for eighteen years, and you will forevermore be inducted into the ranks of your kind. Your royal lineage is now a lie. You are my servant, and shall be so forevermore.

The girl rose to her feet, glistening. There was another lick of laughter crouched in her throat, but this one was black and barbed, and if she let it out, the world would snap in two. A swift severance, a clean seam: magic on one side, majesty on the other. She wanted only to be whole.

You do not understand—I have always been in thrall to you. Tethered to your fear, bound by your hate. I am a princess and a macula both. I have many faces, not just the one I wear day after day, to fool you. I am showing them all to you now. *In the maculate style of making a vow, she put both her hands to her heart.* My magic is like a sunbeam, able to warm and to burn, to illuminate and to blind in equal measure. Under your control I would become a weapon against the forest and the people I love. I will not serve you, and I will not let you use me.

She took a step forward, and the soldiers flinched. Only the king stood tall and firm and unblinking.

From this day on I will be in Graiae Forest, at its very center, under a sleeping spell, *she said, and her father cried out for her not to do this. But the princess pressed on. He couldn't save her now.* The only way to wake me is with a kiss. Yes, just that—a kiss. But know this: Whoever puts their lips to mine must pay a price, and that price is their life. Whoever tries to wake me *will die,* as will anyone whom that person holds dear.

She turned in a circle, staring at the soldiers, who stared straight ahead and did not see her. She turned to her father, who reached for her but could not touch her. Finally she turned to her grandfather. She looked at him, and he looked back. She said, Who will pay the price of a life? Will *you?*

The king said nothing. She knew he would not risk his own life for her, and that was the way she wanted it. She wished only to sleep in peace.

With that, she ran. The soldiers chased her into the woods, but she knew the woods better, and soon she left them far behind.

As she ran she murmured a somnolence spell, one so powerful and old it had a tinge of red magic, like blood spilled on white silk. She whispered all the way to the center, where at last she closed her eyes and collapsed on a bower of brambles and leaves, lush and green. At once they withered to brown and gold,

curling at the edges where her bare skin touched them.
Hair splayed, darker than dirt, hands folded over her
heart, on her back she lay in the quiet, in the darkness,
in a dream.

And in deepest sleep, she smiled.

The Fox Who Is No Fox twisted on his knees to face the Witch.

"Did you like that story?" he said, so gently she thought she might cry, and she did not even know why. She had never cried before, ever. She had no reason to—not in her castle in a dream in the Woods.

The Witch only shrugged. "I enjoyed it some," she said. The ivory enamel of her throne was slick against her spine, wet with her own sweat.

"There's more of the story to tell." He exhaled, shaking the floral crown from his head. "Do you wish to hear it?"

"It grows late," she replied.

"Do you wish for me to stay?" he asked.

The Witch said nothing.

"Do you wish for me to come back?"

The Witch said nothing.

The Fox Who Is No Fox stood, pressed his fingertips beneath the Witch's chin. She did not move. He dropped his hand, but she still felt it, five warm points constellated on her skin. Everywhere else, she was cold.

He left, slowly. Waiting for her to call him back, to bid him to stay.

But she did not.

And, she thought, *I never will.*

A smaller part of her thought, *But maybe, maybe I will.*

The breeze blew and the tree branches shivered and the night was long. It reached on and on and on. The Witch sent the children away. Every single one. Sent them away with empty fists and sores on the insides of their cheeks where melting wishes should have been. Her altar was empty, depleted of scabs and baby teeth and shadows. She could not bear and did not dare to open her heart to them, and she was sickened at the thought of sewing her skin back together. Uneven, ugly stitches, for she had no mirror and she had no help. Save for the foxes, which were loyal but told her no stories, she was alone, all alone, and she wanted to scream, but instead she danced, wobbled, and whirled while the foxes watched. Screams scared people, woke them. Even if the only person around to scare or to wake was herself.

The moon creaked and the stars frowned and the foxes, they lifted their heads and howled. They howled, because she could not.

The Witch of Wishes alone in the Woods could not.

Chapter 12

IN THE DARK

"*What have you done to my sister?*" I demand of the boy in the darkness after everyone else has gone to bed. "Where *is* she?"

"It's all just part of the game," the boy says at once, calmly, as if this is nothing, as if this is normal. As if people disappear from their family's minds and memories every day, yanked like a loose tooth from a bloody mouth, quick and irreversible.

"And if I don't want to play anymore? What then?"

"Then you lose, and you never see your sister again."

My hands trembling so hard that I can barely turn the doorknob, I flee from the attic and slide silently back into my own bed. I toss from side to side, trying to clear my head, forcing myself to think, to *remember*—to remember who he is and where I may have met him before, a boy like smoke clinging to the embers of a fire long gone, with shining black hair and a voice that echoes endlessly in my ears like thunder, soft and sore.

Wait, wait, wait—*shining black hair.* Where did that thought come from? I've never seen him, but suddenly I'm sure—the boy's hair is black and thick and unkempt, and I can picture it perfectly. In my mind's eye I try to adjust my gaze, to force his face into focus, but the space where his features should be stays blank.

Instead, as I grow more and more tired with every passing hour, my mind wanders where it wants, torturing me with *if onlys.* If only I hadn't slept in the attic. If only I hadn't agreed to play the Darkness's wretched game. If only I had told my parents sooner about the sleepwalking, maybe I could've stopped this before I opened the door. Sometimes secrets are secret for a reason, because to know them will hurt us more than to keep them hidden.

Ugliness doesn't need light to exist.

I roll onto my stomach, pressing my face into my pillow. Oh, God—what have I unleashed?

Gabrielle moves from the foot of the bed to curl up next to my shoulder, sharing my restlessness as the night exhales around us, the heat sticking to our skin. Before long I hear Rose stir, and I lie in bed with my eyes closed, pretending to be asleep while she changes into her leotard and tights, coils her hair into a bun, and leaves for class.

When I finally do open my eyes, the room is quiet and the door is closed. Gabrielle yawns and lifts her head from my pillow as I push myself up to sitting, my T-shirt twisted around my waist, only half my hair still tied in a ponytail. The room is dim, and rain runs like liquid fingers drawn down the outside of the window.

Now that Rose is gone, I wish I'd said goodbye before she left.

Before I can stop myself, the thought pops into my head, *Because what if she doesn't come back?*

I grab my phone from the nightstand and send her a text, praying she'll answer as soon as she's done with class, so that I'll know she hasn't been erased from my life, that she still exists where I can see her. When I'm done, I drop the phone onto my bed and go to the bathroom to brush my teeth and wash my face. In the mirror, the line Renata carved into my chest is no longer a line but a gouge, rust brown and bordered by bruises, green and gold. My chest is a moan made visual. A scream.

I stare, but it doesn't vanish; it doesn't morph or molt or melt away. It's real, and it hurts the more I look at it, an itch on an itch on an itch.

"Morning," Raisa says suddenly, squinting sleepily in the open doorway, the thin silver wire of her overnight retainer visible on her top teeth. She slides the retainer out, strings of spit still connected to it as she sidles up to the sink.

"Ew," I say.

"Ew back," she replies, pointing. "That's an *ugly* bruise. What did you do?"

"You can see it too?"

"Uh, *yeah*. Did you think it was one of your visions?"

Despite the soreness, I poke my chest with my fingertips, as if I can remove it by magic. "Um, maybe."

She shrugs, reaching past me for the medicine cabinet, placing her retainer in its sparkly pink case. "Would it have been better if it *was* a vision? Or is it better that it's real, but that you also look like you got punched in the heart a few dozen times?"

"I didn't get *punched*. Renata stabbed me with a sewing needle."

Raisa shuts the cabinet with a magnetic click. "Renata again? Your imaginary friend?"

I stiffen, every muscle in my body tense and aching. Her words, much more than my wound, feel like a few dozen punches to the heart.

"You know what? You're being really rude, and I'm leaving now." I drop my hands and start toward the door, my chest still prickling.

Raisa rolls her eyes. "Well, good, because I need to take a shower."

With Gabrielle following as always, I walk around the house looking for Mom, tiptoeing so as not to disturb the shadows. She told me once that it was okay—cathartic, even—to share when I had a vision that was especially worrisome. My parents' room is empty; only the bed shows signs of life, with rumpled sheets and a scattering of pillows. I poke my head into the tiny laundry room with its starch-and-soap smell, the clunk of wet clothes whirling round and round in the washing machine. The family room is silent, the television turned off and the remote wedged vertically between the couch cushions.

In the kitchen, taped to the microwave is a note in Dad's block handwriting, all caps: WENT OUT FOR ERRANDS. CALL IF YOU NEED ANYTHING. WILL BRING BACK SANDWICHES FOR LUNCH. I LOVE YOU AND YOU AND YOU.

I do the mental math—three *you*s, one for each of his daughters. Although, Rose probably left the house before he did, so maybe the last one is for Mom. There wouldn't be a *you* for Renata, not anymore.

Finally I venture back up the stairs to the bathroom, press my ear against the door, and let my eyes close, an aching exhaustion coming over me even though I just woke up. The water isn't running, so I assume Raisa is already out of the shower. I knock.

"Yeah?" she calls through the door.

"Where's Mom?"

"Hang on." The slap of wet feet on ceramic tile. I barely have time to straighten before the door cracks open and Raisa looks out. She's wrapped in a towel, her silvery-blue hair damp and tangled. "Sorry, what was that?"

"Where's Mom?"

"What do you mean?"

Gabrielle grunts, a half gasp, half choke, and her heart flutters. My own heartbeat begins to accelerate, a compulsive mimicry. Loud enough to be heard over the sudden riot in my ribs, I say, "Do you know if she went out to run errands with Dad, or—"

Raisa scoffs, starts to smile—then stops. "Wait—you're serious?"

I wring my hands in my T-shirt, stretching the bottom hem. "Yeah, I just want to talk to her about—"

"Are you kidding me?" Raisa straightens. "Are you actually kidding me right now?"

"What? No, I—"

"Shut up, Rhea." Her voice is like the audible equivalent of neon lights: garish and mesmeric and ticking with violent color. "I mean, I love you and everything, but you need to shut *up*."

I bring my hands to my face, covering the outer half of each eye, finding it hard to focus on the tantrum of my blood tearing through my body. "Ray, I don't underst—"

"You want to know where Mom is?" she says, and her teeth are as lurid and luminous as car headlights at night on a secluded highway ribboning through the woods, glinting off the deflective white letters of a green street sign: DO NOT ENTER, STOP, BRIDGE MAY BE ICY, NEXT EXIT ONE MILE, U-TURNS PROHIBITED. Her lips are white, white, white. And I am the animal slinking along the shoulder of the narrow gravel road, thinking I am safe and out of sight. Safe, out of sight, until I am awash in her rictus light. "She's in the ground, Rhea. Six feet under. If you want to 'talk' to her, I suggest you either find a psychic medium or start digging."

I'm still looking at her with a gaze half obstructed by my perspiring palms. "Raisa, this isn't funny."

"No," she says. "It isn't, is it?"

No, no, no, no, no.

"Where is Mom?" I shout, stamping my foot, and Gabrielle jumps back. "Where is she, where is she, *where is she*?"

"She's *dead*!" Raisa yells, and I cover my face completely. "She has been for the last six months. Got hit by a car while she was out riding her damn bike, remember? A drunk driver at six in the morning. Does that jog your memory? Now shut up, shut up, shut *up*!"

"*No.* I don't believe you."

"Cool," she sneers. "*Bye.*"

And then she slams the door in my face.

Shaking all over, I stand there and wait for Raisa to reappear, to explain, but she turns on the blow-dryer to its highest, loudest setting, and I know that she will not come back, that the door will not open until she is sure I am gone.

I run down to the kitchen, Gabrielle tripping after me, and rip Dad's note off the microwave. I read it again and again—backward, forward, upside down—then flip it over, as if a secret message will be scrawled on the back.

I LOVE YOU—

Raisa—

—AND YOU—

Rose—

—AND YOU.

Rhea.

"Mom?" I whisper, letting the note fall to the floor and shaking my head.

Wake up, wake up, wake up—

"Mom? Mom! Where are you, where are you, where are you, *where are you?*"

—*shut up, shut up, shut up.*

I walk to the foyer. I could wait, wait for Dad to come home and set things straight.

But how long will that take?

After bursting through the front door, I clamber down the porch steps and skitter across the grass toward the driveway by the side of the house, hurrying toward the detached garage.

124

Dad's car and the van the rest of us share are gone, so I wrangle past the lawn mower, a few folding chairs, and a tangle of dirty jump ropes to get to my bike stored in the back: a fixed-speed mint-green old-timey bicycle with swooping handlebars and a large woven basket affixed to the front. It's dusty and the back tire is a bit flat, but otherwise it's fine. I wheel it out of the garage, into the misty morning air. There are plenty of bloated clouds stuck in the sky, groaning with thunder, but no rain just yet. Though Gabrielle barks a protest, I pick her up and put her into the basket before raising the kickstand and climbing on.

I ride away from the ocean and through the neighborhood where Brett and his friends live, down a main road past a series of shops.

Sweaty, drowsy in the heat and humidity and fog, with steam swirling like ghosts' breath out of the gutters, I try not to notice how the houses sag, how the people in the cars I pass have chunks of their faces missing after every third time I blink.

Like this: one, two, three—*clawed cheek*—one, two, three—*crushed nose*—one, two, three—*torn throat*—one, two, three—

Panting, pedaling, barely obeying traffic signals.

I think, *It can't be true, it can't be true, it can't be true. Can it?*

Where is Renata? Are we all going to disappear, one by one? Will I be the last one left?

I ride along the curb, and my tires splatter muddy puddle water over my ankles and calves. I don't feel real, like I'm wearing borrowed bones and stolen skin. A heart like a rotting apple pinched from a forbidden orchard.

I'm tired, hungry, and everything I pass is dead or dying. Soon it's raining, soft but insistent, and I want nothing more than to turn back, to go to sleep, to wake up again and start over, fresh. But I can't, I know I can't, so even though my knees ache and my lungs strain, I keep going.

I finally arrive at a white church with a slanted steeple and the wrought iron gates of the only cemetery in town, propped open to admit daytime visitors. Gabrielle lifts her head from the bottom of the basket as I pedal down the uneven path that winds through the tombstones and stone angels and marble mausoleums, through the old oaks whose branches bend in the wet wind, thick trees curtsying to the iron clouds. It's not a large cemetery; I can see clear across it, to the busy street on the other side, cars cutting by with their windshield wipers careening across the glass. I ride right for the corner where my grandparents should be buried.

I slide to a stop near their plots, just two square stones set into the ground. More mud joins the gutter sludge already tattooing my legs and arms as I kneel down to the earth and crawl in the sodden shaggy grass. Gabrielle hops out of the basket, shakes the rain off her reddish-orange coat even though more keeps falling. Then I spot it, a nearby grave I don't remember ever seeing before.

I read it once, twice. Again. Again. Fast, slow. Forward, backward, upside down.

Reese Ravenna.

Beloved Mother, Wife, Gardener of Life.

There is no date, but Gabrielle whimpers. I bring the crook of my elbow to my face so that all I can see is a dark crease of skin, threaded with wan green veins.

I keep following my list to avoid screaming: Cover your eyes.

Inhale, slowly.

Exhale, fast.

Blink, three times.

I keep my eyes covered tight, until the scream inside subsides.

But—

The scream, *this* scream—it will never ever, *ever* die.

I bite the inside of my cheeks, hard, as hard as I can, and then—then I dig.

With fists and fingernails, fury and fright, I claw, tear, scratch at the mud, the grass, the grave. I will unbury her if I have to, bone by bone, hair by hair, reanimate her brain and her body. I will bring her back.

Just a little farther.

A little deeper.

A little longer.

My arms become sore and my digging pace slows, but I don't stop. Gabrielle helps, her paws turning tar-black, her teeth gritted, her ears tensed. I want to unscrew the stars and throw them into this mash of grass and earth-guts so that my mother will know which way is up, so she will be reborn in holy light.

I am alone in the cemetery with a mash of mud and worms, with the seething earth. I am alone, and I wish with all my stupid, swollen heart that I weren't.

High overhead there is a choke-spasm of lightning, followed by a cough of thunder, spittle rain bursting from the cloud-crusted lips of the sky. Though it is only early morning, the world is as dark as a moonless midnight. Too dark. Darkest dark. One shadow in particular sticks to the back of my neck, coming closer.

And soon it breathes, and soon it speaks.

"Shhh, my sky, everything is all right."

I slap my fists down into the mud, splattering muck all over myself. "Stop calling me that!" I cry, looking up. As soon as I do, I realize, even though Mom's grave is still in front of me, I am no longer in the cemetery.

I am in the woods.

In the middle of a wide clearing, surrounded by a near-perfect ring of trees, so tall that when I tilt my head back, I can't even make out the tops of them. And I start to think that maybe they have no end, they just go up and up and up, forever, cradling stars like fire-bitten hearts in their branches, and their roots extend from this world into the next and the next and the next. The spaces between them are so black, it is as though nothing, not even air, exists there at all.

But even the trees here are nothing compared to what rises directly in front of me: a castle.

Or, rather, the ruins of one.

A still and sludgy river the color of picked scabs encircling rotted-trunk turrets and a drawbridge dangling on rusted iron hinges, walls of twigs and crinkled red leaves half crumbled and sagging in on one side, crooked crenellations of toppled teeth, yellowed and chipped and spotted with old blood, as if they'd been yanked from the massive mouth of some sickly beast. Large flaps of skin float in the air like dandelion fluff, mixing with the mist hanging like a heavy exhale over my head. A stale, sideways wind blows, as tenuous as a sleepy breath.

Like something out of a dream, a nightmare, both and neither at once.

Entranced, I rise slowly to my feet. The rain thins and eventually stops, but somehow I still hear the rush of traffic just out of sight, tires slicing through slush, the only thing connecting me to reality.

The Darkness's voice comes from behind me now, over my shoulder, next to my ear. I'm not sure if he's really here, or if he's part of the vision too.

"Go inside," he says. "Go and see."

I take one step and then stop, hesitant. Because this, this looks exactly like somewhere a witch would live. A palace in the woods.

"Go on, my sky," the Darkness softly urges. "I'm right here at your side."

"I want to see you," I whisper, my heart beating terribly loud and achingly slow, as tremulous as the hush of the world awaiting a storm. When I turn in the direction of his voice, there is no one there, just a thick, impassable shadow. "I don't want to be alone."

"You aren't," he says. "I'm here; I'm always here."

Blinking rain out of my eyes, I stare at the castle, and I am so, so tired. And soaked. And hungrier than ever. And restless, like I want to tear the whole world apart. But also like I want to sleep and sleep and never wake up, forever.

I walk.

Across the clearing, over the swaying drawbridge, and beneath the raised portcullis.

"Through here," says the Darkness, and I follow the smoke trail of his voice, mesmerized, as he leads me around corners and down hallways with large gaps in the branches of the walls. Rain still drips off my hair and into my eyes as he takes me farther and farther away—from the cemetery, from my mother's grave, deeper into this chilling, thrilling dream, and I do not look back. Not even once.

"Here we are," he says at last, and a pair of double doors before me opens as if of their own accord. "It is okay to be afraid," he says, and I step inside.

A round, open room with columns of twisted vertebrae set into the walls and no ceiling, revealing a sky so low that I can't be sure it's a sky at all. Whatever it is, it glows. It glows, but its light doesn't reach me, and I can't tell if it's morning or midnight or somewhere in between, the whole swath of it a sprained shade of green, and encrusted with dim, deflated stars arranged in a crooked constellation not unlike the tattoo on Dad's back. A spindly hand, reaching for something it cannot have.

It is dark, dark, except for the glitter stuck in the ground like rocks, but more so, like strange almost-diamonds degenerating back into something that is not quite coal, something hot, something that looks and sounds a lot like secrets, secrets in a tangible, physical form.

But there is not only glitter on the ground, I realize—there are also hands. Skeleton hands. Lots of them.

"What happened here?" I breathe, looking down at the discarded finger bones, knuckles, and wrists, brittle and broken, some of them snapped into so many pieces as to be barely recognizable. "What is this place?"

As if in answer, an echo spills from the sky, as soft as spider-steps, words strung like water drops on a web, glistening a moment before plunging to the earth, too heavy for the thin silk to withstand: *Wake up.*

Forcing my gaze away from the floor, I notice then a large, tall tooth carved into the shape of a throne, split clean down the middle, as if cleaved by lightning. I didn't see it at first, so densely is it draped in shadow. I drift toward it slowly, bones cracking beneath my feet.

"Careful, Rhea Ravenna," the Darkness says from near the entranceway, as if he's willing to venture only so far into this forsaken space. "Do not touch anything."

"Why? It's not real anyway," I say, stopping before the dais. I had some vague idea of sitting down, but now that I'm in front of the throne I don't even want to be near it. Its enameled surface is as smooth and shiny as the whites of an eye, and I feel instinctively that if I were to touch it, something in me might burn, might blister, might die.

Running my hands through my wet, mud-splattered hair, I turn away, to face the center of the room.

And what I see is this, something that was not there just a moment before: a coffin.

A coffin raised on a wooden bier, and made entirely of glass.

And it's not empty.

"Mom?" I move toward it, cautious at first but then fast, faster, fastest, sprinting to reach her. "Mom!"

As soon as I come close enough, I see that I was wrong. There is no figure inside. Just flowers.

The lidless coffin is filled with roses, and every one of them is red.

"You didn't tell me," I hiss at the Darkness, my eyes on the roses and nothing else. A screech of thunder like a grinding jaw, and the branches of the walls begin to writhe, entangle. "You didn't tell me that playing your game would make my sister disappear and make my mom suddenly be dead."

Silence.

"This is not my doing," he whispers. I reach for a rose as if hypnotized, my heart slamming against my sternum in warning. "It's— Wait, Rhea, *don't*—"

Too late. I wrap my hand around a stem and pull with all my strength.

But the rose doesn't budge.

Instead a row of five thorns digs into my palm, pricking me so hard, it draws blood, a crescent of pain. I wrench my hand back, with a curse and a cry, a ribbon of blood dripping down and encircling my wrist.

That's when the screaming starts.

More feverish and urgent than I've ever heard it. I clap my hands over my ears, smearing blood against my cheek. The walls twist and grate in earnest now, and the ground seems to clench like a muscle, tautening beneath my feet. The sky tears down the middle, and the glitter chips in the ground turn blue, then violet, then black. The columns lean and crash into one another, gouging holes in the frenzied walls. I watch all this with wide, wide eyes, dizzy and entranced.

A dream can't hurt me.

Can it?

An arm slides behind my knees, and another wraps around my back—and then I am being lifted, up off my feet, tucked tightly against a chest I can't see. The Darkness holds me against him, and then—he runs.

Through the doors and down the halls, over the wildly undulating drawbridge and out of the dead and dying castle, back to the clearing where he found me. I expected him to feel like stone, inflexible, but his skin is warm and soft, his bones protruding in little knots and lines beneath a thin layer of muscle. I press my face into his neck, and his pulse there feels more like a flinch than a beat.

Why does your heart sound like an apology? I think. *What are you sorry for?*

He sets me down, and I sink to my knees, Gabrielle licking my cheek. *Gabrielle*—why didn't she enter the forest with me? I wrap my arms around her and pull her close, water in my eyes, and I realize that it's raining again. I wipe the tears with the back of my hand and blink at my surroundings, at the neat rows of tombstones and sculpted angels watching over them, the black fence separating the cemetery from the sidewalk and the road beyond, the perpetual rattle of traffic.

Somewhere nearby there are loud footsteps splashing in the unrelenting rain, and I wonder what other lonely soul is out here in the storm, crying tears that are immediately washed away.

"Are you here?" I whisper, hoping the Darkness is still near, gripping Gabrielle's fur as I wait.

"Rhea?" a voice yells, but it is not the Darkness. Someone splashes through the cemetery, and even though I knew it was him by his call, it's still a shock to see Dad standing there, holding up a big blue umbrella. "Rhea, what are you *doing*?"

I open my mouth but nothing comes out.

"Raisa called." Dad crouches down, shielding me with the umbrella, his shoes drowning in mud. "She said I might find you here. She said you were upset."

"Mom is . . . gone?"

Dad nods, resting a hand on my shoulder and squeezing.

"No," I say. *"No."*

"Let's talk about this at home," Dad says gently, lifting me by my arm. "You can have a nice hot bath, and relax."

I let him lead me away, my clothes suctioned to my skin, cloaked in muck from head to toe. When I inspect my injured hand, uncurling my fingers from a fist, the wounds are still there—five little punctures, curved like a wolf-bite, bitter and red as a rose.

Dirty pajamas, stiff with dried mud. Damp hair, runny nose. My legs are scrunched to my chest. The rain has stopped but the clouds remain, the sky looking the way my eyes feel after

I've cried—salt-stiff and puffy and shining. I sit on the ground in the center of Mom's small garden, facing the sparse trees rimming the backyard, staring at a crow perched on a high branch. He blinks back at me as if he recognizes me but is hesitant to say so until he is sure. Gabrielle sits at the base of the tree, her gaze stuck to the bird, tail tensed with elated voracity, even as the crow ignores her completely, unthreatened. I clench my jaw to keep my teeth from chattering.

To call this a garden is generous. It's now just a patch of naked earth, marred by scars of prickly green weeds, the bristled heads of dandelions bobbling on skinny stems. I keep waiting for them to transform back into flowers, into bright leafy gems, but they don't.

I keep waiting for the dream-haze to drain out of my head, to feel like I'm real again, but it doesn't and I don't.

The only thing keeping me from falling asleep is the sting in my chest, like fresh jabs of the needle, ripping me open again and again.

"Rhea?"

The crow flaps away, making no sound, and I turn toward the house. Dad stands in the doorway, peering out. He's been checking on me every twenty minutes since he found me in the cemetery and drove me home, the promised sandwiches on the backseat. He crammed my bicycle into the trunk while Gabrielle sat curled in my filthy, damp lap.

"You'll catch your death," he says now, crossing his arms over his chest.

"I don't care."

Raisa steps up behind him, her chin jutting just over his

shoulder. Rose is there too. She's on tiptoe, peering at me over the top of his untidy head.

"She made waffles." I scoot my legs in tighter, thighs pressed to my chest, trying to be as small as possible. "Just two days ago. You ate some, Dad, right at the kitchen table. And then you had a sword fight with the silverware."

Raisa groans. "Come on, Ree. Stop it now."

I have eyes only for my father, who pinches the soft skin on the underside of his chin and looks at me. "Did you win the duel, Dad, or did she?"

He says nothing.

And nothing.

And nothing.

I shrug, turning back around so I won't have to see that gaunt, haunted look on his face, or the warning in Raisa's lifted eyebrows, or the idle distraction I don't know how to construe in Rose, who bites her lip and glances away.

"Oh, well," I say. "I guess it was a draw."

Chapter 13

IN THE WOODS

Spider-bite midnight: an infected emerald sky strung with clumps of silk-woven stars, a cobweb moon. The Witch of Wishes had conscripted an army of arachnids to decorate the universe for her that night.

She rested on her back on top of the empty stone altar in the glade, with the Fox Who Is No Fox sprawled beside her, a soft, thick blanket beneath them. Their knees were bent like pyramids pointed straight up, so close that they touched and held each other up, her right thigh against his left. A piece of her hair was pinned beneath his bare shoulder, the rest of it spread around her head like black fire.

"Tell me," she said, "about what happened after the magic princess put herself to sleep."

The Fox Who Is No Fox blinked up at the poisoned green sky and continued his story, quiet and clear:

Deep in Graiae Forest, the princess slept, on and on and on. She lay in the deepest and darkest part of the woods, where even the stars would not allow their light to flow, and for a long time, no one came.

The Immacula who had spoken to her in the north wing might have gone to her side, but he had been sentenced to languish in the dungeons indefinitely. Unbeknownst to the princess, he had been there that day, in the woods, when she had cast the sleeping spell. Roused by the commotion of the guards, he'd followed the king and his soldiers all the way to the woods' edge. When the princess had fled into the forest, he had given chase with a mind to stop her—to help her, to hide her, anything but that she should place an irreversible curse upon herself. But the soldiers had snared him before he could catch her. Accused of conspiring with the princess against the crown, he'd been spared only because he excelled in the enigmatic magic of necromancy, and the king knew that his only known necromancer was far too valuable to kill.

All this time the necromancer had wished only for freedom—freedom he'd thought the princess could grant. But now, because of his foolishness, he would never know freedom. Neither would his sister, who'd lived in hiding in the Heartless Hollow with their magicless parents since the day they had been caught a year before.

He would never forget the choice they each had

had to make, the way his mother had clasped her
palms to his eyes while the king's ichoromancer had
plunged her shimmering hands into his father's chest,
reaching through skin and muscle and bone, through
his human heart, and then closed her fist around its
center. But not even his mother's trembling hands
could conceal his father's screams, or the tang of
burnt blood he could somehow taste on his tongue.
And he remembered how, when it was done, his father
had clutched the boy's shoulder for support while the
ichoromancer had performed the same mutilation on
his mother. The boy had watched without shield this
time as the ichoromancer had yanked his mother's
small macula heart out, for a moment shining like
silver in her slick palm before it had crumbled into
dust, gone.

Forever after, he could not understand nor accept
his parents' decision to surrender the chance for
freedom. For though he was now an Immacula,
living in a glass tower with a whole host of other
Immaculae, being used by the king when he needed
something—a bewitched weapon for some skirmish
with a foreign territory, or to heal a stubborn illness,
or to resurrect the dead loved ones of those who could
afford to pay for a private session—well, at least, even
then, he still had his magic, even if he could not use it
for himself.

He knew he might never see his family again,
except for his sister, an oneiromancer hiding in a

musty attic, who had managed to escape on the day
the others had been caught a year before, and who had
sought refuge with the Forest Forgotten until it had
been safe to join their parents in the Heartless Hollow.
Every night since he'd become a prisoner, they'd met
in their dreams. She reached out to him while he slept
and wrenched him away with her to a place where
they could be alone, if only for a few hours.

A dream-walker, that's what she was—not to
be confused with a dream-designer, a rare kind of
oneiromancer with magic so powerful that they could
create new *dreams—*

Here, the Witch huffed, short and sharp. She'd been listening closely, concentrating so hard on his words that her forehead wrinkled, an ache creeping from temple to temple.

"Enough of this boy and his sister," she said. "I want to
know what happened to the *princess*. This is a story about
her, yes?"

"Not *only* about her," said the Fox Who Is No Fox. "There
are many others who—"

He stopped at another terse sigh from the Witch. He tilted
his chin back to the sky and continued:

Right away the king sent his men to watch the
princess's sleeping form, so if anyone wanted to

revive her, they would find their path through the forest considerably more dangerous than usual, as the soldiers' orders were to kill on sight anyone who attempted to approach.

Even her own father dared not wake her. If he were the one to interrupt her rest, then the princess would die too. Whoever tries to wake me *will die*, as will anyone whom that person holds dear.

Days passed, and the crown prince did nothing but pace the castle corridors from dawn to dusk, gnashing his teeth and sliding deeper into grief. He neglected his royal duties and ignored the king, who tried in vain to calm him, to control him. The crown prince had known all along that his wife and his daughter were maculae, keeping their secret hidden with the promise to change things as soon as he sat on the throne. But now that what he had feared most had come to pass, with both his wife and daughter beyond his reach, he could not even convince the king to make an exception for the princess, to let her live a free life as if her secret had never been revealed.

Erasing minds is beyond my power, *the king said.* Even if I pardoned her, the people would never accept her as their princess. Not now that they know what she is.

Then banish her to the forest, release her to the wilds! *The prince paced before the throne, fuming. He was the heir, wasn't he? And yet, he was powerless to*

*save his own family. How would he someday defend
a whole country when he had failed to shield his
daughter from his own father?* Disown her, deny her,
send her away—anything but this.

But the king only sighed. It is too late.

*So the prince raged and mourned and walked
a thousand miles without ever leaving his castle,
wandering the halls like a phantom. But soon his
despair began to look like something else, something
like determination. All this magic had him thinking
strange and sticky thoughts:* I can't save my daughter
right now, but what about my wife? *The dead queen
lay entombed in the castle temple, before the altar of
the Wandering One, a god whose left hand symbolized
life, and the right hand death. Under cover of night, a
week after the princess's curse, the prince summoned
the necromancer from the dungeons.*

*The necromancer said his spell, and the dead
queen opened her eyes—but something was wrong.
Her lips were rose-red again, her skin flushed and
her lungs gaping, greedily gathering air. Though her
awed husband stood by her as she awoke, clasping her
unstiffening hand, she could not focus on him, did not
even seem to know he was there. Her eyes closed, and
her heart slowed—but did not stop.*

*Before the prince could even kiss her newly warmed
lips, she slipped into sleep, dreamless and deep. And
though he tried, he could not wake her—not with a
touch or a cry or a mighty shake of her shoulders.*

A sleep like living death had taken her, just as it had taken their daughter.

The prince was distraught, but the necromancer had suspected something like this might happen.

She needs magic, *he said.* Without her natural magic, she will never truly return to herself.

The prince did not divert his gaze from his wife, not once, not ever. How does she get new magic?

The necromancer hesitated. She will need time to restore it. *And this was true—but only for a healthy macula. If someone used too much magic in a day, they would fall tired, and only a long sleep would return them to normal. But if, like the queen, they'd been drained of their blood and their magic entirely— then they were dead. The only hope of the queen coming back to life relied upon new magic being given to her. The necromancer also thought of the very rare spell to transfer magic between maculae—but the spell made the allocation permanent, and he did not know if such a spell would work, so he pushed all these thoughts aside. He feared the prince would command him to gift his magic to the unconscious queen, and to defy the prince was to defy the king—neither was worth his life.*

So the prince, without knowing the whole truth, sent the necromancer away, re-clasping the boy's chains before the guards led him back to the dungeons. The wearied necromancer met his sister in a dream that night and—

"Is that it, then?" The Witch pushed herself to sitting. "What of the dead queen? What of the cursed princess? Is that the end of the tale? With everyone falling asleep?"

The Fox Who Is No Fox sat up too. Their shoulders touched, just barely, and his skin felt like smoke against hers, smooth and singeing. "That is not the end."

"What, then? Does anyone even try to wake the princess?"

The Fox Who Is No Fox stared straight ahead, sucking in his pallid cheeks. She eyed the swirl of scars on the backs of his hands.

"Yes," he said, "yes. Two, in fact. The nymph and the gray gorgon. But for that, we will need another night."

The Witch said nothing, only staring at her homespun sky. The web of the moon had sagged under the weight of a captured comet, a squirming skein of fire hissing like a fly in a snaggle of shimmering strings. The envy-green venom was fading, like a bruise almost healed. The spiders themselves skirted the horizon, slumped with exhaustion.

The Fox Who Is No Fox looked at her. "Do you wish for me to stay?"

The Witch said nothing.

Finally he sighed, and stood. "Do you wish for me to come back?"

Still the Witch said nothing.

"Until tomorrow, then."

He walked to that place at the edge of the forest where the children and the foxes whirled between worlds. It was so *easy* for them, wasn't it? To bounce back into the kaleidoscopic crush of their own lives, worlds with a sun that rose on its own; and trees that did not talk to the wind; and a sky so high, they were unlikely ever to touch it.

For her such a dizzying quest was not possible. She could not leave, and she did not want to. No, she did not.

But she could have stories, and it was almost the same. It was almost like leaving, just for a little while.

"Wait," the Witch said. "Please."

The Fox Who Is No Fox stopped.

"Yes?" he asked.

And the immutable, curious, indefatigable Witch said, "Stay."

Crossing the clearing, he knelt down before her. Without looking up, he murmured, "I will stay as long as you wish."

Chapter 14

IN THE DARK

After a long warm bath and hours of staring at the ceiling in bed, I decide that the only way forward is to win this mad game I've agreed to play. And for that I will need a hint.

I wait for everyone else to sleep, and then I climb up to the attic, the rain gentle against the roof and the windows, barely audible, sounding the way a tingle feels as it slides along your scalp. A liquid lullaby, and I wish it would stop; I wish the whole world would stop for a moment so that I could catch my breath.

But the world never stops and wishes don't work that way, not without candles or a star or a dandelion.

Everyone in the house is asleep, even Gabrielle. Only I am awake, and the Darkness is too. Before I've even reached the top of the stairs, I hear him, breathing. Breathing and pacing, back and forth across the small space in the attic, waiting for me.

I stop before I cross the threshold.

"Hello again, Rhea Ravenna." A pause, and then, much more quietly: "I wasn't sure you'd come."

"How could I not? You are the only one who can help me." Lingering in the darkened doorway, I jam my thumb into each of the five little punctures in my palm, hard, over and over, and the pain feels like the opposite of hunger, the annihilation of it, filling me up now and for always so that I need never eat anything but my own anger ever again, as addictive and delicious as an apple marked *For the fairest one of all.*

"I know this is terrifying for you," the boy says gently. "But it *will* end. All things end, eventually. Even the very best of stories. And the worst of them too."

"Were you there with me today?" I ask, tucking a clean strand of hair behind my ears as a covert gesture for wiping away a tear. "In the cemetery? Were you with me in the woods?"

"Yes," he says, "and no."

"Which is it?"

"I am part of you, Rhea." The knob at the end of the bedpost shrieks as he twists it in its loose socket, around and around and around. "I go where you go. I stay where you stay. I'm lost when you're lost, and I'm found only when you find yourself."

"But what *are* you exactly? Are you like me? Do you dream when you're asleep, or when you're awake? Are we the same?"

It is a few seconds before he responds. "It is like this: If I am a single star, in a single galaxy, then you—you are the whole endless sky."

"You are no star," I snap, and I can barely speak around the incredulity clogging my throat. "The very last thing I would call *you* is *bright*. Tell me the truth."

He sighs. "Can I tell you a story? Then you will see. Then you will know."

Instead of answering, I take a step toward him.

"Can you see death?" I whisper, wondering, hoping, dreading. "Do people decay before your eyes? Have you ever had a vision of your own corpse, rotting at your feet?"

He says nothing.

Not even a sigh.

Not even a breath.

"No. I do not," he murmurs. "The opposite, actually."

The unexpectedness of this confession knocks me off balance. I step back, wrapping my arms around my waist as the anger drains out of me, leaving me exhausted. I have no idea what he means, but I know by now there's only one way to find out.

"The story you want to tell," I say. "What is it about?"

His words come fast, faster than I've ever heard him speak, as if he's afraid I'll change my mind and run away. "It's a story about the Witch in the Woods."

It hurts to breathe, and it hurts not to.

I thought I dreamed her.

And I did.

"So there *is* a witch?" I ask.

"There was," he says.

"I've heard her," I whisper. "Screaming."

The Darkness shakes his head. "The Witch never screams."

"But I heard her."

"No. That sound was coming from inside you."

At this, I take a tiny step back. As I do, I hear a sound coming from below, like dull footfalls slinking down the hallway.

"Okay," says the Darkness, oblivious. "Let's start with—"

"Wait." I hold up a hand, gesturing for him to be quiet. The sound isn't *like* footsteps—it *is* footsteps. Not loud enough to wake anyone else in the house, but clunky enough to reach me through the hush.

Could it be Renata? Mom?

I drop my hand. "I have to go."

The Darkness shifts. "What?"

"I'll be back."

Before he can protest, I find the top step and close the attic door behind me, then dash down the stairs as quietly as I can. My socks slipping off my heels, I rush into the hallway.

A dark figure at the far end startles, turning. I blink, my gaze sifting through the mundane darkness, and soon I see that it is not Renata or Mom but a silhouette with hair parted into two tight braids, a long silver chain glimmering around her neck in the weak light from the hallway windows. Wearing a tank top and skinny jeans and a frayed backpack.

Raisa.

"Where are you going?" I tug at my T-shirt, feeling that peculiar skin-sliding sensation again. "Are you sneaking out?"

I think she might start yelling at me like she did earlier, might tell me to shut up, shut up, *shut up*—but she only looks at me like she doesn't know me. For so long she looks and looks, until I start to think that both of us are dreaming and we've somehow stumbled into each other's heads.

And then she raises her hand, taps her fingertip against her temple. Once. Twice. Lets her finger curl slowly into the rest of her fist, hovering there next to her cheek.

"When—" A thistle of dread scratches and tears all the way down my throat as I swallow. "When will you be back?"

"Never," she says simply. "Never ever."

I almost expect her to disappear in a puff of pink smoke, to spin three times and vanish, to evaporate in a flash of light. Something dazzling, something dramatic.

She doesn't, though. She simply turns and clomps down the stairs, backpack bouncing against her tailbone, her hand sweeping the banister. The click of the front door unlatching and then refastening echoes through the house.

I sprint after her, nearly tripping headfirst down the stairs. I will bring her back. I will make her stay.

But when I open the door, she's gone.

I hurry onto the porch, careful not to tumble down the steps. The rain has stopped but the ground is still wet. Out on the lawn, I look around, straining to see.

"Raisa?"

No one answers.

"Raisa?"

Never ever.

It should not be this easy for people to vanish. Disappearing should be difficult, rough and bloody. They should have to claw, tear, rip their way out, enduring some of the torment felt by the person left behind. There should be firecrackers bursting in their eyes; and stars snagging in their skin; and lightning bolts tangling in their hair, thrust under their fingernails. Explosions, abrasions, shudders, and shouts.

Disappearing forever should not just be the quick and quiet opening and closing of a door.

I stand on the front lawn, curling my bare toes into the wet grass, and stare into the stupid, ordinary darkness that has stolen my sister from me, maybe forever, darkness that has opened its moon-toothed mouth and guzzled her whole.

I gaze into the darkness, and this is what I see: two shadows edged in silver, twisting, twirling, mist trailing from their fingertips, from their glazed and open lips. Pulsing, joints popping, a rush, a release. Floating, spinning to the rhythm of the heartbeat they share, breaking apart and coming together again and again.

Not a vision, exactly, nothing so garish, so convincing. More like a memory.

An echo.

A scar.

They dance on the air in front of me, their glow growing crisper, clearer with each step, and I reach out to touch them, curious whether they are made of liquid, or wind, or light, or something else altogether, something that cannot be changed or contained or destroyed. But just then the porch light snaps on, and the figures fade into the night as I jump, turning so fast toward the house that I nearly fall over.

Someone stands in the open doorway. It takes me a second to work out who it is, still half dazzled by the dancing shadows.

"Rose! You scared me!" I cry, my heart skittering as I regain my balance. "What are you doing? How long have you been standing there?"

Peering around the doorframe, she blinks once, twice, still half asleep. Her hair is long and loose, and there is a thin sheen of sleep-sweat on her chin, her cheeks, her forehead. "Only a second or two."

A tingle twines up my spine, and I wait for her to leave; I'm impatient to glimpse the ghostly figures again, certain that I could never tire of watching them, so long as I lived.

But the seconds drift by, and Rose doesn't leave.

Instead she holds out her hand, her elbow cracking as her arm extends. She says nothing, but she doesn't need to. I sigh, quietly so she won't hear, and then I cross the short space between us, step up onto the porch, and slip my hand into hers.

The pain is immediate and immense, much more than it should be from such a simple touch. It's the sores on my palms—they itch, and they *hurt,* searing like stars set into my skin, a true and ancient omen in the shape of a scythe fated to cut my world apart. A sudden, strange thought: *From now until the end of time, will I burn everything I touch?*

I look quickly at Rose, but if she takes notice, she doesn't show it; she doesn't seem to even feel a thing from this un-likely wound I received in a dream that was not quite a dream.

A dream can't hurt me, though.

Can it?

A realization like a hiccup, convulsive: I never thanked the Darkness.

I never thanked him for carrying me safely out of the not-woods.

I have to go back, I think, tremulous with something like sleeplessness, something like the urgency of hunger. *I have to hear his story. I have to—*

"Come to bed," Rose says, squeezing my hand as I try to pull it away. She keeps on squeezing and does not let go. "Please—I don't want to be alone."

One last time I glance back at the ordinary darkness, in the direction Raisa went—but now there's nothing there. I nod to Rose and let her lead me inside, shutting the door behind us. It closes without a sound.

Up the stairs and to our room; Gabrielle is snoring at the foot of my bed. The window curtains are closed tight, and Rose's night-light is practically as bright as a second moon.

"Can we unplug it?" I ask, pointing. "Just this once?"

"Okay," she whispers, and watches while I yank it out of the socket, drop it onto the carpet. Better, but still—it is not enough. It is not *my* darkness.

As soon as she's asleep, I tell myself. *Back to the attic.*

But then: swiftly, silently, she slides into bed next to me, the way she used to before we were both too big to fit comfortably, drawing detailed pictures on the other's back with our fingernails, scratching messages into soft skin for hours, too restless to sleep; or during a storm, giggling and whispering, *That was an angel tripping up the stairs,* after each thunder-scrape that sounded the way a skinned knee feels. Or when I woke shivering with visions already fading, Rose pulling a blanket over both of us as she climbed in beside me. Somehow she always knew when I needed her.

And sometimes she insisted even when I didn't.

I scoot as far to the edge of the bed as possible without tumbling overboard, on my back with my face straight up to the ceiling. The side of her bare calf touches mine, smooth and cold, so cold that I don't know how she stands it.

In this dark I see color, smears of it, red and blue and violet, iridescent. Exactly like a butterfly's wings.

"Do you believe me when I say that there's the boy in the attic?" I whisper, wanting at least one person I trust to tell me it's all going to be okay, to reassure me that whatever I released when I opened the door can be contained and locked back in again. To tell me that I can win this game. "Do you believe me when I say that our family is disappearing?"

She doesn't answer, and I start to think maybe she's already sleeping.

But her breathing is jagged, and her legs are so tense and motionless, like she doesn't want me to sense that she's still awake.

"Do you?" I ask, but again there is no answer.

Until morning we lie here, my sister and I, side by side, each waiting for the other to fall asleep first.

Chapter 15

IN THE WOODS

The Witch of Wishes took the Fox Who Is No Fox by the hand and led him into her castle, pulled him onto the dais.

"Sit," she said, pointing to her throne.

He sat. He stared up at her, waiting for her next command. It didn't come.

She stood beside him and said nothing for so long, looking up through the open roof at the spiders as they clambered home to the trees, that finally he hooked one arm around her waist and settled her sideways on his lap, her legs draped over his knees. The Witch stiffened, and he held his breath.

This, the Witch thought, *is the safest place in all the worlds.*

And then she sighed, sighed and let her head fall against his shoulder. The scream in her throat relented, retreated, and the bone bloom in her heart closed its red petals. The Witch breathed against his skin, in and in and in. He smelled like a wish that you think is finally about to come true. Sweet and sharp. Apples and cinnamon. She crushed herself more tightly against him, edging ever closer.

"Speak," she whispered into the cradle of his neck, breathing out and out and out.

Except for the necessary rise and fall of his chest, the blink of his eyes, the beat of his heart, the Fox Who Is No Fox did not move, as if the slightest disturbance would be enough for the Witch to change her mind and order him away. His arm around the small of her back, he told the next stretch of his story.

While the prince was sequestered in the temple, waiting by the queen's side, the first inklings of revolt percolated outside the palace walls. The dissenters gathered near the center of Graiae Forest, just on the other side of the narrow river where the princess slept.

We must find a way to break the curse, *said the manticore who had introduced the princess to the woods.* We cannot abandon our friend.

She made a choice, *said the sylph who had taught the princess the incantation to change the direction of the wind, a fast whorl of words that the obstinate air would often ignore.* I think we should respect that choice, even if we disagree with it.

But what of the king? Perhaps this is a chance to depose him once and for all, *argued the manticore.*

This is not our war, *said a deep-voiced sphinx.* We don't bother the king, and he doesn't bother us. Why should we insert ourselves into the affairs of humans?

The manticore lifted her head. If we have a chance to make the woods safe for *everyone*, then I think we should take it.

Eventually it was decided to let sleeping sovereigns lie, but they would plan a first attack against the king. Meanwhile the princess's best friends, the gray gorgon and the nymph, were devising schemes of their own. Because they were young, they were left out of the war council, and so they rebelled in the biggest way they could think of: they were going to take back their princess.

They skipped and they giggled and they leaped and they sang, hand in hand, all the way to the place where the trees had teeth and the thirsting brambles slashed their shins and licked the blood dribbling down around their ankles.

When they reached the floating bridge spanning the narrow river, they stopped. Twenty men guarded the glade. The girls turned to each other, their eyes perfectly adjusted to the undying dusk surrounding them.

Half and half? *suggested the gorgon with a nod toward the guards ahead, and her friend the nymph nodded, combing her long sea-foam hair with her fingers.* Meet me by the princess when you're through.

They crossed the bridge and separated, the nymph with quiet footsteps and a shy smile, while the gorgon took great care to let the soldiers know exactly where she was as she approached: cracking twigs, breaking branches, humming a melody somewhere between dismay and desire.

Who's there? said the men, blindly spinning in her direction as she weaved through the trees, raising their guns. Who are you?

Oh, be quiet, *she said sweetly, and the soldiers went silent. The lightning-glint behind her eyes was the last sight they saw before they dissolved into harmless shadows, blending in with the dim.*

Have you ever heard of calenture? *asked the nymph on the other side of the glade, and the men nearest her quirked their heads and listened, delirious in the dark. She picked one first with a cut across his nose, fresh ruby red. He couldn't have been more than seventeen, and as soon as she saw him, she thought her heart would rupture.* It's when you spend so long at sea that you start seeing things that aren't there. It's the same in the dark. And there is nowhere on earth darker than it is right here.

She began walking backward, boldly but slowly winding through the trees. And he followed, of course, drunk on the satiny stream of her voice.

What are you seeing, silly soldier? A maiden with ceramic skin and hair like the wind, silky and warm? Or a creature with saltwater veins, and teeth so sharp, they could split diamonds into dust?

She led him to where the black river rushed in a ring around the clearing, surging swiftly and silently. Murmuring all the while, she stepped backward into

*the water, wrinkling its sable surface, treading deeper
and deeper until her scaly feet no longer touched
bottom. The soldier drifted after her.*

What are you seeing, my sweetmeat, my love? *She
laughed and laughed and laughed, and the soldier
opened his mouth as if he could eat the sound. Once
the water was up to his heart, the nymph stopped and
treaded toward him instead of away. She pressed her
body against his, wrapping her legs around his hips.* A
glossy-cheeked girl with plump lips and a thin waist,
or a famished little fairy with pearl-ivory eyes and
clamshell knees? Tell me, my dear, what do you see?

*Then she clasped the back of his head with
both webbed hands and dragged him down until he
drowned.*

It doesn't matter which one you see, *she said after,
as she laid his limp form along the shore. She leaned
down near his unhearing ear, and she wept and she
wept and she wept with such glee.* It doesn't matter,
she whispered, because *both* girls are me.

*When she had a collection of slick bodies lined up
on the shore, the nymph joined her friend, who was
kneeling by the princess.*

She's so beautiful, *the nymph breathed, tears dry
on her cheeks, reaching to touch the princess's black
tresses tangled up in the leaves of her bed. But then
the nymph retracted her hand, as if the curse might be
contagious.* But she looks so sad.

The princess's eyes twitched behind her lids at the

sound of their voices. The gorgon rested her head on her friend's shoulder and sighed. We won't kiss her, as that's not what she wants, *said the nymph.*

The gorgon nodded. Yes, we won't wake her.

What shall we do? *mused the nymph.*

We'll stay here. We'll watch over her while she rests.

The nymph grinned. This time when she reached out, she did not withdraw at the last moment. She touched her fingers to the princess's wrist, to the feverish flutter of her pulse.

We are your guardians now, *the nymph vowed.* We will keep you safe.

And they did—for a little while.

When the first set of guards stationed near the princess failed to return to the castle, the king dispatched another corps, and then another when neither the second nor third came back. And though he did not trust the boy, with the fourth set of soldiers, the king sent the infamous necromancer.

The girls tried to stop him, but the boy was quick and clever. At once he raised the decomposing bodies of the drowned soldiers and reassembled the scattered cells of the shadow-men, rendering the girls outnumbered. The gorgon's eyes could not flash fast enough, and the nymph's voice was not quite sweet enough to subdue so very many men at once. Soon they were caught, and a blindfold was tied over the gorgon's eyes as they were led in chains to the crystal castle. The nymph begged for water, her lips crinkled and white, but her pleas went unacknowledged.

The king knew now that sometimes the dead had a habit of rising again, so he did not have these girls murdered for their crime—but they were imprisoned. For them he fashioned a unique kind of incarceration, one that could not exist without magical aid. And there was no way out, and no one to rescue them.

It was here that the Fox Who Is No Fox stopped.

Jarred by his sudden silence, the Witch opened her eyes, and was met with the sight of a smooth, empty sky: colorless and clear, wiped clean of comet-catching moons and crooked silk-snare stars. She did not seem to know when her eyes had first closed. She did not seem to know when her eyelids had then clenched, squeezing so tightly that they had trembled, hypnotized by this fairy story that was no fairy story, just as he had promised.

"Well," said the Witch, blinking fast, "and how did they get out?"

The Fox Who Is No Fox tilted his head toward her and spoke softly into her hair. "They didn't."

The Witch swallowed around the scream resurfacing in her throat, wedging there like powder in the barrel of a gun. "What do you mean?"

The Fox Who Is No Fox watched her, and tightened his arms around her waist. "They did not escape."

The Witch exhaled. "So they died there."

"No—it's just not my story to tell."

The Witch pressed her hands to his chest and pushed herself away so that she could look at him. "Do you mean to tell me that this story you started has no end?"

"No, no, there is an end," he assured her. "I just don't know what it is yet."

"And what about the queen and the princess and the necromancer and all the people in the forest?" She reached out to thread her fingers through his hair. He let his eyes shut halfway as she combed his hair back from his face. *Safe, safe, safe,* she thought with desperate vehemence. But she no longer believed it.

"Well," he said, licking his dry lips, "there was an attack on the king, as the forest folk had planned. A shape-shifter assumed the shape of the princess and lured the incredulous king near to the forest's edge, where the people attacked. But it did not work—they did not kill him."

She twisted her fingers into his hair and pulled, just enough to make it hurt. He let his head fall back into her grip, the cords of his neck curving, protruding like the roots at the base of a tree.

"And?" the Witch prodded.

"The queen—she slept."

"And?"

"The princess—she slept too."

"And?"

"The necromancer—after he saw the princess in the

glade, he thought of a way that she might be saved. A way to reach her."

The Witch released him. The folded flower in her heart finally flourished, opened like a mouth: petals and pollen, blood and bone, a reawakening so violent that she was surprised when he did not so much as flinch at the eruption.

"And—and did he?" asked the Witch, shivering. She stood and faced her throne, lifted her chin and gazed down at the Fox Who Is No Fox.

"Yes," he said.

She knotted her hands behind her back. "And he woke her?"

"No," he replied. Leaning forward, he rested his elbows on his knees. Slowly he looked up at her.

The Fox Who Is No Fox let out a long sigh.

"Not yet," he said.

Not yet. The Witch smiled. Smiled so hard that her teeth hurt, an infinite ache that tunneled right down to her dizzy, wide-open heart, a garden of glittering veins and shining chambers where a wish waited to be plucked and devoured.

She said, "Little fox, little fox, get out of my throne. It is almost time for you to go home."

Chapter 16

IN THE DARK

It's Saturday, the day for bird-watching out the window and fox-crawling around the house to see what Gabrielle sees. Saturdays are for crunchy cereal and constructing forts out of books and blankets on my bed. Saturdays are for gathering the paint swatches Dad brings me from the hardware store, dozens of them, then standing on the sidewalk and holding them high overheard, finding a match for every color of the daylight universe, and taping the swatches to the wall over my bed, a spectrum of sky-dyes. Saturdays are for dust and daydreams.

But not today.

Today I will not let Dad out of my sight, even if that means following him around inside as he tidies up, then out to the front lawn to walk right behind him as he mows the grass. I hover while he makes sandwiches for lunch. I trail him back outside so he can trim the bushes in front of the house.

"Don't you want to relax, maybe have a cup of cinnamon tea?" he asks as I kneel next to him with dirty gloves on my hands, ripping weeds from Mom's now neglected garden. The sun shines, unrestrained, no clouds left from yesterday's storm. "After the, ah, *breakdown* you had yesterday, I thought you might want to, you know, take it easy."

Silence and silence and silence. I grab a particularly spiky, gnarly-looking weed and tug at it.

Why can't things just go back to the way they were?

"Dad." I lean back on my heels, staring at him. He has a huge smudge of mud on his stubbly cheek. "Listen, please. I'm going to tell you something, and all of it's true."

His jaw clenches; his neck tenses. "Rhea—"

"Please, just listen. Okay? *Okay?*"

I wait until he nods. I wait until he sighs. I wait until he turns his attention away from the mushy ground and says, "Okay. I'm listening."

Words like boils bubble in the back of my mouth, popping pustules that need to get out, out, out.

"Okay," I say. "Let's start with yesterday. Yesterday I had a sister named Raisa. She's fifteen, almost sixteen years old, and she's stubborn. She's snippy sometimes, and she's always telling me to shut up. Are you with me so far? Last night she snuck out, and I didn't stop her. I tried to, but she was gone. I think . . . I think she stopped existing as soon as she left the house."

He frowns. "That doesn't—"

But now that I've started, I can't stop. Gabrielle continues to tear weeds out with her teeth.

"The day before that, Mom was alive. *Alive,* Dad. She was *here*. She made us waffles and you dueled with the silverware.

The day before that, I had another sister, Renata, fourteen years old. Dad, are you listening?" I blindly grab for a lone dandelion nearby, as if everything will just melt away around me if I don't hold on to it. I have to fight for what's mine, even my memories. "Renata, she—she had fantastic dreams that she thought were real, and she would always hide when she was upset. The last time I talked to her, she told me to wake up and—are you following any of this? Do you understand?"

"Uh—"

"And throughout everything, I've been talking to this boy. No—it's not like *that*. Don't make that face. I don't know his name—I just think of him as 'the Darkness.' Because I can't *see* him, Dad. He's just a voice, and he wants me to guess his name. He says if I guess it, then he'll—then he'll take my curse away. He'll make it so that I don't have visions anymore." I pause, catching my breath. "But the thing is, the thing *is*, even if the Darkness could do it, if he truly could take my curse away, if he's even *real* and not just in my head—I'm not sure that that's important anymore. Because the *real* curse is that my family is being taken from me, one by one." I stare at him and I don't blink, even as my eyes water, even as they burn. "And I think—I think you might be next. You or Rose. What if she doesn't come back from ballet? In fact, maybe we should go there, to the studio, right now. Just to make sure. Because what will happen then, when both of you are gone? Will I disappear too? Will I see you again? Will we still be together, just somewhere else?"

Dad shoots to his feet. "*Rhea!* I have no earthly *idea* what you're talking about. No one is disappearing, all right? Except your mother, but—it's just your imagination talking, okay? Your strange but beautiful imagination. With that big brain of yours, you can create whole worlds, Rhea—or you can destroy them. It's up to you how you use it. There is always, always a choice." He sighs. Tired, tired, tired. "Just start with something simple—think happy thoughts."

Happy thoughts. Right, of course. How hard could that be? Um, *very*.

Like trying to catch sunshine in a cup. It's not liquid; it's *light*. You have to let it be what it is. Don't fight it.

"That's not simple," I say. "That's starting with the hardest thing."

"Just try."

"But my head hurts."

"I'll get you some ibuprofen."

"No!" I stand now too, wrenching off the stupid gardening gloves, my hands sweating. "I mean, it's—it's not that bad. I'll do without."

"Really, it's not a problem." He moves across the lawn. "I'll be right back."

"I'll go with you."

"You need to stop this. Stop following me around like a shadow. You're driving me crazy. I'm just going inside the house. Right over there. I will be back in a few minutes, okay? Stay here!" he snaps when I start to trail after him again. "I *mean* it. Don't. Move."

"Okay," I whisper, and watch him go, my gaze fixed on the back of his head. Dad raises his voice so rarely that it's a shock when he does, and I don't like making him upset.

Besides, Raisa disappeared when she walked *out* of the house. Dad is going *in,* and I have a clear view of the door from here—I'll see him as soon as he comes back.

Seconds pass, and then minutes. I shield my eyes with my hands, watching the house. Panic like a rash radiates down the back of my neck, twines around my spine, crashes across my chest. Slowly at first, then faster. My thoughts burst like bug bites across my brain, itchy.

Dad, I think. *Come back.*

Please, please, please.

I tally my heartbeats, counting down from one thousand. At zero, I begin again.

And again.

And again.

And again and again and again and again until I know.

He's not coming back.

He's not coming back, and I let him leave.

"Never ever," I whisper in a voice like dry skin, wrinkled and rough. "Wake *up.*"

No. All I have to do is wait. Wait right here, just like he said. Maybe he just can't find the ibuprofen. Maybe he had a phone call. Maybe he's making me tea.

I sit down facing the house, crossing my legs. I barely blink. Gabrielle comes and sits very close to me. We wait.

Just like he said. Just one minute more. He'll be back.

He *will.*

I wait.

* * *

I can't wait anymore.

I run toward the house. I throw the front door open, let it flap on its hinges as I dash into the foyer. Then I circle around to the kitchen, the laundry room, the living room.

"*Dad?*" I bellow, so loudly that it is almost a scream, but not quite. "Dad! *Where are you?*"

I tear up the stairs, with Gabrielle sprinting ahead of me. I tumble in and out of each empty room, opening the closets, ripping aside shower curtains, even stooping to peek under each bed. Twice. Just in case I've missed something.

"Dad, *please*—"

In the hallway I stop, slumping against the wall.

There's one room I haven't checked. Just one room left.

But I will not look there. Not yet.

Gabrielle blinks up at me, her pink tongue hanging out.

"Are you going to disappear too?" I shout at her, and she recoils, backing away from me so fast that she almost falls down the stairs.

"I'm sorry." I wipe a sweaty strand of hair off my cheek. "I'm sorry," I say again, trying to make it true, because suddenly I want to break things, and the only thing near enough that would make the kind of *crack* I crave is her heart, and mine. We stare at each other, breathless and wild.

I wish—

I wish—

I wish I knew exactly what to wish for.

If I got only one, what would be the wish to reverse this mess? Should I wish that I never opened the door, that I never dreamed that dream? Or should I wish for the Darkness's name?

If I knew, then maybe, just maybe, I could make it come true.

My family is gone. All but Rose, I think. And me. I'm still here. Stuck at the point where madness meets miracles, immovable. Me, the goddess of all shadows that shimmer, of all souls burdened with a bottled scream.

I have never felt so strange. Like I'm not real. Like nothing I say or do will matter. There's a distorted sort of comfort in that, in the absurdity of my own smallness, in all the space I do not occupy.

Leaning my head back, I close my eyes, willing myself to disappear too. And then to reappear, in the place where they have gone. But all I see behind my lids is darkness. And I don't want to be stuck in darkness. If my family is there, I must find a way to pull them back into the light.

"Rhea? Are you home? Are you here?"

I open my eyes.

"Ree?" Rose calls again from the bottom of the stairs. "Are you—"

I don't move as she ascends, her canvas ballet bag hooked over her shoulder.

"Hi," she says, stopping with one foot in the hallway and the other on the last step. She blinks at me, shifting her bag. "Uh, what're you up to?"

"What am I up to?" What an ordinary thing to say, when nothing at all is ordinary or okay. "Do you remember Dad?"

She clamps a hand around her bun considering, holding onto it like a doorknob, like she could open her skull and lift a memory out. "Dad?"

"Yes, Rose. *Dad*. Our father. Rafael Ravenna. Six two and a tattoo of a made-up constellation on his back." My chest itches. "He was here this morning, wasn't he? You remember seeing him before you left for ballet. Right? Please? You *remember*, don't you?"

She says nothing.

She stares, and then she says, "I remember."

"You—do?" My throat tightens, and I think I might cry. She remembers, and I am not so alone as I'd thought. "And Raisa? And Mom, who's not really dead? And Renata—you remember her too?"

"Yes," she whispers, and even Gabrielle's little fox body relaxes in relief. I feel her contented sigh in my own lungs, like a phantom breath that does not quite belong to me. "*Yes.*"

Rose lets her bag fall to the floor as she strides toward me. She presses the back of her hand to my forehead. As always, her fingers are cool, soothing.

But she won't look me in the eyes, even though her face is mere inches from mine.

"You knew this whole time," I say, and though I meant only to whisper, the statement comes out as a hiss. "You *knew*, and you said nothing. They disappeared, and you just—*went along with it*?"

The way she avoided me after I asked about Renata while my family ate ice cream; her silence after we scoured the attic for the voice; bouncing on her toes and staring over Dad's shoulder at me in the garden as I lamented Mom's implausible passing. Pretending to be asleep when I asked her last night if she believed me. The whole time she knew and kept quiet—but *why?*

She scrunches her mouth from side to side, and it is a moment before she speaks. "Is it really so bad, though, if we're here together, just the two of us?"

I wrench away from her, slap her wrist when she reaches for me again.

"I didn't mean—" she says, but I hold up a palm to stop her. After a moment she says, "I miss them too. But I want—"

"No. *No.* You are wrong, Rose. You are wrong, wrong, wrong. It will never be just the two of us. There is one more here. We are *three,* not two." I grab her elbow and tug her down the hallway. "Come on. I want you to meet him. I want you to meet the darkness that lives in our attic."

She presses her heels into the floor and won't budge. "Wait! Please—*no*—"

"Come *on.*"

She drops to the floor, dead weight, and I can't drag her. She crosses her arms like a child. "I don't want to."

"Fine," I say, and Gabrielle flattens against the wall, trying to make herself small. "If you won't go, then I'll make him come to us." I tip my head back and shout, even more loudly and more urgently than when I was searching for Dad. *"Darkness!* Boy? Are you there? Will you come out?"

My pulse ticks off the seconds. He has to obey, doesn't he? For some reason I cannot yet understand, he is mine, mine to command. He is a part of me, he said. But only this test will tell: Is he like my lungs, breathing either with or without conscious thought, or like my heart, which beats on and on in whichever rhythm it wants?

The silence changes, like a shifting of weight from foot to foot, like something being decided. There are no telltale creaks of the floorboards, no squeaks of the stairs, as if he glides instead of stepping, as if he weighs nothing. One moment there is perfect quiet, and the next the knob on the attic door starts to turn, slowly, twisting like a broken kneecap, grinding bone.

The door opens, and the darkness oozes out like oil, sucking up the sunlight coming into the hallway from the windows in the bedrooms. The murk of midnight seizes the space as the boy steps sideways through the slit between the door and the stairwell beyond, snatching my sight away entirely. As always, I feel him there rather than see him.

"Darkness," I say as Rose scrambles to her feet, backing away, her blue eyes wide, petrified. "Darkness, boy, whoever you are—I want you to meet my sister."

And he says, "No, Rhea Ravenna." Then he breathes, "I want you to meet *mine*."

Silence, silence like a mirror, reflecting Rose's anguish, my astonishment, the Darkness's grim anticipation.

"You've met?" I ask, confused. "You—you know each other?"

Has she made a deal with him too? How many players are there in this game?

"I have known Rose Ravenna her entire life," the Darkness declares, stepping toward us. "In *every* life, by *every* name. I know her better than you do."

"That's not true," Rose whispers, backing away. "Don't listen to him, Rhea. You don't have to listen to him."

"I don't want to listen to either of you," I say, "unless someone would like to explain what we're all doing here! How do you know each other?"

I feel the Darkness grin. "Come, *Rose,* tell her. I'm curious to hear as well, since the last time I saw you, you betrayed me."

I don't miss the emphasis he puts on her name. "Rose? Is that not your name? Who are you?"

Rose is just a silhouette in the outer rim of the darkness. I watch her tip her head back, as if she'll find solace in the ceiling. As if she could just disappear in an instant, like the rest of our family. She opens her mouth—but nothing comes out.

I walk toward the boy in the darkness, raising my hands, thinking that if I can only touch him, I will know him. His name, his face, his heart, his soul—one touch and I'll know everything.

"No—" Rose grabs my arm, but I jerk out of her grasp, so hard and fast that she whimpers and jumps back. *"Please—"*

Another step and another, and the Darkness doesn't move, waiting for me to come. Close, closer, closest—I stop before him, immersed in his shadow, eclipsed. I put my hands to his chest, and he flinches at the sudden touch.

But then, after a long moment, he relaxes, his muscles unclenching as his shoulder blades slump against the wall. I press my hands over the stammer-song of his heart, his pulse still punching out an apology. Slowly, slowly, I move my palms toward his neck, the tendrils of tendons at his throat, his square chin. I crawl my fingertips up the curve of his cheeks, brush the outer edges of his thick eyebrows. I tangle my hands in his soft hair, running my fingers to the back of his neck. He sighs, and I am safe. Nothing and no one can find me here.

Is this, then, how I disappear? Devoured by purest, deepest darkness, curled in the belly of the wolf?

No—not a wolf, I think. *A fox.*

Always, always a fox.

"Rhea," he whispers, taking my hands and twining his fingers with mine, his grip sure and indomitable. "How long will you sleep before you tire of your dreams?"

"Let go of her!" Rose yells from outside the darkness, but I don't want the boy to let go. Because, in a weird way, I want to be crushed, the way he's crushing my hands now. Like cracked glass, melted and remolded into something else. *Someone* else.

Who am I, really? I want to, need to, *wish* to know.

If only I had magic.

I close my eyes, and what I see is this: A princess. A wood. A castle. A king. A sea and a city and a secret and a curse. Humans with two hearts, one inside the other. *Maculae.* A strange word, a lovely word, one that feels like a kiss fading from swollen lips. Waltzes and backless dresses and moons like skulls scattered in the forgotten tomb of the sky. A mother who was meant to be queen but died too soon. A father who was staring straight ahead when he should have been looking side to side, at the woman whose hand he held and the daughter who smiled as though nothing were wrong, when all along nothing was right. A faceless grandfather with hot iron in his grip.

And a girl who was chosen but who chose to avoid it.

When I have remembered all of these things, I open my eyes.

The Darkness and Rose—both gone.

Chapter 17

IN THE WOODS

I am no longer in my house but instead am sitting on a throne.

Someone speaks, and it takes me a moment to realize it's me, it's my mouth that's moving.

"Now," I say. "I am the Witch of Wishes. What would you ask of me?"

I can't see her, this so-called Witch, because I *am* her. I look through her eyes; I see what she sees. Before her stands a boy no older than herself, with burnt red lips and hair as black as charred wood and skin so paper-pale that she—I, we—can nearly peer right inside, through the temple of his ribs to the gasping garnet of his heart.

Your bones quiver and sigh my name at night, I think, staring down at him. *Let me see them, let me see your bones.*

For a long moment he says nothing. I notice then the scars on the backs of his long-fingered hands. No, not scars, not exactly—*brands.*

I do not like to ask twice, and my voice, the second time, is not so nice. Grating, impatient: "What do you wish?"

"I wish—"

He licks his lips, and smiles. Something inside me snags, rips. He opens me, and I bleed. I know I will give him anything, everything. He needs only to ask, and it is his.

And all at once I know what he is going to say before he says it. The Witch, she knows too, though not with the same certainty that I do. His wish is hers too, a wish that has been blooming between them since the very moment they met, and now all he must do is speak it aloud, and she'll make it come true.

I have seen this scene before. The Witch and I are one, and I know exactly what is to come. *Just this.*

"Just this," he says. "A kiss."

Wake up, wake up, wake up.

He waits, and it is very quiet, not even a breath to splinter the silence. With trembling fingers I reach into the split in my sternum, pluck a petal, and place it in his waiting, open mouth. He swallows, and then he wraps his shaking hand around the nape of my neck and brings our lips together.

This, I think, *is what it must feel like to wake up. Never let it end.*

I will stay here, suspended, stuck in a kiss, somewhere between a life and a dream.

I am the Witch of Wishes and want for nothing. I have everything.

Behind us, someone shouts, "Varon, leave her alone!"

Shut up, shut up, shut up.

The boy pulls away, his hands still twisted in my hair.

I lift my chin and look around him, beyond him. A tall girl with gold hair scrambles into the room, green leaves swirling around her as the walls begin to shed, slowly at first and then faster, the leaves crisp and brown by the time they hit the ground. The boy still standing so close to me does not seem surprised, neither by the leaves tumbling as the dream dissolves, nor to see the girl standing there. He is only watchful. Wary.

Rose? The Witch's lips don't move as I try to say her name. In this memory, the Witch whose body I'm borrowing does not know her. This girl is at once my sister and a stranger.

The Witch startles as she sees her, and so I startle too. "And who—who are *you*?"

It is only now that I realize what I've done, what he has done to me. All at once, there's a sound like the sizzle-snap of power lines, my veins cracking with electricity. No, not electricity—*magic*. Hot, hotter, hottest, and soon my skin is sticky with sweat. Violet lightning severs the sky in several directions; the tooth crenellations crowning the castle topple, and thunder as they hit the dry dirt. The branches of the walls unravel and fall to the floor, where they writhe like snakes. Far above, the stars melt like a mint, and plump yellow maggots devour the moon.

Every muscle in me is clenched, resisting. The curse has begun to break. This is how the world ends: in a kiss cut short, a storm of sleeping synapses, in murder mistaken for mercy. My dream is dying, dead.

You have wasted your wish.

I look at the boy before me, his hands still wrapped around my neck. I want him to let go of me, but I can't summon the words, so I push up on my toes and with my teeth nip the skin over his jugular, sudden enough to get his attention but not hard enough to hurt.

"What—?" He hops back, his arms falling away as he brings his fingers to his neck, rubbing the spot where my teeth just were.

The girl reaches us and leaps onto the dais, sliding her palm into mine, holding tight. I let her. It is comforting to have her here, even though I don't know her. Not in this memory. She is so beautiful and so bright, and by her touch I know at once that I am safer than I have ever been.

"You cannot keep running," the boy says, and he has to shout to be heard over the moans of the world breaking apart. "You cannot keep sleeping. Not while we need you. You have to wake up, Princess. It is time to wake up."

Princess.

Panic, like a thousand tiny paper cuts in my brain.

"What have you done?" I whisper. *"What have you done?"*

"Please—" The Fox Who Is No Fox reaches for my wrist, pleading, but as soon as his hand touches my skin, he retracts it, his fingertips blistering as though he's been scorched.

I propose that we play a game, you and I. A guessing game.

"Do not touch me," I say, and stumble back. I let go of the girl's hand, but she stays close to my side. "You cannot keep me here. If I must wake, I wake to another world, another life. I will not go back to the place that would not have me."

"All worlds live beneath the same sky," he says, clutching

his burned hand to his chest. "And I will *always* find you. I will always know you."

I will take your curse away.

"But I won't know you." I pause, knowing I need to design a new dream, fast. But first—a new curse. "And if you tell me, I won't listen. I see now that you are doom. You are death." I stop again, looking down at my hands, at the brands now seared on the back, so red that they are almost black. "You wish to take me back to the crystal castle between the forest and the sea, to a world that cannot hold me." I lean close to him and whisper a new spell. "I curse you now to darkness. And only I can release you by uttering your name."

As soon as I've said it, I wish I could take it back. All of it. This spell, it leaves the taste of tar on my tongue. All wrong. He did not kill this world, this dream. I did that. There is no one to blame but myself.

But it's too late. What's done is done.

And all you have to do, my sky, is say my name, my name, my name.

"Take me with you, please!" cries the girl, squeezing my hand, hard. Her eyes are wet. "I don't want to wake up, just like you. I want to dream with you forever."

I turn to her, and I know her now—not as Rose, my sister, who shared a bedroom with me. But the Witch knows her, remembers the girl who came not so very long ago to the Woods—my Woods—and wished to stay with me here, always.

I reach for her arm and sink my nails into her skin, but Rose does not cry out, and she does not flinch as I look deep into her heart, a rushing reel of images, of memories: Rose hidden away in an attic in the Hollow with her slowly shriveling parents. Using her oneiromancy to reach out to her brother sleeping in the crystal castle; waking up after meeting the Witch, the wish she was given sitting like an insoluble stone in her belly. *Let me stay with you. I am nothing but a dream too.*

My nails bite down harder, and I see how the girl suffered the chill of panic and paranoia each time she cast a spell, how she despised the poison inside her, this magic that was the reason why her parents were dying and why her brother served a spiteful king and why she had been locked away so that she would be safe. I see how Rose rushed to the mirror in her tiny room, stood before the glass with frozen lungs and tremulous hands, asking her reflection, *I'm still beautiful, aren't I?* How she tried in vain to reach the Witch again, this time alone; how her brother grew secretive and strange, telling her to rest, telling her that there was a war coming and she had to be strong and ready when it came. How he told her not to worry, that they were going to win.

How can you be sure? she asked, and I feel how his reply clamped like crystal teeth around her brain: *I think I know how to wake the princess up.*

What are you thinking? she cried. *If you kiss her, you will die! I will die! You—you love me, don't you?*

You can't die in dreams, he said with a confident smile. *Everyone knows that.*

But she didn't obey; she didn't rest. Instead she followed him through his dream, skulking close behind as he transformed himself into a fox and entered the Witch's castle. And there she saw him, asking for his wish.

Asking for a kiss.

And Rose gasped, for suddenly she knew who the Witch of Wishes was.

Who *I* was.

And with all her little quivering heart, she did not want her brother to wake me up—to end the dream, and her wish with it.

When I have seen all this, I release her arm, and she exhales. We are alike, she and I. Dreamers both.

"I wish to go with you," she begs, and the Fox Who Is No Fox reaches for her. But her flesh is flushed now, smoldering like mine, and just as untouchable. We are safe—from him, but not from ourselves. In this moment we don't know who the monsters are.

Not us, we think. *Surely it's not us.*

I look at her and I smile, and the world shatters in a final gush of gray sky-guts and broken branches, a torrent of teeth sharp enough to scratch diamonds. "It will be done."

I shut my eyes.

I say, "I am not afraid."

Once is enough.

Chapter 18

IN THE DARK

With a crash and a cry, I come back to myself. Somewhere nearby Gabrielle yelps, helpless, watching me. I trip backward, unseeing, but I don't fall. Because the Darkness—the Fox Who Is No Fox—is there to catch me. This time I let him.

It's a dream. It has always been a dream. I am a princess, a macula, a witch. I am an oneiromancer, a dream-designer—that is my greatest magic. This boy came for me in the Woods while I slept, wanting only to wake me. Instead I slipped away again, and I brought all those I loved with me: Gabrielle, my fierce guardian in the Woods. Rose, a girl who refused to forget me or give up on ever finding me again. Raisa and Renata, the gray gorgon and the nymph who watched over me while I slept, my two best friends in Graiae Forest.

And my parents, of course, my father the crown prince and my mother the future queen, raised again by this boy who has followed me to the ends of this earth, disguised as darkness because I cursed him to be that way. I cursed myself, not to know him. Not to know myself.

It seems so unfathomable to me now, that I would ever want to forget. The desperate actions of a frightened girl. A girl so full of hunger, a specific kind of hunger, the kind that curls between your bones when you look up at a cloud-dusted dusk. A girl like a half-moon visible in the late daylight, a pale specter in the sky, like the smell of smoke after the fire is long gone. A loose eyelash on a dry cheek, the chime of a cracked bell. A girl whose face is the first you see right after you fall asleep, even if you don't remember. In fact, for certain you *won't* remember, because I'll already be long gone. I am fickle and ephemeral and I flow, from one dream to the next. The opposite of stasis, even while I sleep.

What have I done? I think as I regain balance, the boy's arm around my waist. *This has to end.*

"I know who you are," I say to him around the rushing roar of my pulse. Rose shouted his name when she interrupted our kiss. "I know *exactly* who you are."

He tightens his hold on me. "Who am I, then? Tell me, Rhea Ravenna. Tell me."

"No, Rhea, don't do this." Rose rushes forward but stops short of the edge of the darkness, unable or unwilling to go any farther, to leave the safety of the light. I turn toward her, and I can see *through* the darkness to where she stands, but I see nothing within it, not even my own hands. "You don't have to. Mom, Dad, Raisa, Renata—I know how to get them back."

The sun itself could have fallen at my feet, soft and quietly burning up, burning out, and I would not have been as surprised as I am by what Rose has said. "Wh-what?"

"This is my dream too. You designed it, but *I* brought them here. I reached out to where the crown prince slept at the future queen's side, and where your friends dozed in their prisons. I pulled on their magic, or at the very least their dreams, and I brought them here. For *you*. So you wouldn't miss them, so you'd never want to leave." She dashes her fingertips across her cheek, a quick, angry gesture, wiping away a spill of tears. "But my magic isn't strong enough—I held on for as long as I could, but they started to wake up, one by one. But now that you know, we can start over. *Together.* We'll build a new dream, stronger this time, and with our powers combined, none of us will ever wake up."

"Rose! What are you saying? You want me to build a new dream with you? I don't even know who you *are.*" I've started to shake, my whole body shuddering, but I keep my voice steady and clear. And loudly, so loudly that I'm almost shouting, I say, "You crave beauty even though you already have it. You want love, even though you have plenty of that too. You are a key with no lock, nothing to open or close. You are a quick kiss on a cold smile. You are longing personified, longing without end."

Rose raises her chin and doesn't bother now to hide her tears. "I'm your *sister.*"

I shake my head. We *were* sisters, and maybe we can be again—sisters in spirit if not in blood. But right now all I see when I look at her is the blister-shine of betrayal, pale and raw and about to burst.

"I've lived in the Hollow for too long now," she says, her

voice low but strained, a vein standing out on the side of her neck like the branch of a cherry tree under ice. "Locked away in the attic for my own safety, with no one to keep me company but my mirror and my dreams. What kind of a life is that? I can't go back. *I won't.*"

At this my anger softens. Not all the way, but enough that the sheen of betrayal dulls and my jaw unclenches. We've both made mistakes.

"I can't keep running." I bring both my hands to my heart. "But I promise that I'll make things right. You won't have to live in the attic anymore. You won't have to hide."

Her eyes fall to her feet, and she does not look up again, her chest rising and falling rapidly. "We could go back to the Woods," she says, so quietly that I have to lean forward to hear. "We could make the wishes of every child in the world come true. We could grant wishes to those who need them most."

"That world is *gone*," I say, gentle but firm. "It collapsed when the spell broke. And this mirage will too."

I turn so I'm facing the boy in the darkness, his arm falling from around me. I can't see him but I imagine him there, tense and listening.

"Instead of helping you, I ran, I slept, I dreamed. But still you came for me in the Woods when no one else would. You followed me *here,* even though it meant drowning in darkness until I was ready to find you. Until I knew your name."

I exhale.

"You are breathlessness," I say, and I am all skin and nerves, and every inch of me glitters, every inch of me groans. "You are cold fire. You are wonder, and curiosity that cuts through bone. You speak to Death and convince him to give you what's rightfully his. You promise him diamonds in exchange for souls, but give him coal and time instead. And Death, he falls for it again and again, because your smile is a sword that no one, not even a god, wants to feed with his blood. And your name—" I stop and step back until his darkness no longer touches me. "Your name is Varon."

The darkness falls from him like chains unclasped, shackles of thick shadows tumbling to the floor and disappearing in a hissing swirl of black steam. His face is familiar to me now, and I can't fathom how I could have ever wanted to forget him.

When the darkness is gone completely, Varon reaches for me, but he stops when he sees me standing still, confused about why I won't come to him. *Kisses are nice, but they won't work twice.* No, a kiss won't kill this curse, this spell within a spell. Not this time.

Something savage spreads in me like a yawn, a girl within a girl, and she stretches herself to fit into my skin. All my life I have been waiting and waiting for her to come.

Now, she says. *You are the Witch of Wishes. What is your wish?*

I look first at Rose, who glances away when our eyes meet, and then at Varon, who licks his red, red lips, waiting for whatever comes next.

Then I wish just this: to *scream.*

I clasp my hands to my ears and close my eyes, and I open my mouth to purge my body of this boiling, itching agony I have clung to for so long. And it hurts, it *hurts,* but I do not stop. There is relief in destruction.

Part Two

Chapter 19

IN THE KINGDOM

The stars—they're different here. The way they're arranged. They make pretty patterns, and one of them I recognize: an upside-down skeleton hand. And the color—faintly violet. Puckering. Pulsing. No, not pulsing—choking. Choking on what?

Wishes.

Wishes, and every one of them tastes like, feels like, apple slices shoved down the throats of the children who make them. That's what it is to wish, to sacrifice breath for possibility. Waiting for a wish to come true—it hurts.

The stars are the first things I see when I open my eyes. I look at them, and they look at me, and then—they fall. They shrink to the size of a needle-tip as they come, hot and glittering, stitching the darkness with silvery threads of light. They stick to me, to my palms and wrists and shoulders, my knees and shins and ankles, my neck and my cheeks and all around my eyes. I glisten, everywhere.

For what seems like too much time and no time at all, I lie there with stars on my skin like goose bumps, and I don't know who I am or what I've done. I'd like to stay here, unhinged, floating and drifting, like a shadow—but then I remember that that's how this all started in the first place. The wish to be left alone, the wish to be a dream instead of a girl. But then a boy came to me, and he showed me what real fear looks like. His fear was that life would always be misery. My fear was that I could not truly help him, and had no real power to change anything.

"Darkness?" I sit up slowly, half buried in a pile of leaves. "Varon?"

But there is no reply.

The trees here are stuck in the soil upside down—roots in the air and branches underground. The darkness here is very still. It doesn't speak or smile or sigh. I am alone.

Mom, Dad, Raisa, Renata—they didn't disappear like I'd thought they had. They were asleep like I was, and now they're awake. *We* are awake.

It's strange, though, that now I'm awake and I remember who I am, I still feel like my old self. My dreaming self, Rhea Ravenna. Except my name *is* Rhea Ravenna, but Princess Rhea Ravenna here, and my father is Crown Prince Rafael and my mother was the future Queen Reese. This is the Kingdom of Ravenna.

My life there in that other place was a dream, but not. We were all there, all sleeping, dreaming the dream together. I will find them, and we will be reunited, a family never to be torn apart this time. A strange family of trembling hands reaching for each other in the dark, not all of us blood-related, but a family just the same.

And Varon. Where is he? Still in the dungeons, chained and slowly dying?

I'm coming, I think, wishing he could somehow hear me as I blink up at the star-swollen sky. *I'm coming for you.*

And though a part of me is still angry with Rose for lying to me, that part is small and growing smaller. I made her a promise, and I intend to keep it. I'm not sure how just yet, but I *will* find a way.

Still covered in tiny cooling stars, I untwist the folds of my dress from around my waist, the red dress I wore for my mother when I was in mourning. Every movement is painful, metallic pain like clusters of bruises roped all along my body, blue-gold and shining, jabbed over and over by invisible fingertips.

No, not pain, I realize. *Magic.*

I am a princess.

I am a witch.

I am Rhea.

I have many faces, and I want to wear them all.

With a cry that is somewhere between a laugh and a scream, I jump to my feet, setting the leaves around me to spinning. My head is full of fireflies, and my heart is a flashing light. This magic inside me—it is like the sun in your eyes from every angle, careless to the burns it leaves on bare flesh. I hold my hands high and let a burst of flickering light loose from my palms, sending the stars on my skin back to the sky.

And then the shouting begins.

"It's her. It's the *princess*!"

"She's awake!"

"Come quickly!"

"Wandering One, save us!"

At the sound of the voices, the stars pause their skyward scarpering. They linger just over the treetops, scything the night with their thin, pointed light, as if checking back over their shoulders to see that I'm all right.

But.

I am not all right.

Several armed men surround the clearing, and I realize too late that I probably should have been a bit more discreet upon waking, instead of immediately and cheerfully blasting the stars back up into the dark. The stars are now hovering overhead like a thousand tiny spotlights, every one of them pointing straight at me.

Me, the wanted, watched-over princess. The one who's now been cornered by the king's soldiers. I wonder if this finally means I'll be carted away, kicking and clawing, to the king. It almost makes me laugh—but then I see the soldiers' fingers tightening, and the sound shrivels in my mouth, sticky on my tongue. They won't kill me. This I'm sure of—but that doesn't mean what will happen instead will be pleasant. I have to be quick, and as long as they take me alive—alive and *awake*—then it probably doesn't matter much to the king what means they use to subdue me.

I reach far inside myself for words I haven't spoken in a very long time. In a language at once familiar and strange, I look at the men and say, *"Astynta."*

They freeze, blinking, bemused. They are tipped slightly forward, with their weight on their toes, ready to run again at the slightest ease in pressure from my stilling spell.

"Put your weapons on the ground—carefully!"

They hesitate: their hands relax, but they do not let go completely. One of them steps forward, and speaks. "Please, Your Highness. We're not—"

"Drop them!" I cry, but nothing happens.

Not to them, at least.

My palms cramp, and the brands on the backs of my hands burn, itchy and inflamed. A tingling twinge surges up my arms, wraps around my second heart, and squeezes. Using my magic again after being asleep for so long is like popping a dislocated bone back into place—it's not broken, but it hurts. I flex and roll my wrists, as if I could simply shake away the ache, but it's too late anyway. The spell splinters completely. The guards rush toward me.

I turn and run, as fast as I can, toward the Grimly River, to hurl myself into it, to count on the nymphs to ferry me across the current, to hope they'll capture and drown anyone who dares follow me down into the cold black water.

As I draw nearer to the river—*so close, so close*—one of the soldiers speaks from behind me. Not a spell—just an ordinary command.

"Stop."

No, I think.

"Stop," the soldier repeats.

No, I think, again.

"*Stop!*" the soldier pleads.

No, no, no, no, no.

On the edge of the river, about to throw myself to the mercy of the death-hungry creatures below, I push down the pain of waking, scraping the stupor of sleep from my eyes, from my mind and my heart and my veins. I turn around, raising my cramped hands, and try one last time. "*No! Astynta!* Do not follow me!"

The soldiers obey. Their footsteps go suddenly silent; their exhalations loud and lurching as they catch their breaths.

They stop, and I'm relieved—but then I see that it's not entirely because of me.

One soldier has lunged ahead of the rest, and I'm stunned to see that this soldier is not a man like I'd thought, and not even a boy—no, before me stands a *girl,* a short, thin girl with red hair pulled into a knot on the top of her head.

"Witch," she says, more softly now, and I go still as I realize that the other guards are not men either—they're *children,* every one of them. Skinny and dirty and wearing guard uniforms as if they were playing dress-up, their hair tangled, and deep purple bruises beneath their eyes. I watch, bewildered, as the red-haired girl who has somehow managed to evade my tenuous spell inches closer to me, cautiously. She called me Witch, not Princess, so I stay and wait for her to come. She says, "They are more afraid of you than you are of them."

Above us, the stars tremble and flash. "Who said I was afraid?"

She shakes her head. "You didn't have to say anything. I *feel* it."

I peer at her, amazed at the way her apprehension foams in

my bones, how her heartbeat skips forward and skids faster to align with mine. I gasp, stepping toward her. *"Gabrielle?"*

She nods, smiling eagerly, and I notice how young she truly is, barely fourteen.

"I followed you, Witch," she said, "and I did my best to keep you safe."

There are still a dozen weapons aimed at me, at us, and I'm growing dizzy with the effort of keeping the spell from breaking. Gabrielle notices me straining.

"It's okay," she says gently, and for some reason I want to cry. It's *Gabrielle,* and she's still on my side. "They won't hurt you. They were just spooked before, when you suddenly awoke and started sending up sparks."

"Delita," I say. The spell snaps, and the fluttering, flickering stars continue their upward slide. The children slump, dazed, and don't raise their weapons again.

"You are the Forest Forgotten," I say, marveling at the memories those words conjure, of nights spent roasting fresh game around a fire, of tucking the orphans into their tents after the meager feast, of tapping them each on the temple and whispering, *Go to sleep, and may your dreams be sweet.* And Gabrielle, a wiry, smiling child who followed me everywhere, who refused to go to bed until I had told her a fairy story, demanding to hear only those that had a happy ending. Her magic was like a whisper, like a blurred breath in an open ear, soft, and slinking always just out of sight. "You are the Forest Forgotten and—and you protected me? All this time? But where are the guards? How did you get those uniforms, the weapons?"

"We used our magic, of course." Her voice is more gruff than I remember, like a fox's growl, like claws raking bark. As if she were a fox so long that she's forgotten how to be human. She points at a tall boy whose uniform is short in the arms, his wrists poking out of the sleeves. "Don't you remember? Leo can turn invisible, and little Imelda there in the back is a pyromancer. As for me, I'm a shape-shifter, mostly. I followed you into the woods as a fox—that's all I can really turn into so far—and I brought along several others. Everyone here helped stage our own coup against the guards, after the gorgon and the nymph were taken away." She turns back to me, her cheeks flushed, exuberant. "We're here to keep you safe, and so you wouldn't be alone. It was harder to get to you in your second dream—I couldn't bring the other children that time."

"Thank you, Gabrielle." She smiles at last, all her teeth showing, and now I really do start to cry, just a little. I wipe my eyes with the back of my hand and take a breath. Turning to the children, I raise my voice so that I'll be heard. "How long was I asleep?"

"One turn of the crow moon."

My stomach twists, though that's not as long as I feared. After all, eighteen years passed in my dream. I was born; I grew up. I lived an entire life while I was asleep. Two lives, really, counting the Witch. But oneiromancy doesn't adhere to a linear flow of time. In a dream, you could live a thousand lives in a single second.

"Well." I try not to choke on the bile creeping up my throat. "A crow-month isn't *so* long, is it? That's only, what— thirty days?"

Leo steps forward. "Thirty days, or seven hundred and twenty hours, Your Highness," he says proudly. "That's two million, five hundred and ninety-two thousand seconds."

I stare at him, both impressed and unnerved that he has this information so readily.

"Are you going to help us, Princess?" Imelda says, drawing my attention away as she rises on tiptoe to be seen through the crowd. "Now that you're back?"

At this I straighten my shoulders and lift my chin, doing my best impression of a princess, of a fearless leader. I don't feel like one. Yet.

"Yes," I say.

"How?" asks Imelda.

"Oh." My shoulders slump. "Um, well, I'm not sure *exactly . . .*"

A girl with short, dark curls crosses her arms over her chest. *Glenna*—I recall her name with a start, and remember too that her magic is strong in divination. "We thought maybe you were dreaming of a solution. And that's why you were gone so long, because you were thinking and thinking really hard."

Dreaming of a solution.

At once her words jar something loose inside me. *Of course,* I think, letting my head fall back, my throat stretching long, feeling relieved and incredulous and furious all at once. I laugh, a high, sharp sound, and the stars above rattle and shake, clattering against each other like teeth.

If my reality before was a dream, then maybe my *dream* there was real. I remember now: a crumbling wing of the castle, a door at the top of a spiral staircase, sneaking away to explore during the balls, testing the doorknob and finding it locked. *A forgotten place, a forbidden place.* Something is behind that door, something the king doesn't want anyone to see. If I find the door and open it, for real this time, I'll discover some secret that will help me destroy the king's legacy.

At the very least, this is a place to start. By the end of this day, the right Ravenna will sit upon the throne—or else I will be dead. The king will not let me go a second time. This is my last chance to fight, and I won't waste it.

I *won't.*

"I've just remembered something. Something I think can help us," I say, and the children exchange glances, some of them smiling while others fidget, unconvinced. "I promise, I'm going to make your wishes come true. But first I need you to do something for me."

The children gather close, and I ask them to find everyone they can in the forest and tell them that I'm awake, that I'm traveling to the city to confront the king. "Ask them to meet me there, if they are willing."

When I'm finished, they clutch their weapons and hurry away into the woods on silent feet. A few throw their arms around me in a tight hug before they go. The only one who doesn't move is Gabrielle.

"Come, Witch," she says, taking my hand. "I will show you the way home."

Together we leave the darkest place in the forest, and cross over the bridge to where the pale glaze of the moonlight blushes through the shadowy gaps between the trees.

"Where are the soldiers you overthrew?" I ask as we hurry away, hopping over fallen branches, brambles scratching our ankles. "What happened to them?"

"At the bottom of the river," says Gabrielle. "We had some help from the nymphs," she adds without remorse, leading me over a rotting toppled trunk.

The nymphs remind me of Renata, her glistening salt-song that makes no distinction between mirth and mourning. These trees are starting to look familiar, and soon I lead Gabrielle instead of the other way around. I know exactly where to go. I start to walk faster, my breath snagging in my throat—all I want right now is to see Renata and the others again, to know for sure that she is safe.

Gabrielle and I run away from the darkest part of the woods, the stars above watching me warily. Now that they've touched me, I feel their ancient fever; I hear their crisp whispers.

They say, *Hurry, little princess.*

Hands ready, little witch.

Go, little girl, and take *what belongs to you.*

"I am not little," I say to them.

To us, they say, *you are.*

But little things, they say, *grow into big things.*

And big things, they say, *must not forget they were once little things too.*

Gabrielle and I trip over brambles in the semi-dark until I mutter a flat-footpath spell to clear the debris as we come to it. The terrain becomes more and more familiar: there to the left is the blue-barked Fir of Fates. Pinch a drop of your blood onto its roots, and it will reveal your future when you press your ear to its trunk. Or, depending on its mood, it will simply stretch its pine needle branches down behind you and scratch your unsuspecting spine, begging for more blood.

And up ahead is the glowberry bush where I hid once from a human hunter with a gun at his hip; just past that pond is the place where I mastered a wind-changing incantation for the first and only time. Over there is the trodden trail to the manticores' cave, and right around that willow is—

Wait.

"Gabrielle?" I slow, my lungs aching, and duck beneath the drooping branches of the willow. Here the trees are right-side up, not like in the clearing, where the roots are avaricious for air and the branches are banished to the worms. "What—"

I peer around the tree and stop. I blink three times, fast, but the picture before me does not dissolve or disband. I'm not haunted here by visions of death, but I almost wish I still were. Because then the destruction before me wouldn't be real. I could blink, and it would all disappear.

Or, rather, what was once here would *re*appear. Because there is nothing left of the trees beyond the willow, save for some still-smoking sticks, a spread of shrubs, and underbrush spitting sparks into the sky, aiming for the eyes of the seven moons I can now see without the veil of the trees, tiptoeing across the cosmos as if they aren't sure if they should stop and help or just pretend they haven't seen the devastation that's ravaged the rest of the forest.

The world is hushed, and a gray haze hangs in the distance, occluding my view of the city beyond. What has become of those who lived here? Have they fled deeper into the forest? Left it entirely? Or—

No. No, no, no, no, no.

Don't even think it.

I bend down, uttering a flame-resistant spell, slowly touching my fingers to a smoldering patch of moss.

"Don't—" Gabrielle cries, gripping my shoulder to yank me back. "Do you have a death wish?"

"It's okay," I say, showing her my fingers. My flesh is fine. But I know that if I had let my hand linger, I would have gotten burned, even with the spell. "That's no ordinary fire, though."

"What is it?" Gabrielle asks.

"Star Fire." She looks at me blankly. "Star Fire spreads quickly but burns slowly. It could take years before the last of it is gone. See how those trees are still standing, in an almost perfect line? Someone put up a defensive spell there. But whoever it was, they were too late to save all of it."

I remember the old, sacred stories that Varon as the Fox Who Is No Fox told me while I twisted flowers into his hair, stories of great heroes who boasted they were strong enough to command the stars to hop right into their hands. Every one of those tales ends in disaster. In death.

Who would willingly pluck a star down, searing and blinding, and then use it to raze the forest, to murder all its creatures?

I can think of only one person.

"But how did he even do it?" I wonder aloud. "How did the king get himself a star?"

"He commanded one of his servants to do it?"

"A single Immacula would never be able to accomplish something like this. But maybe—maybe it was a whole group of them. Maybe he got them all to do it together."

Gabrielle scowls. "And then let them burn here when he was through with them."

I clench my jaw, trying to picture him, to see his face in my mind, but I can't. I can't remember him. He is a vague shadow skulking around my skull, and nothing more than that.

For just a moment longer, Gabrielle and I do nothing but survey the wreckage: reddened roots peeking out of the earth, sputtering scrub that once provided prickly padding for the forest floor, diverting those who did not belong there from entering its wild and blood-hungry depths. I keep expecting the flames to vanish with each blink—but they don't.

All at once, I miss my curse. Well—not so much my curse, exactly. I miss my family, and our quiet house by the sea. I miss all of us, living together. I miss the neighbor boys pedaling past, teasing, *Look, guys. It's the Raving Ravennas! How you ghouls*—girls—*doing today?* I almost laugh now, thinking about Brett and his friends. How would they feel if they knew they'd been taunting a nymph, a gray gorgon, a macula, and a witch princess, all of us so powerful that together we could turn them into frogs, moldy amphibians to keep as pets in a jar, only kissing them back into boys when—and *if*—we felt like it?

I wish Raisa were here with me right now, to rage at our enemies, to tell them who we are and what we will do to them if they wish to stand against us. She has always been the best at succinctly saying exactly what she means, fearless—though sometimes careless—with words. I wish Renata were here, to seek out the places where nobody thinks to look. Those hiding places, those sighing places—they are saturated with a strange and wonderful sort of magic, and with it, I know Renata would be able to fashion a happy ending out of all this madness and mutiny.

And Rose, Rose—I wish only that she would press her cold, cold hands against my forehead. I wish she would stomp around this ruined forest and crush the flames beneath her feet.

Because, this place? It is not beautiful anymore.

"Should we continue on?" Gabrielle asks eventually. "There's not much we can do here."

"Actually," I say, "there is something we can do."

As much as I might miss my house by the sea, my dream within a dream, there is something here that I never had there.

Here I have magic.

I take a few steps forward, gesturing for Gabrielle to hang behind. She watches me, curious and a little wary as I look up, up, up and I revolve in place, scanning in every direction. But there is not a single cloud in sight.

I stop spinning, and close my eyes. Concentrating very hard, I send out feelers with my magic, searching for a nearby cluster of clouds, a hint of a hurricane, the start of a storm—anything already formed so that I don't have to do it myself. I feel in the direction of the forest behind me, the city before me, and the ocean beyond.

Finally I find something—a small but violent thunderstorm

about a mile or two out from the coast. I form magic hooks that sink into its edges, and when the connection seems secure, when I am so thoroughly bonded to it that the lightning is snapping and the thunder is snarling inside my own head, I stretch my hands high and drag the storm across the sky.

Gabrielle moves toward me, the heat from her body at my side almost distracting. "Um, Witch?"

I say nothing. I pull and pull.

"Witch, what are you—"

"Shhh." To her, it probably just looks like I'm tugging at an invisible rope. "You'll see in a minute."

It takes more than a minute, my arms shaking from the effort, but soon the storm is on the horizon. I still hear it in my head, but now I hear it with my ears too, gnashing both inside and out. Only once I feel a splatter of cool rain do I open my eyes and sigh. I release my hold, dropping my arms and sagging against Gabrielle's side.

"*Ah,*" she says, putting an arm around me for support. "I see."

We watch in silence for a while, periodically wiping the rain out of our eyes. The flames on the ground hiss. They don't vanish completely, but it's something, at least.

"Let's go." I push away from Gabrielle and resume walking toward the misted city, the palace. "It's time to move on."

All around us the field that was once a mighty forest sputters and writhes with the last remains of slow-smothered Star Fire as the rain falls. But soon I notice there's something odd about these clouds. They're *wrong,* somehow. Their lightning is mechanical, flashing at intervals of five seconds exactly. And the thunder—it's the same every time: a long, low howl followed by a quick crash and then deepest silence. Again and again and again.

We pause, the rain coming straight down at the same even pace. Snick of lightning, two-part thunder. Five seconds. Snick of lightning, two-part thunder. There is no wind.

The storm makes me think of Raisa, who always ran to the front porch to watch whenever one blew through. *Sometimes I feel like I'm trapped in the eye of a storm,* she said once as we stood together in the open doorway, just out of reach of the rain, clouds like thick, frayed gauze bandaging a broken sky. *Like I'm the only quiet, still thing in a world that won't stop spinning.*

"*Raisa,*" I breathe, and then I'm running, tearing across the simmering field, not toward the city, the castle, but to the eye of the storm. Neck craned back, hunting for a tower made of enchanted vapor.

The rain lashes into my eyes as lightning surges and thunder churns, never breaking its five-second pattern. It seems to go on forever.

And then, just as I'm about to give up, to convince myself I was mistaken, I see it: a cylindrical swirl of peculiar silver clouds, a whipping vortex of condensation roughly in the shape of a turret.

"Raisa!" I shout, jumping up and down and waving my arms as if she could see me. "Raisa, I'm here!"

"Can't you, uh, magic her down?" Gabrielle asks.

My face flushes, but not from the fire.

"Oh," I say. "That would probably be more effective, wouldn't it?"

Gabrielle grins, and I see the fox within. A sly, slanted sort of smile that I feel on my own lips like a froth of warmth.

"I should think so," she says.

Mock-scowling at her, I raise my hands yet again, calling on every last reserve of energy. "It's taking some getting used to, is all," I add, steeling myself.

Her smile falters. "What is?"

"Having magic again."

Just as I moved the storm, I send out hooks to grab hold of the whirling column of water and air. It stretches like a tornado, the tip touching the ground, and with all my might I focus on slowing it, and then stopping it completely. Breathing fast, my elbows overextend as I push, as I pull, as I bend the wind to my will.

Like the careening of an out-of-control carousel, the gust comes to a gradual halt. Its exterior seems almost to crack—as much as wind *can* crack—and slough away in wisps of gray.

"Raisa?"

I sift through the curling miasma, my heart growing a thousand tiny teeth with each step. Poised to eat itself raw if I can't find her or if I've hurt her. If she's—

No, no, no, no, no.

Through the fog, a voice says, "Ree?"

"Raisa!" Relief is like an injection shooting through my veins, pushing me forward, urging me toward her. But I don't quite know where her voice is coming from. "Raisa, oh my god—where are you? Where—" Inspiration strikes. *"Aflema,"* I hiss. "Disperse."

The steam immediately surrounding us clears, and suddenly my sister stands before me, not three feet away. She's still *her,* but more so: her teeth are whiter and her skin is brighter, faintly luminous, and her hair is naturally silver-blue. I don't get a good look at her eyes before she claps her hands over them.

"Rhea! Don't look at me!" She hunches over and twists away. Her magic is bubble-gum bright, flashing beneath her skin. The shape and size of it is different from mine—hers is gorgon magic, and mine is human. They have the same source, but not the same form.

I walk over to her, puzzled and pleased at once. "You—you know me, then? You remember? You remember the house by the sea?"

"Of course I remember! We were all dreaming together, weren't we? We—"

I put a hand on her shoulder, but she jerks out of reach, hiding her whole face behind her hands. Her nails are hot pink and pulsing with light.

"Don't look at me!" she says.

"Why not?"

"I'm a gray gorgon, stupid! If you look into my eyes, I'll turn you to shadow."

"Oh, right. But you never turned Renata into a shadow, did you?"

"She's a nymph. She's not human!"

"Neither am I, exactly," I say, but I rip a strip of red fabric off the hem of my already ruined dress. I tap her on the shoulder until she straightens, her eyes still covered. "Here, try this."

She fumbles blindly, then snatches the strip and ties it around her head. The fabric is opaque enough that we can't see her eyes, but thin enough that she can still see through it. She turns to look at me, and we wait. When I don't turn to shadow, she smirks, as if she were the clever one who came up with the idea.

"Excellent." She shifts on her feet, and though I can't see her eyes, I feel her avoiding my gaze. "And, uh, thanks for, like, saving me. I guess."

"You're welcome." I smile. "Thanks for—you know. Staying by me while I slept. For guarding me, even if it was only for a little while."

"Well, I mean, we were just bored and stuff." She shrugs. "We just wanted something to do."

I shake my head, feeling, for the third time, as if I might cry. Because this is exactly, *exactly* the Raisa I know. We're here, we're home, and she remembers. "I'm sure you could have found something else to do other than babysit a selfish princess."

"Whatever," she says, and I can tell she's rolling her eyes. "And for the record, it may have been a bit selfish, what you did, but—it's what I would have done too, if I were you."

We slip into silence, the rain still splashing rhythmically all around us. Lightning and thunder, every five seconds.

"Wait—who's *that*?" Raisa says, sensing Gabrielle behind me. She peers around my shoulder. Raisa quickly combs her scraggly hair with her fingers, nails winking. "Are you going to introduce us?"

"Oh, of course. Raisa, this is Gabrielle." I wave Gabrielle over, and she holds out her hand. "Gabrielle, my sister, Raisa."

"It's *very* nice to meet you," Raisa says slowly, as if she's turning the words over in her head.

Gabrielle's cheeks flush. "I, uh, yes. It's nice to meet you too. I mean, I've already met you. Sort of? You met me when I was a fox. But now I'm not. A fox, I mean. Now I'm human and I—um, nice to meet you."

Raisa's mouth is open, but no sound comes out.

"She's a shape-shifter," I say, as Gabrielle edges backward to lurk behind me. "I'll explain later. Right now we need to find the rest of our family and then get to the castle."

"And win the war and find the king who put me up in that spinning vortex of doom in the first place and make him stop," she says. "Got it. Let's go."

She stalks away, her chin high. As I start to follow, Gabrielle speaks, quietly.

"Rhea?"

"Yeah?" I pause, looking at her.

"You know what you said before, about how you're still getting used to having magic?" she says, and I nod. "Well, you *always* had magic. In every life, in every dream."

I smile, and there is no trace left of the scream that was once coiled so tightly inside me.

Chapter 20

IN THE KINGDOM

Raisa insists we need to swing by the sea before we go to the city. *Swing by,* as if we're simply making a quick stop at the supermarket for a carton of milk.

"Renata is trapped out there!" Raisa says as we emerge from the foggy field near the shoreline. "We have to get her first, then deal with everything else," she says, waving a hand as an indication of everything that's left unsaid. "Safety in numbers and all that. Plus, you need to rest."

"I don't know if you've heard," I say, "but I've been sleeping for a *month*. More sleep is the last thing I need."

She groans, adjusting the mask over her eyes as it starts to slip. "I don't mean sleep; I mean *rest*. You need to sit down for a bit, reenergize. Sorry to say, but you look terrible. Your skin is, like, *gray*."

"Apologies, Witch, but you *are* a little pale," Gabrielle adds, then recoils as I turn to glare at her. Whose side is she on, anyway? Mine, I thought, but because of the way she keeps glancing sideways at Raisa, I'm not so sure.

"All you need to do is stop the surf around her little island, and she'll come," Raisa says, hopping over a particularly fiery bunch of broken branches.

I frown. "Shouldn't we physically go get her?"

"No. I'm *telling* you. Just calm the water, and she can swim to shore. Those scary waves are the only thing stopping her. She's a really good swimmer."

"But—"

"You're forgetting, Ree—she's not *human*. She's a nymph. Swimming a mile or two for her is like what running a mile or two is for you."

"Running a mile or two is *torture* for me! Why do you think I prefer to ride a manticore through the forest?"

"Whatever. It's like running a mile or two for a normal person who's actually in shape." Behind her mask, I just know she's rolling her eyes. "Just do it! And if she doesn't show up in an hour, you can magic up a boat or something and we'll go rescue her. Okay?"

"*Fine.*"

So we head not to the city but to the sea. Just short of where the waves curl and crash, I kneel on the shore, pressing my hands to the sand, and close my eyes. I send my magic into the ground beneath me and out into the silt bottom of the sea, then let it rise up through the water like fingers reaching toward the surface, whispering the words to settle, to soothe. My voice starts to waver as energy pours out of me, and Gabrielle puts one hand on my shoulder. A little of her magic seeps through my skin to steady me. Eventually the waves flatten and slow—though I'm not sure how long this calm will last.

While we wait for Renata to reach us, I sit on the shore with Raisa and Gabrielle on either side of me, our legs stretched in front of us and the cold waves embracing our bare feet

"The tattoo on, um, the prince's back," Raisa says while we wait. I look at her, confused—both as to why she's bringing this up and as to why she called Dad *the prince*. "The one, um, your mother became so obsessed with?"

"You can call them *Mom* and *Dad*, if you want," I say quietly. "I mean, you don't *have* to. I know they're not your real parents. But I think—I think they'd want you to."

Raisa smiles, and it's like a leap of lightning, sudden and bright. "Yeah, okay. Mom and Dad." I try to reach for her hand, thinking the moment calls for it, but she slaps my hand away, and I laugh. "Anyway, the tattoo on Dad's back. It *is* a real constellation. It's just real here instead of there, in that place where we used to live."

"You're right." My memories are rushing back practically faster than I can remember, catalog, and assess them—stories and snippets, riddles and names and places and faces, all discarded in my dreams. And the constellation—I know now that it's the symbol of life, the left hand of the Wandering One. "Mom wasn't making it up."

I'm supposed to rest while we wait, but I'm not resting. *I can't.* How can I possibly relax, when I still have yet to find five more people, including Renata, who may or may not be swimming to us right now? How can I be calm when I still have to wrestle a kingdom away from a king?

To the north of us the enchanted storm still tosses, anchored in place and slowly but surely quenching the last vestiges of Star Fire. Lightning flits at the edge of my vision every five seconds, but we are too far now to hear its cadenced loop of two-tone thunder. I start to worry that moving the storm may have been a bit too conspicuous—surely someone has noticed that an *entire storm* raced suddenly across the sky and is now completely stationary over the field until it dissipates. Will the king know I'm here now?

Will he guess what I'm after?

"There she is!" Raisa jumps to her feet and rushes toward the water. Startled, I leap up and follow her, gaze raking the gentle waves. "Ren! Over here!"

I stand on tiptoe, squinting. "I don't—"

"Right *there*." Raisa points, but all I see is black water marbled with moonlight. "That's her hair! The rest of her is underwater, obviously."

"That's just a tangle of kelp. Or algae or whatever. I— *Oh!*"

As it turns out, the kelp or algae or whatever really *is* hair. Greenish-brown hair attached to a head that's attached to a body that just so happens to belong to one of my oldest friends. Her skin has a slightly blue tinge, and where she used to have freckles, she now has scales: on her shoulders, her knees, the bridge of her nose, and around her eyes like a mask, the sides of her neck. Thin and delicate rather than jutting and rigid, the scales look almost like aquamarine petals. If I were to reach out and touch them, I think they'd be soft, pliant.

When she's close enough, gliding serenely through the water, I toss my arms around her and squeeze. Her gauzy blue dress is drenched and her hair is dripping. I'd just started to dry off from the storm, but soon I'm soaked all over again. I don't mind, though. Not at all.

"I knew you'd figure it out," she whispers, and her breath is cool and brackish against my ear. I feel the stream of magic beneath her skin, clamshell clean, slick and salty. "I knew you'd come back."

I let go, taking a step away so that she has room to embrace Raisa. "You were the only one who actually remembered, weren't you?" I ask Renata. "You made the conscious choice to wake up, while the others just disappeared."

"Well, it wasn't easy. Your spell was so strong," Renata says, with admiration rather than admonishment. She kisses Raisa's cheek before releasing her, and turns back to me. "But, you know, I've always had trouble sleeping. And the sea told me. And the rain and the clouds and the snow. They always know everything, because they're *everywhere*. Water is the same in all worlds." Her gaze moves past me to Gabrielle, who lingers nearby, quiet and as vigilant as ever. "Hello. Who's this?"

"This is Gabrielle." I wave her over. "My guardian."

"So pretty," Renata says, smiling as Gabrielle nods in greeting. "Shall I drown her?"

At once Gabrielle gives a wordless grumble while bending

her legs, ready to pounce at Renata's slightest advance. But Renata only continues to smile, blinking at me expectantly.

"No, you may not!" I stamp my foot on the sand, and a tiny tremor grips the earth. Just large enough to rattle our hearts in our chests. "In fact, there will be no more killing unless I say so. I heard about what you did to those guards, Ren. And while I appreciate your helping me, you can't just go killing people all over the place, okay?"

She pouts. "But she looks so soft, and it's been so long since I last sang."

At this Raisa grabs hold of Renata's wrist, squeezing the brittle bones there. "Touch her, and I'll drown *you,* you silly girl."

"Impossible." She giggles, and her lips turn blue, almost violet. "But never mind—I can see she's important to you. Maybe you'll drown her first."

"Enough of this." The skin over my sternum is beginning to sting, to itch. A phantom pain, because when I look down, there's nothing there anymore. No slash or seam or scar. Does that mean the rose of wishes inside my macula heart has vanished too? I can't feel it blooming, swaying on its skeletal stem. My heart doesn't hurt. Not anymore.

But still—I want my witchy rose. I want my toothy palace. I want to bestow wishes. I want an altar piled high with warts and blisters, sores and torn toenails. I am willing to hurt, if it means no one else has to. If it means a wish can come true.

I look at my friends who are my sisters, and at Gabrielle. The sea is quiet, listening. The moons are faint, yawning.

They'll sleep soon, when the sun comes up. And at the same time, everyone else in the world will be waking.

"Well, we're not accomplishing anything by standing here," Raisa says. "Should we go?"

"Yes, but I don't think we should walk." I turn so that I'm facing the remains of Graiae Forest. I raise my hands and say, "*Cymst, mantichora. Cymst ot mec.*"

We wait and wait, but not for too long.

A cluster of moving shadows appears at the forest's edge, quickly coming closer. The shadows become familiar, and then they aren't shadows at all.

Four manticores, each with the lithe body of a lion, the head of a woman, and a curved tail tipped with a scorpion's stinger. They approach on padded feet, their gait smooth and silent, their shoulder blades bobbing. Renata gleefully waves to them, and Raisa yanks her hand down, holding it firmly. Gabrielle shifts in front of them, protective. Even the sea seems to shrink away, waves curling back on themselves to ensure the beasts will not touch them.

"Hello, Shay," I say to the largest of the four, who steps forward and bows with her front legs. Her breath smells like apples and cream, like dirt after rain, and mint tea leaves. It is a scent spun specially for me. Regardless of who I am, I am prey, and manticores lure prey close with the amplified aroma of the things one wants most.

But I know Shay would never hurt me, even if she were mad at me. I peer at her, trying to find any hint of fury or forgiveness in her face. But she only blinks at me, waiting, and I recall Renata's assurances from my dream life.

Shay wants me to tell you that she forgives you. I hope that's true.

"Shay, I'm so sorry I left you and the others. I was afraid of so many things—that I couldn't help you, that the king would turn me into a weapon against you, that I would never be free again." I wring my hands as the words tumble out of me, but I never avert my eyes, I never shy away. "But I'm here now, and I'm ready to fight. Will you come with me?"

For a terrible moment I think she'll say no. She stares at me, and her breath is hot as it steams in the chilly air whisking in from the ocean.

Finally Shay nods, tossing her messy mane of golden hair. She grins, rusted blood between her teeth. Her voice is spider-web sticky, just as I remember.

"Yes," she says, "of course."

A beat passes before she adds, "But our help comes with a price, my sweet, and the price is this: next time you run off, you must bring us with you, no matter where you go. We will *not* be left behind again."

In the maculate style of vows that must not be broken, I put both my hands to my heart.

"*I promise,*" I say in the old language. "It will be done."

Chapter 21

IN THE KINGDOM

We circle around the city, from here just a smear of distant light on the horizon, blurred by the speed of the running manticores and by the morning mist rising in the east, mixing with the last skyward dribbles of smoke from the fading fire in the forest to the west. The castle is not our destination yet; we are still one girl short.

As I ride on Shay's back, she tells me of the attack that happened while I was gone, the one that set the forest burning with Star Fire.

"It took weeks to plan, nearly the entire time you were away," she says, my fingers twined in her tangled hair. "A shape-shifter took the form of—well, of *you,* my sweet, and approached a guard, beseeching an audience with the king alone."

I frown at this. "That was risky."

"I know," Shay sighs. "It was not a good plan, and I was

against it. But it was also the only plan we had. So we did it. And—it worked."

Varon told me as much when I was still the Witch in the Woods in a dream, but it still baffles me. "The king really came to the woods? *Alone?*"

"Yes. I still don't quite understand it. He came, but before he could even speak, there was an explosion, and everything was burning."

"Do you know who started the fire? Did anyone see?"

"No, my sweet. It happened so very fast. The king turned and ran while a group of maculae produced a protective wall to stop the fire from spreading. But by then a quarter of the wood was already gone. Some of us wanted to keep fighting, come up with a new plan, but others decided it would be best to hide, or to leave. To start again somewhere else."

"But not you."

"But not us," she echoes.

I glance to my left at Gabrielle, who's cringing as she bounces on her manticore's back. To the right Renata sits calmly, smiling, while Raisa periodically looks over her shoulder at the stinger curled behind her.

"Can you point that thing in another direction, please?" she shouts, but the manticore either can't hear her or doesn't care.

"I don't understand," I say to Shay, her muscles rippling beneath me. I unstick a strand of hair from my lips. With no rubber band to tie it back, my hair writhes all around my head. "What did the shape-shifter say to the king to make him come?"

"I believe she said, *I know your secret.*"

"Secret? What secret?"

Shay shakes her head. "I do not know. It was all a ploy."

My eyes begin to water in the scrape of the wind, my cheeks raw and flushed. Again I try to remember everything, anything I can about my grandfather. The king, the king. He is . . . a man. A man with . . . dark hair? And . . . olive skin, like mine? Black eyes and . . . a beard? Suddenly I'm so dizzy, I nearly topple off Shay's scissoring shoulder blades.

I can't remember.

He is like the gap between two teeth, the infinitesimal space between a fingernail and the flesh beneath, the thin space between skin and soul. Life and death. Here and there. Everything and nothing.

What I'm certain of is this: whatever secret he has, hidden behind the door in the abandoned wing of the crystal castle lies a clue, a clue I can use to depose him.

And the secret is only half of this mystery. What happened when he reached the forest? Who set everything burning?

Then again, maybe it doesn't matter. Maybe all that matters is that I wasn't here to stop it.

The sun rises now above the sea, and its bleary light begins to burn away the fog from the fire and the rain. Soon Shay and the other manticores slow to a stop.

"What's this?" I say, sliding off her back. The ground is soft and springy. "Where are we?"

"The Heartless Hollow, Princess," says Shay, standing close beside me. Renata and Raisa hesitate; only Gabrielle gets to her feet and walks over. "What is left of it."

Dread drips down my spine like candle wax, my heart like a flame that someone has just blown out. I lift my hands and sweep them outward, helping the sun banish the gloom. *"Aflema."*

There are no houses here. No buildings crammed together like musty books on a shelf, sloped porches and splintered windows. No flickering streetlight orbs bobbling in the breeze. No sounds but static emptiness. No people. No life.

Only this: bricks and sticks and bones, piles of them. Slabs of glass and blackened rubble and bits of trash, a smell of melted plastic, burnt rubber. Sludge and blood and quiet flies flicking over the remains. Ashes, everywhere.

To the left, the skyline is vaguely visible now, cutting through the murk, arranged like a cluster of oversize knives stuck in the ground by their pointed tips. Like I could grasp the handle of the sharpest tower and plunge it into the rancid heart of whoever did this.

For a moment I am back in my dream life, confined again by my curse, and I wait and wait and wait for the damage to disappear, for the bricks to mortar themselves back up into buildings, for the bones and blood and ash to stitch themselves back into people.

But I am no longer cursed. And this is no dream.

I round on Shay, my fingernails flashing as spits of sparkling magic leak from my hands. *"This is not the Hollow."*

"You are right, my sweet. It is not, not anymore. But it used to be."

"Why didn't you tell me?"

"I think it is important for you to see."

Gabrielle puts her hand on my shoulder, but I wrench away from her touch. Renata and Raisa linger off to the side, silent and staring. Staring at *me*. I kick at the ash, sending it puffing into the air for all of us to choke on, wishing this were all a game. *Guess my name, Rhea Ravenna, guess my name.* That quiet, dazzling terror of contending with the Darkness was only a pinprick on my fingertip compared to the sword-slash in my stomach of this new panic.

"Use this anger, Princess," Shay says with the same spiderweb-sticky voice, "to do what must be done."

I freeze. "And what is that?"

She lifts her head, straightening her front legs. She is poised and proud. "Whatever it takes."

I raise my hands and sweep the ash out of my way as I stalk away from her, my despair disintegrating into desperation. I need to find Rose. *Now.* But if there is nothing here, then—where *is* she? If she was under a sleeping spell while whatever battle was lost here seethed through the Hollow, then what has become of her?

Plowing the ashes out of my path, I begin to run as fast as I can, the others close behind. Somewhere to the side, that infernal thunderstorm cranks like clockwork.

"Rose?" I cry. *"Where are you?"*

"Wait—Ree, over there!"

I look where Renata points, off to the left and about a hundred feet in the distance beyond a small hill of soot and cinders: a blinding glint like sunlight on a lake.

"But—" I say, and Renata rises to tiptoe as they all watch me, as if waiting for my permission to hurry forward. "But there's no water here. That's what it looks like, doesn't it? Sunlight on the surface of a pond, or . . ." I trail off.

Raisa shrugs. "Why don't we just go look?"

"It could be dangerous," Gabrielle says, stepping in front of me. "It could be some kind of tainted magic, a trap."

Shay nudges the ash on the ground beneath her, kneading it with her paws. "We do not know quite what happened here, it is true. And Rhea is right—I do not remember there being any bodies of water in the Heartless Hollow."

"Then it's *not* water." Raisa throws up her hands. The manticores remain quiet, looking to me for what to do next. Shay seems to want me to make my own decisions, and then to stick by them. "Or it *is,* and you just never knew it was here. I mean, how many times have any of you come to the Hollow to go swimming, hmm? How many of you have come here at *all*? Why would you? This place was horrible, even before all this."

Again there is a flash of light coming from the ground, shooting upward like a searchlight or a reflection or—

A reflection.

Maybe it's not water at all.

Without a word, I start toward the spot, ignoring Gabrielle's groans of protest. I run through the debris, and soon I can see that it's definitely not a lake. It's very small, and continues to gleam in the sunshine. I crest the little hill, keeping my hands slightly lifted in front of me, a thousand spells tucked under my tongue and wedged between my teeth. I'm ready to use any of them at any moment.

Almost there—

It's about twenty feet away when Gabrielle speeds up and grabs my elbow, stopping me. "Hold on," she says. "Maybe I should go first."

Renata steps forward before I can speak. "It's nothing sinister. I can tell. But—" She closes her eyes, lifting her chin. Her voice goes sort of slippery, and her head falls to one side. "Someone lost hope here. Can't you feel it?"

"I lost a little bit of hope, when I saw that the Hollow had been completely obliterated," I admit.

"You did not lose hope," says Shay firmly. "You *gained* anger."

"Wrong. I was already angry."

"Were you?"

"Of course!"

She shrugs her sleek lion shoulders. "It was not enough."

"Rhea, you need to shut up and focus," Raisa snaps before I can reply.

Shut up, shut up, shut up.

"Witch, wait here." Gabrielle rockets toward the object. Immediately I follow.

"It's—an old mirror," she says, arriving half a second before I do. She stands a few yards from it, wringing her hands and looking down. "Not magic, Witch—just a mirror."

Just a mirror?

No.

Nothing is ever *just* anything, is it?

Magic mirror, on the wall, am I beautiful—or not at all?

As the others come up behind us, uncertain, I lower myself

to my knees and crawl across the remaining few feet to where the long oval mirror lies, its ornate bronze frame slightly chipped in places but otherwise whole. I look down, fully expecting to be greeted by my own unsmiling face. But it's not there.

I don't see my own image, or that of the others gathered around me, all of us peering down at the surprisingly pristine surface, free of dirt and cracks and nicks in the glass. No, the girl who blinks back at us has long blond hair secured in a high bun, ice-cap eyes that melt and drip tears down her cheeks, a strange sheen to her skin like the side of a blade, glinting each time she moves. Like a portrait, she's visible only from the shoulders up.

"*Rose?*" Something small and sharp, pebbles or bits of shrapnel, burrow into the dry skin of my bent knees. I grip the ground, curling my fingers into the mud. "R-Rose?"

Silence and stillness and suffering. Like waiting for a voice at the end of a phone line, wondering if they've already hung up, if they've already gone.

Then, Rose's voice: "Go away."

Her lips move and she blinks. I actually twist around and look up to the place she should be in order to be reflected in the mirror. But it is only Gabrielle and Raisa and Renata and Shay huddled over me.

How is this possible?

"Rose? Is that really you?" I lean closer, pressing a fingertip to the glass. Cold, cold. For a second, I believed I might be able to reach right through and touch her. Might be able to grasp her and haul her out. But no—the mirror is solid, real. "Um, what am I seeing exactly? Are you—are you *in* the mirror?"

She shies away, half turning, so that all we see is her profile. She seems to come up against some invisible barrier, and can't quite maneuver herself completely out of the frame. Finally she hunches her shoulders, not looking at any of us. Her voice is stifled, as if she's talking through water. "Leave me alone."

"Aren't you happy to see us?" Renata says.

"I almost lost my life to a manticore sting while trying to find you," Raisa adds. "The least you could do is say hello."

Rose says nothing.

"But it *is* you, isn't it?" I seize the frame, adjusting the mirror so that it slants at an angle instead of lying flat on the ground. She wobbles a bit but doesn't lose her balance. "You're really here?"

She sighs. "Yes."

"This is strange magic," Shay says, taking a few steps back. The other manticores follow, stamping their front paws. "I do not like it."

"Don't worry. I'll just—get her out, I guess." I cross my legs, propping the mirror against my calves. "There is no spell that cannot be undone."

I don't know, actually, if this is strictly true, but it *seems* true, so I raise my hands and try to touch the edges of the magic that has bound her living body inside the mirror. As I probe, I realize that Shay is right—this magic is uncanny. It feels like a sore in the corner of your mouth, stretching and chafing each time you part your lips even a little bit, to laugh, to breathe, to bite, to scream. This magic hurts to touch, and it will probably hurt to terminate it too.

"*Liesinge*" is the only counter-curse I can think of. *Release her.* I open one eye, peeking at the results.

Nothing.

I try again. "*Cymst.*"

Nothing.

"*Abeata!*" I cry in frustration. "*Abeata, breca!*"

Nothing and nothing and nothing.

"Be careful, Princess," warns Shay. "You do not want to hurt her."

"Is this some sort of trick?" I ask Rose, wiping a fresh drip of sweat from my forehead with the back of my hand. "How did you get in there? Who put you there?"

"Well." She takes her time in answering, squinting her eyes in the mild morning sun. "I put *myself* here, Rhea. For protection. This is an unbreakable mirror. It's been in my family for ages. Each night before I went to find you, I said a spell and crawled into the mirror to sleep, where I knew I'd be safe if anything happened. You can't dream when you're dead."

"That is very *clever* magic," says one of the manticores, impressed, and Shay exhales, stamping her paws.

"Thank you," Rose murmurs. "Only *I* can undo the spell, though."

"Well, great," I say, slightly annoyed that she didn't just say this outright. "Then are you coming out now?"

"I'd rather not, thanks."

"What? Why?"

"Because."

It's like we're four years old again. "Because *why*?"

"I have my reasons."

I give the frame a sharp shake. Not enough to injure her, only to rattle her, just a little. *"Come out of there right now."*

She stumbles. "No."

"I command it."

"No."

"As your princess, I command it!"

"No."

"As the Witch of Wishes in the Woods, I command it!"

"Look around!" she cries, her voice thumping against the glass. "This doesn't look like the Woods to me."

I shake the mirror again, wanting to hurl it halfway across the world. "You're being stupid, Rose!"

"I don't care."

"So what are you going to do? Stay in there and sulk forever?"

"Maybe." Her eyes flick up to the others, then back to me. She speaks quietly, and I have to lean in to hear. "I am not beautiful anymore."

"That's ridiculous."

"No, it's not." She doesn't look me in the eye as she speaks. "My magic—it isn't wonderful like yours. When I use too much of it too fast, I get dizzy, I get *sick*—my chest hurts, and I feel like I can't breathe. I get tired so easily, and my head starts to feel like it's being squeezed by huge hands that won't let go. It's not—it's not pretty. It's messy, and it makes me feel like I can't handle things. Like I'm not—I don't know. Worthy."

"Rose," I say, my heart breaking for her, all my frustration driven away. "I'm not a doctor, but I don't think any of that is because of your magic. It sounds like anxiety. It sounds like you have panic attacks. And that's nothing to be ashamed of. It doesn't make you weak or not able to handle things, and it doesn't make you any less of a macula than me, or anyone else. I mean, look at me—I'm the *queen* of anxiety. Or, rather, the princess! It comes with a crown I can never take off, but some days I don't even notice it's there. And during the times when it became too heavy for me to hold my head up, in our life with the house by the beach when I had visions and nightmares, no one in our family ever called me crazy, even though my crown was invisible to you. Worth has *nothing* to do with it. You know that, don't you?" Rose says nothing. I stand up, taking the mirror in my arms. "I'll just take you and the mirror with me. And you can let me know when you're ready to come out, okay?"

"I may never be ready."

I try to smile, but the corners of my lips don't quite curl the way I want them to. "Then I'll carry you forever."

Her gaze flits up to me, then back down again. She nods once, and says nothing more.

"Here. I'll carry her," Renata says. "You should keep your hands free. In case of a magical emergency."

"Yes, good thinking. But hang on just one second. . . ." Still clutching the mirror, I hurry away from them, scattering ash with my feet. I don't go far—just far enough to be out of earshot. "I wanted to ask you something. Your name—is it really *Rose*?"

"Um, no. You didn't know my name as the princess, so

Rose is the one you gave me in the dream. My name's really *Vittoria*." She gives me a sheepish shrug. "But I think I like *Rose* better."

"But are you sure? *Vittoria* is so pretty."

"I don't feel like Vittoria anymore."

"Okay," I say, nodding. "Then *Rose* it is."

"Thank you."

I start to turn, but stop when she speaks again.

"Have you found Varon yet? Is he all right?"

Varon, Varon, Varon. The boy in the darkness, my Fox Who Is No Fox.

I bite the inside of my cheek. "No, he's not here. I think he's in the castle, where he was before my second sleeping spell."

I straighten my shoulders, gazing over the frame of the mirror to the sea glass skyline beyond, my heart clenching with something like determination.

"But don't worry," I say, grim and eager all at once. "It just so happens that that is *exactly* where we're going."

Chapter 22

IN THE KINGDOM

The city stands, but it is empty.

Massive and winding, with shiny black streets that always look freshly paved and edged in scalloped cement, sidewalks like lace. Enchanted orbs that float at night like tethered balloons, conjuring shadows that drip like rain down the sides of the seven-story houses, tall and narrow and tightly touching each other, heavy doors adorned with all manner of gothic flourishes: corrugated steel columns and chrome corbels, copper gargoyles and stained glass windows ranging from tongue-pink to bloodless-lip lavender to apricot blush. The houses grow wider and sturdier and taller and newer the closer you come to the palace, which is set far from the inland entrance and sits proudly on a cliff overlooking the sea.

The crystal castle is really a cluster of skyscrapers in the shape of a castle. It's sprawling, enormous, with towers like turrets rising one hundred stories high, connected to each other by long, slanted bridges with rounded glass roofs.

Behind the keep at the castle's center, out of sight, is the abandoned wing made entirely of stone, with only little holes cut into it at intervals to let in trickles of light. There is no moat or battlements or anything like that; this is not a fortress. The king was confident that the castle would never be attacked.

And he was right. Even now it's still polished and perfect and impermeable, like a city in itself.

"I feel sick," Raisa complains as we walk down a deserted street, the castle high on the hill before us. "All your life you've had to live in this nauseating monstrosity, Ree. How did you stand it?"

"I didn't really have a choice."

"Do you feel it now?" she asks. Even Shay and the manticores appear paler than normal, nauseous and cringing.

"I don't know." I'm a little dizzy, but I'm not sure if that's due to the steel storefronts and iron facades of the mansions, or to the anticipation of what I might find when I get to the top of that hill. Dad, Mom, Varon—they are all there, and that thought comforts me, the thought of seeing them soon.

But.

The king is there too.

I look down at myself, at my palms and my elbows and my knees, just visible beneath the hem of my ripped dress. My glow has dimmed. Maybe it's the metal, or maybe it's something else. Something like fear.

Misty sunlight illuminates the stained glass in the houses on either side of the street, casting us in colored shadow. Soon we pass into the heart of the town, which is as quiet as a graveyard, with only the sound of whispers and breathing and footfalls skimming the sidewalk somewhere out of sight. A prickling starts at the top of my spine, and my heart starts to beat very fast.

"Is it always like this?" Renata whispers, clutching the mirror to her chest, her arms wrapped around the bottom of the frame so that Rose can still see out. "Is it always so . . . dead?"

"No," I say, thinking of the first crowds usually forming in front of the shops along these streets even at such an early hour, and the elevated trains that slid high above the street, floating along on unseen tracks. "It used to be very much alive."

Raisa shudders and sidles closer to Gabrielle's side. "Then where is everybody?"

"Hiding," Shay says, nodding toward the nearest building. For the first time, I realize there are people inside all these seemingly empty houses and stores, their noses pressed to the windows. They're watching as we walk by. "Most fled the castle when the burning of the Hollow and the forest began. But some stayed, Princess. The ones who had nowhere else to go."

I look back behind me, and there are faces there too, out in the open, eyes on the ground that tentatively flick up to me and back down. The people dart into alleys when they see me seeing them. I stop, and my sisters and Gabrielle and the manticores stop too, and together we watch as the people emerge from their hidden places behind posts and corners and front doors. Some of them have brands on their hands and red sores on their wrists where iron chains once chafed their skin, while others have large X's inked on the backs of their hands to show their solidarity. The rest of the Forest Forgotten are there too, the children still in their stolen uniforms, weapons in hand.

"The whole world did not wait for you, Princess," says Shay as others join the crowd, sighing sylphs with dragonfly eyes and wet-haired nymphs and sphinxes with scarlet-stained paws. Winged wyverns with slick, thick scales, and gray gorgons wearing black veils over their faces so that they can see us but we can't see them. So, so many creatures, some with two legs or four legs or no legs or wings. Creatures that laugh and creatures that lie, creatures with hearts small and strange, hearts that spill magic and others that don't.

I can hear every one of them, every heart, and all of them sound like hope, quiet and hungry and trembling and divine.

"But those who waited are now the world," Shay says. "They are everything that is left, everything that matters."

Gabrielle takes my hand, and Raisa takes hers, and Renata takes Raisa's, forming an unbreakable chain. I swallow, lick my lips, and stare, and now is not the time for crying but I want to anyway. I don't cry, though. I don't.

Can't.

Won't.

They seem to be waiting. Waiting for me to say something.

"I promise only that I will try my best," I say. "I promise I won't leave you again."

They say nothing.

But they're not waiting for me to *say* something, I realize as I resume our trek toward the castle, still holding Gabrielle's hand, my other palm pressed to Shay's furry flank. They're waiting for me to *do* something.

So I walk.

And.

They follow.

Through the narrow streets, silence skulking in front of and behind us, stretching from side to side. More people slip out of their houses to join us, and the sun fully opens its eyes after a long, restless night.

Soon the palace is right there, right in front of us. Rising up and up and up, glimmering steel, sparkling windows. My feet ache, my head aches, but adrenaline or love or fear or maybe all three have their jaws clamped in me, and I know I couldn't lie down and sleep just now even if I tried.

"Witch?" Gabrielle says, her voice low. "What now?"

They're all waiting for me, everyone who has followed me to this vacant, quiet place. Why is it so vacant, so quiet?

I set my hands on the heavy iron doors in the place where the knobs should be. At my touch, curlicues of dark green and violet light spiral swiftly along the surface of the metal, spreading until the entire double doorway is illuminated in loops and whorls. The doors then slide apart without a sound.

I step inside. Into the castle, into the palace where I grew up. But though I have lived here for the entirety of one of my lives, it does not feel like home.

The others squeeze in around me, Raisa and Renata and Gabrielle and Shay the closest, with the three hundred or so others clustered behind. Once everyone has passed through the doors, they slide closed on their own.

Empty, empty, empty. And cold, so cold that braids of goose bumps quiver all across my skin. The walls, the floor, the ceiling—everything is made of the same smooth, opaque material. We call it crystal, but it's not; it's magic, in its pure and solid form. An emerald sunburst pattern in the floor at the center of the cavernous foyer shoots out to form a single stripe down the center of each of the four hallways. The windows set at even intervals along the corridors let in only frail light—they've been charmed to obscure the harshest rays of the sun and the moons, rendering the interior permanently dreary.

I turn to those who followed me here. I put on my princess face.

"Search the castle. Disarm any guards you come across. Find anyone who might be hiding or in need of help. Once you've found them, get them out. I'll join you once I've found my family." *And the staircase,* I think. "Okay?"

No verbal reply, only the soft shuffle of eager footfalls as they steal away, prowling together through the shadowed halls. Except my closest companions, all waiting for me to announce our next move.

"Gabrielle, go to the dungeons and look for a boy with black hair and—"

"Varon." Gabrielle scowls, crossing her arms over her chest. "I met him in the Woods, remember? And the attic too."

"Oh, right." I give her a stern look. "Be nice, okay? I would go myself, but I need to find my parents. Please release him and bring him to the rooftop temple. Shay, will you go with her?"

Shay lifts her head and locks her knees. "Princess, I will not leave your side."

"But—"

"I'll be fine on my own," Gabrielle says, already turning and running down the hall. "Don't worry about me!"

"Be careful!" Raisa calls as Gabrielle disappears. Then she snatches a piece of her silvery hair and nervously chomps it between her teeth. When Renata giggles and playfully pinches her shoulder, Raisa smacks her hand away.

"The rooftop temple," I say, reaching again for Shay's mane, curling my fingers into her hair. "That's where Mom and Dad will be. I'm sure of it."

"This is so creepy," Raisa whispers as I pull them along, treading carefully down the corridor straight ahead.

At every moment I expect someone—the king, his guards, anyone—to come crashing around the corner, weapons held high and voices raised. The hallways are dotted with doorways leading to various rooms, but none of them open, and no one springs out at us. "Where is everyone?" I say. "I don't like this at all."

"Shhh," Renata says. "Someone broke their own heart here. Can you feel it?"

"Kind of," Raisa admits.

"You should really free your hands, my sweet," says Shay as I lead them down another hallway, identical to the first, letting my memory guide me to the spiral stairs that will take us to the roof of the keep. She gently shakes her head, trying to get me to let go. "Just in case."

I tighten my grip.

On and on and on we go, through the clinically clean corridors with the eerie echo of our footsteps and our scrambled heartbeats, with sweat dripping down our spines.

We finally reach the temple stairs, tucked on the other side of an open archway. I'm forced to relinquish my grasp on Shay's hair, moving forward, with Raisa just behind, and Renata behind her, cradling the mirror to her chest. Shay is in the rear, her warm breath fogging up the passage with a mess of sharp scents. I try to breathe through my mouth.

As the crystalline windows light up the stairwell, I know this isn't the stairwell from my visions. Except, I see something skim quickly into and out of view, an errant shadow on the high ceiling. And I hear a voice, saying my name. But the voice is all wrong, not the voice I've been longing to hear. It's like flaking rust, unraveling at the edges, instead of smooth and solid and certain.

"Rhea Ravenna . . ."

Before I can think it through, I lift my hands and hiss, *"Forla!"*

An iridescent ball of crystal blasts through the wall above Raisa and Renata, a ball made of the same substance as the castle, solid magic. The fracture-snap of splintering glass echoes through the stairwell, and even Rose flinches, safe inside her unbreakable frame.

Raisa clasps her hands over her ears until the ringing fades. "What was *that*? Are you trying to kill us?"

The wall is covered in contorted cracks that have turned wine red. With the hard knot of magic lodged at the center, it looks like a bloodshot eye, unblinking.

"I thought I saw something," I gasp, wrapping my trembling arms around my waist. "I thought—but I guess it was just a shadow."

"Leave strange shadows to me, Your Highness," Raisa snaps. "I'm the shadow expert here."

She folds her arms over her chest, while I look apologetically at the others.

"Someone lost their patience on these stairs," Renata says gravely, and a laugh boils in my chest but never quite makes it out of my mouth; it scalds my ribs, trapped inside.

"Come on," I say, and the others follow me as I start to run, hastening to reach my parents. My calves throb, and I'm so dizzy that I stumble a dozen times, but I do not stop or slow, my hands raised and tingling.

But we come across no one. Not even a shadow.

Why is this so easy? I think. *It should* not *be so easy.*

Finally we come to the temple's door with its big, iron filigrees, and when I press my hands against it, it shudders and slides sideways into the wall, just like before.

The sun—it's everywhere, everywhere. I shield my eyes and step out onto the open roof.

"We're here," I breathe.

Steel columns soar on all sides, and overhead are several arched iron beams, between which slices of sky are visible, bright, bright blue. I see the Wandering One, the god with two faces whose golden hood is peeled back, revealing its horns, hands stretched out, carrying life in its left hand and death in the right. I wonder which palm he will press to my chest today.

The last time I was up here, Mom was dead. The time before, I pricked one of the fingers on my left hand, knowingly letting blood from the wrong hand dribble onto the altar for death. I had been working myself up to it for a while, for years, telling myself that it was silly to be afraid, because if I had been performing this ritual all my life under the guise of normalcy and had yet to be cleansed of the "taint" of magic, then it was all empty anyway. It meant nothing. The Wandering One was just a man in a fancy cloak with white and black smoke stuck between his fingers. What was he compared to me? I had magic, and kindness, and cruelty, and a heart that reflected sunshine at night, so bright that the ocean answered my call.

Nothing happened.

Little did I know what would happen two weeks later—it was not just Mom but the reveal of my magic that followed, which weighs heavily upon me now.

I turn away from the altar, and suddenly the open sky, the metal, the intensity of the light—none of this is as magnificent and distracting as the glass casket in the center of the temple, one that was not there the last time I was here. A casket with a sleeping woman inside, curled on her side with her knees to her chest and her hands under her cheek, her skirts twisted around her legs. A starburst-bloom of black hair spread over a white pillow, bare feet with long toenails curling like dried leaves. And a man hunched over her, a man with his sleeves rolled up to reveal a tattoo on his forearm in silver ink—silver, not black like they once were in a dream. Here, silver is considered the color of the soul.

"Dad?"

He looks up. "Rhea?"

I rush across the temple and around the bier to where he stands, and I tumble into his arms. After several long seconds he releases me and reaches out to embrace Renata, who carefully sets the gilded mirror on the ground before tossing her arms around his neck. If he is surprised by her blue-tinged skin and her scales and her wet hair, he doesn't show it.

"My girls, my girls, you're here." He lets go of Renata to reach for Raisa, who balks, scrunching her lips and staying very still, like a confused but polite pet who does not understand this human inclination to squeeze to death the things we love.

"I know you're not technically my dad here," Raisa says when he finally relinquishes Renata, "but I'm still basically your daughter, and I, you know—I love you or whatever."

Dad laughs, and it makes my knees go squishy with relief. Relief that we are all here now, together. Dad is laughing, and that means everything will be fine, everything will be fixed.

"Oh, Ray, I love you—or whatever—too," he says. "Our time in the beach house was the happiest I've been in a long while. Not because we were living in a dream but because I was there with all of you, being a father instead of a prince." But then his smile slides sideways and my knees stiffen again. "But wait—where is Rose?"

Renata picks up the mirror and holds it high for him to see.

Rose says nothing, only angles her chin to the side, as if there is something more interesting there, just out of sight, than our reunion. But she doesn't fool me, not for a second.

"Rose?" Dad peers into the mirror, touching his fingertips to her reflection. As soon as he does, swirls of ice crystals bubble and blister on the surface, and he snatches his hand back. "What's going on?"

"She says—" I begin, but while we stand here, the sun that

should be warm isn't anymore. I have a sudden thought that I'm standing in someone else's shadow, someone standing just behind me, but when I check over my shoulder, no one is actually there. My magic recoils from it, from the shadow that is no shadow, reversing in my veins, and it feels like a fingernail bent backward. "She'll come out when she's ready."

"Uh, all right." Dad looks up from the mirror, and over his shoulder to Shay. She smiles, displaying her blood-speckled teeth, and I know he probably smells roses, roses and lilacs and lavender. His eyes jump to me. "Rhea, what's all this?"

"If by 'all this' you mean the manticore, her name is Shay and she *won't eat you*," I add, giving her a pointed look as I leave Dad's side to pace around the coffin. I'm still in the sunlight, but I don't *feel* it. Something is there, something is saturating the air, absorbing the warmth before it reaches me. "And what we need to do right now is wake Mom up and get out of here."

The wind changes direction abruptly—first it comes from the east, and then from the west, as if driving the sun across the sky, impatient for night.

"What's happening?" Renata says, and we all look up. "Why's the sun going away?"

And I realize: the wind really *is* pushing the sun, shoving it back below the horizon, stuffing it down, the world receding back into night.

On its way to jostle the sun, the wind delivers a whisper, another one, same as the first except louder, insistent, a voice that could be coming from a thousand miles away or, just as easily, from right behind me.

"*Rhea Ravenna,*" says the unseen someone, and it is like a prophecy, a promise: *You were, you are, you always will be.*

Something is here, something sticky and stale and slithery, and I don't want it anywhere near me. Near *us.* I have found my family, and nothing is going to take them away from me again.

"I don't know what's happening," I say, and since no one reacted to the strange voice saying my name, I'm fairly certain I'm the only one who heard it. "But I know we need to leave."

"Slow down," Dad says. "We should—"

"No." I press my hands to the coffin, looking in at Mom. I knock a few times, open-palmed, as if the sound might jar her back to life. "How do we get her out?"

"Don't bang on the glass like that!" Raisa rushes over and pushes my hands away. I flit out of her grasp, around to the other side. "You'll disturb her. You'll deafen her!"

"Ray, she's not a fish."

"I don't like it here." Renata hugs the mirror to her chest again. "I don't *like* it here."

Shay walks over to the open edge of the temple and lifts her front paws onto the ledge so she can look down. "There are people gathered on the ground, and more are pouring out the front door," she tells us. "It might be wise, Your Highnesses, to adopt a sense of urgency."

I run my hands over the casket, searching for a clasp, a hinge. "How do you open this?"

"I want Mom out of there," Renata says, nearly shouting. "I want her out *now.*"

Leaving the ledge to rejoin us, Shay huffs and coils her

stinger more tightly over her back. The shadows from the steel columns are slanted now, the sun pushed lower and lower. In the west, a few sleepy stars blink their eyes, confused. "I don't know what to do," Dad says quietly. "She's not under a spell, as far as I know. It's more like she's in a coma."

"Let me think." I turn to the altar of life to my left, then swing my gaze to the right. Offerings of flowers and wine, of silk and blood. Death, the ultimate riddle. And there is only one person I know who knows the answer. Who knows how to reverse it, to stall it, to trick it.

What was it that the Fox Who Is No Fox said, when he told me how the necromancer—how *he*—had brought my mother back from death? That her magic—that her *veins* had been scraped clean of it, and that—that there was little hope of reviving her entirely without injecting her with more.

I close my eyes and whisper, "Varon?"

Nothing.

"Darkness?" I try.

I open my eyes. Still nothing. The sun is nearly sunken, and is splashing us with rosy golden light. Bright and sharp and wrong, wrong, wrong.

Please, I think. *Where are you? I need you.*

I stamp my foot. *Aren't you supposed to come when I call?*

Then, finally, an answer: *"Rhea Ravenna,"* says the wind, the walls, the other side of the world, and though it has his cadence, this voice does not belong to the boy I seek.

But neither is it entirely unfamiliar.

"Mom needs magic," I say, everything in me shivering, clattering, everywhere aching. Slowly, so slowly that I didn't notice until now, the others have been creeping forward, so that we're all gathered close around the casket, a private vigil of restless mourners.

Dad sighs, rubbing his eyes, both relieved that the problem has been identified and stymied by the solution. "How does she get some, then?"

"It has to be given to her." *I am not afraid*. "I'll give her mine."

"Rhea, you can't!" Renata cries. Shay, startled, blows a cloying cinnamon breath across the coffin and into my face. Raisa combs her fingers through Renata's long wet hair to calm her. "We need your magic. We need *you*!"

"Wait," Dad says. "Rhea, wait. If you do that, then won't you fall into a coma too?"

"I'm not sure," I admit, my heart tripping over itself in my chest. I'm willing to do this, of course, but still there is a part of me that wishes I didn't have to, that there was another way. "But donation isn't the same as depletion. Her magic was taken from her, whereas mine would be given freely."

Dad stares at me. "How much magic are you planning to give her?"

I shrug, trying to hide my anxiety. "A lot? At least enough to jump-start her second heart."

"We shouldn't wake Mom at your expense," Raisa says. "She wouldn't want that. Can't we strap her to Shay's back to take her with us and then figure out what to do later? I mean, we kind of need your magic right now. In *you*."

"*No*. I have to—"

"I'll do it."

We turn. The sun is gone now, and except for the stars and the seven moons, the sky is black. But still I can see her there, a little removed from the rest of us, eyes downcast and small sprigs of gold hair escaping from her bun and curling around her face.

Rose.

Her magic—it's different from mine. I feel it at once, plunge my hands into it, cup it in my palms and let it drip through my fingers: sloshing and saturated, her magic is like slogging down a wintery sidewalk in boots and a dress while the wetness gradually spreads through your tights, creeps up your calves and the backs of your knees, your thighs. Uncomfortable, soggy. It doesn't sit well inside her.

"I'll do it," she repeats when no one says anything. "I'll give Mom my magic. *All* of it."

Everyone starts talking at once. Only I am quiet.

"Rose, you're here! We—"

"No, no. Rhea will—"

"Wow, look, the mirror is empty!"

"Let's just—"

"Can't we—"

"But if—"

"If each of you give *half*—"

"Mom wouldn't—"

"Stop!" Rose cries. "*Please.* It should be me. I hate my magic—I've always hated it. It makes me so sick whenever I use it. I don't want it. I don't *need* it. But Mom does. And if it makes her sick too, then when she's strong enough again, she can donate it to someone else, someone who won't get sick from it." She drops her hands and walks over to me. "Rhea, do the spell. I'm ready."

"I'm telling you, Rose," I say. "It's not your magic that's hurting you. This isn't going to solve anything."

"Rhea, come on," she pleads. "You *know*. You must know how this magic hurts me."

"But—"

"We have to get out of here," Raisa interrupts, her gaze on the darkness swelling through the sky. "Like, *now*."

I turn to Rose. "You say your magic hurts you. But what if this spell hurts you more?"

"I'm prepared to accept whatever comes. I want to do what's right. And I know she's not really my mother, but I love her too." She smiles. "I can do this, Ree. I came out of my mirror, didn't I?"

Seconds go by, fluttering past, and panic prickles my chest so that I can't breathe or sigh or cry or think. Or scream.

"Okay." I need to calm down, to think clearly. I have to open the casket. But there's no hinge. And that's because—*of course*. Because it's magic. I place my hands on the glass, as much bracing myself as preparing to invoke the spell.

Rose puts her hands beside mine.

"*Fofalda*," we intone. Not precisely in sync, but close enough. "*Fofalda, ze.*"

At once the glass vanishes. The others watch in mute wonder as I gently but quickly prod one of my mother's hands out from underneath her cheek, then lift her limp arm until her wrist is on top of Rose's, my hands holding theirs together, one of mine on top, and the other below. I breathe in and in and in.

And then: *"Alenia se dricraf awell."*

Immediately the spell manifests, a mixed-up midnight star-swoop, a planetary parade of whiplashed light, concussed constellations, knock-kneed nebulae, and two girls wearing tiaras of tangled starlight, loops of asteroids around our necks. It's like the whole universe is surging through us. It pours out of Rose, through my fingers, and into our mother.

Let the magic flow.

Rose closes her eyes, while Mom's slowly, slowly start to open.

When the last drips of magic have been funneled from one to the other, I let go of their hands. Rose's cheeks are blanched. When I ask if she's okay, she says, "I don't know. I think—I think I'll be okay, though."

She doesn't look okay, or at least not her best, but since she's still speaking and breathing and her heart is still beating, I take that as a good sign. Once I'm certain that she's really all right, that she won't faint or throw up or worse—every one of us presses closer to the coffin, human and maculae and nymph and gorgon and manticore. We look anxiously at Mom, who has rolled onto her back, blinking and breathing and utterly silent. Dad crouches down and takes her hand, presses a kiss to her brightening cheek.

I say, "Mom? Are you awake?"

Her eyes swivel to me, shiny and lucid, but before she can part her lips to speak, someone else speaks instead: *"Rhea Ravenna, come to me."*

Dad's head snaps up. "What was that?"

This time, we all heard it.

Renata twines her arms around her waist and hunches over, as if the voice has cut her, slicing her in the stomach. "*Who* was that?"

Raisa brings a hand to her makeshift mask, ready in a moment to lift it up and turn the intruder to shadow if she has to. Shay's dirty mane bristles.

"We have to go," I say, and without protest Dad hooks his arms underneath Mom and lifts her to his chest. Groggy, muddled, she wraps her arms around his neck. I wave for them to follow and say, "Come on."

We sprint toward the door on the north side of the roof, the only exit. Raisa gets there a second before I do, but we all stop as she jerks the door open.

Something is different now; something is wrong.

There is nothing but empty blackness beyond.

Chapter 23

IN THE KINGDOM

Darkness. Laughing. The darkness itself is laughing.
Or.

Someone is laughing in the darkness.

I don't know which is worse.

I step farther into the hallway, but there is nothing to see. Nothing to hear, except the soft laughter. Or is it merely breathing? Or weeping? Or nothing, nothing at all. The others follow me. Do they hear it, feel it, too?

"Litus," I say, to no effect. *"Alita,* please. *Alita."*

I try a different luminosity spell, but it doesn't work. I drop my hands, blinking fast. "This isn't ordinary darkness."

"We will just have to manage without sight, then," Shay says. "We have other senses, other strengths to guide us."

"At least I don't need this mask anymore," Raisa says, pulling the fabric off her eyes, careful not to look at us directly until we are completely submerged in the shadows. "Come on, Ree. Let's *go.*"

Gulping, inhaling, as if I'm about to plunge into a pond and not into silent sightlessness, I take a step, and then I run down the stairs. My family trips after me, and only the stamping of our feet smothers the cold, rough laughter. I long for my attic, for *my* Darkness, because this is someone else's Darkness, and I'd rather be eaten alive by my own fright than by this new terror that laughs but does not grin.

We finally stagger to the bottom, pile into the hallway, and press close together. I startle at the sound of Gabrielle's voice.

"Witch? What's going on?" she says, her breathing uneven. "I went to the dungeons, but—they were empty."

"Empty? Are you sure?"

"I got a good look before everything went dark. No one was there."

I chew the inside of my cheek, thinking. I *hoped* he would be in the dungeons, but maybe that was only wishful thinking. Because if I *really* think about it, what comes to mind are the staircase and the door from my dream. If I find that door and open it, will Varon be behind it, waiting for me like he waited in the attic? I picture him, remembering the first time I met him—in *this* world, not in the attic. He found me, told me he knew I had magic, and I led him to the north wing of the castle, where I'd been told never to go.

Where I'd been told.

Never.

To go.

And who had told me that? *The king.*

I put my hand on the wall both to steady my nerves and

so I won't lose my way. Addressing my family, I say, "Exit the castle and join the others. I'll be there soon."

"Where are you going?" Dad says, and the air around me flutters as someone reaches for me. "We are *not* splitting up."

"I have to. I'm sorry; I have to." *I must find the staircase and Varon,* I think, and am already walking down the hallway, feeling along the wall. I'm guided by the laughter that sounds more and more like howling, like weeping, as I hurry along. I shout back over my shoulder, "There's one more thing I have to do."

"I'll come with you!" Rose already sounds far away, and her footsteps falter as if someone grips her wrist and yanks her back. "No. Let go, Ray—I mean, Ren—I mean, whoever you are. Wait for me, Rhea!"

"No!" My voice echoes, and I wish everyone would be quiet so that I can follow the sound of this new, unknown darkness. "I'll be all right. I promise!"

Except.

I can't really promise that. I can't, because I don't know. I don't know if I will be all right.

I skitter and slip on the glossy floors, and I close my eyes even though it makes no difference if they are open or shut. It's difficult to leave my family behind, especially because I've just found them, but I sprint across the castle until I can no longer hear their reverberating protests. There is a door in this darkness, and I need to know what's behind it.

Jamming my feeler-fingers against doorknobs and sconces as I pass room after room, rounding corners, listening for the source of the magic that created this spell. Created by an Immacula, I assume, the very one I seek, forced to cast it by the one who seeks me now as well.

Thoughts push their way into my mind, thoughts of my grandfather holding Varon against his will, forcing him to create this darkness, to be smothered by it, tortured—*no*. I have to believe that Varon is okay, that there is still time to save him, that the king is only using him as another tool to bait me.

"Rhea Ravenna, come to me . . ."

Finally the wall gives way to a set of double doors, and I intone an unlocking spell as I push against them. A brief swirl of silver cuts through the gloom as they unlock and glide silently aside.

And then I am in the old stone north wing of the castle, and I sense, rather than know, that there's a thick glamour hiding this place, and has been for a long time, so that no one would know about it. A glamour the king took no steps to strengthen even after Varon and I were able to see through it.

But *why* is this wing kept in shadow?

The thought sends chills down my spine, and I press on.

It takes me only a minute to run down the corridor. A steep staircase is at its end. Though my lungs seize, I never slow, climbing up and up and around and around. The tower is short, only a story-and-a-half high, and the ocean laps at its northern wall, splashing halfway up the outer stones at high tide. When I reach the top, I pause to catch my breath, the doorway from my dream-not-dream rising before me, shimmering around the edges. It's almost a relief, seeing it there, knowing for certain it's real. But my relief is soon dampened; it is not enough to find the door. I have to *open* it.

To my right is a glassless window, a narrow, arched slit in the stone, and through it I get a glimpse of the stars doing their best to burn through the darkness stretched like a pulled muscle from horizon to horizon.

The stars say, *This is it*.

The moons chime, *Mind your magic*.

Together they tell me, *It is okay to be afraid*.

I reach out, ready with a spell, but the door isn't locked. Maybe it never was, and I was just too wary to open it, too frightened of what I might find.

I'm frightened now too, but I do it anyway. The door swings heavily, a screech of rotted wood and iron hinges. When I step across the threshold, the door slams shut behind me. I jump.

"Hello?" I whisper, shivering in the cold and the stillness and the silence. An odor rises, nearly unbearable, like stale rain on an overturned grave. Even the ocean is quiet, listening. "Grandfather? Varon, are you here?"

Not even the stars can break through the heavy darkness. Holding my hands out in front of me, I take a step forward. And then another and another. I keep walking until I finally hit something with my toe, slamming my foot hard against what I think is stone. I lower my hands, reaching, and my fingers brush something that feels like skin.

Like a mouth.

Moving.

"Rhea Ravenna," says the king's reverberating voice as I recoil, stumbling back with a cry. It has always been him, murmuring and mocking me with my name, the surname that we share. But it's louder now, clearer. Coming from right in front of me.

I move quickly in what I think is the direction from which I came, but I soon collide foot-first with another hard object, and another beyond that, and each time I reach my hands up, I feel something different: matted hair, a wrinkled cheek, a smooth and pointed knuckle. Finally I cross my arms over my chest, squeezing my eyes closed and backing up, backing away.

What is this place? I want to shout, but all I manage is a whisper. "Where am I?"

"I will show you," comes the reply. "But you must promise not to scream."

I almost laugh. Almost. "I can't promise that."

"Well, then, something must be done."

Another voice comes from somewhere very near, and this one is familiar even strained with desperation, a cracked masterpiece. "My sky, I—"

His voice cuts off, and my breath with it as a hand wraps around my throat from behind me, forcing my head back. Warm flesh and ironbound wrists, magic like the snap of a pulled wishbone. I would know him anywhere, my Darkness, my Fox Who Is No Fox. He has his other arm around my waist, immobilizing my arms, crushing me against him, spine to sternum, and I want to ask why he is doing this, but I can't speak, I can't scream, I can't—

"I am so sorry," he says. His teeth grind with effort, whether to hurt me or not, I can't be sure.

"Do not choke her," commands the king. "Just hold her."

Varon's hand relaxes only slightly, his fingertips pressed over my pulse at the side of my throat. I gasp and blink. My neck is stretched back so far that I fear my skin might split.

The darkness begins to lift, gathering like a storm cloud, high, higher, highest above our heads, and suddenly I can see everything.

Everything.

Everything.

The room in front of me is wide but shallow, with no walls and no roof save for the Gothic arches connecting overhead like steepled fingers, supported by columns made from the vertebrae of impossibly enormous beasts. A chandelier of sickly white antlers hangs from the center of the arches, the bones giving off a faint blue glow.

But none of this is enough to startle me, even though it is disconcertingly reminiscent of my castle in the Woods, as if the king had peered into my dreams and designed this place specifically for me. No, what makes me want to scream is a row of thrones carved out of giant teeth, arranged around the room in a half circle like the steep curve of a jaw. And in every throne sits a body, all in varying states of decay: some with their eyes open as if they've only just awoken from a deep sleep, others with their skin scraped away in places to reveal the bone beneath. But all with their heads bowed, all with a fist-size hole in their chests, crusted with old blood. Wrinkled cheeks, maggots in their hair. Knees pressed together, hands clasped, blue-violet lips parted as if begging for one last breath.

It takes me a moment to realize that of all the bodies before me, one isn't dead, the man in the center of the crescent. His flesh is wrinkled as if he's had all the water sucked out of him, and the veins of his hands bulge as he grips the edges of the tooth. His chest rises and falls, quickly and shallowly. His head is adorned with a gold crown, and the scarlet cloak wrapped around his shoulders sweeps down to the floor. His eyes, a pale, shivery blue, lock onto mine and stay there. Only his mouth moves as he speaks.

"Rhea Ravenna. Blood of my blood, my littlest crown jewel. Here you are, at last."

I try to speak, but still I can't.

"Do you know what it is like to be the ruler of a land wherein half your subjects wield more power than you?" the king rasps, indifferent to my disgust. "When they could cut you deeper than any knife with just one word, when they could humiliate you, laugh at your weaknesses and spit in the face of your laws? Do you know what it is like for a king to kneel to others? No, you do not. You were born with magic, and so you will never know. But *I* knew, once."

"Wh-what are you t-talking about?" I gasp as Varon's hold on me loosens, but not completely. I wriggle against him, trying to get free, but he won't let go—and I don't understand *why*. Is it possible that he's on the king's side?

But then, why would he have come to me in the Witch's Woods, night after night after night, telling me stories and wishing for a kiss to break my spell, only to turn me over to the king? Why would he follow me into the darkness in the attic, only to betray me now? It would have been easy to let me stay asleep, forever and ever and ever.

The king blinks once, slowly. "Magic comes from the heart, you know—the second heart, the hidden one. Magic is in the blood. Drain a man of his blood, and you drain him of his magic also." A pause, a dragging inhale. "*Drink* the blood of a man, and you drink his magic also."

If Varon weren't holding me, my knees would give out. The skeletons, the thrones, the wounds where their hearts should be—oh, no, no, no, *no*.

With this wrench of revulsion comes an unbidden vision of the king's rotted teeth slicing into *my* skin, into *my* heart, of him drinking and drinking until I am drained. A horrible waking nightmare, there and gone, and I promise myself from this moment on that I will not let him steal macula blood from me or anyone else. I will do whatever must be done to make sure of it.

The vision fades, and another one takes its place, not of the future this time but of the past. I remember my mother, how I found her in the temple, a gouge in her throat and her veins drained dry. I remember how I screamed, and how, in that moment, it felt like if I stopped screaming, my heart would stop beating. Like the scream was the only thing left alive inside me.

"Your mother was an accident," says the king, as if he knows exactly what I'm thinking. "One of the Immacula I drank managed to regenerate enough magic to come back to life, and he descended upon the first macula he found, ravenous. It is a rare thing, but some maculae can detect the magic in others. It calls to them—they can feel it there, under the skin, through a simple touch. But perhaps you knew that already."

I swallow, my throat aching. How could the king know that I can feel the magic in others? Even now I sense Varon's, the shimmer and the strain of it: apples rotting on a golden branch, stars peeling like scabs from the sky. It's like he's fighting against something—but what?

The king continues. "Those without magic have always tried to steal from those who have it. A sip of blood for a mere minute of magic, before it fizzles and is gone." A long sigh that seems to go on forever, until it doesn't. "I knew it would not be enough. Not blood on its own. No—the source must be consumed. The heart within a heart."

At this, my own heart stops. It stops, and for a second I'm not sure it will ever start again. But it does, it does, and the sound of it is louder than anything else, louder even than a promise breaking, than a secret snapping, than a storm skinning the sky of its colors. *Not my heart,* I vow. *He will* not *have my heart.*

Varon's grip loosens a little bit more, and I shake my head, dizzied but determined not to let the king know it. "That would *never* work."

"I disagree, my dear. A heart eaten every few years, taken from those who wouldn't be missed. There are many ways for a macula to serve the crown, and sacrificing oneself is the highest of all honors."

I look up, but I can no longer see the stars. The darkness billowing there obscures everything. "Such an act—it would tear you apart."

"And what is it that you see there above you? My deeds, made manifest. Ever since the first bite passed my lips, I have been deteriorating, piece by piece."

"But I saw you a month ago. Before I cast my spell. You were there. You were—"

"A proxy, glamoured in my image."

A shudder passes through my entire body.

"Soon I'll be nothing but darkness, a roiling mass of it. Glorious and unbounded. A kind of magic no one has ever before seen."

"That's never going to happen," I hiss. "Any of it."

"Oh, you'll see, Rhea Ravenna."

"Varon, let me go," I plead. But his grip only tightens, even as his heart flinches an apology against my back. My hands are pinned to my sides, but I rotate my palms so that they are facing behind me. *"Alenia mec liesana.* Varon, please. *Alenia mec!"*

Nothing.

"You are so powerful," Varon says quietly, "but you do not have that kind of magic. The kind that controls."

The new Darkness, the king—he laughs. Humorless, colorless, dry.

"Necromancer," he says. *"Alenia sec liesana."*

Varon releases me.

And it is then that I truly comprehend the depth of this horror.

For years the king has had magic—sticky magic, stolen magic—and all the while, he's been persecuting each macula for committing a far lesser crime than every one of his combined. The crime of merely being born with magic.

I know your secret, the pretend Rhea said, to lure the king into Graiae Forest. *Your secret, your secret, your secret.*

But for him, his journey into the forest was never about his macabre magic, even if the creatures *had* known about it. No, he went to them knowing what they had planned to do, striding through the trees with a plan of his own. The rallying woodland people didn't expect anything, because they didn't actually know the secret they claimed to hold, that the king was capable of such a thing. Of seizing a star, and letting them all burn.

And they *still* don't know—but I do. I do, and there's no going back now.

"What do you want with me?" I ask, holding my hands behind my back and letting a knot of hard white magic swell between my palms. "Why did you want me to see this place?"

"You are mine, Rhea, the true heir to my throne, even over your father, who does not know what it means to have magic. And despite all that has happened, you can still have the throne. The brands on your hands, the renouncement of your title—it was all for show. You would have known that if you had not run off. I was going to keep you hidden, keep you safe, until it was time for you to take my crown and rule as I have done."

Terror sickles apart the chambers of my heart as I imagine being locked away for years and years, learning how to become him.

I pretend to consider his words for a second. Then I bring my hands out from behind my back, and throw my glass knot of magic toward him as hard and as fast as I can.

The king lifts his decrepit fingers and flicks my blast aside. It shoots off into the night and shatters in the wind, shards bursting in a flash of gold light. As it does, the darkness comes crashing back down around us, a billowing cloud, obscuring the king and the ruined bodies slumped in their thrones, negating any further attacks.

Well, I'll just have to get close enough to press my hands against his chest and whisper the words to stop his derelict heart. I know the spell, though I've never used it before. I never thought I'd have to, and to do so might cause my own darkness to fester. But I have to try.

I grasp Varon's hand. Our fingers entwine and our pulses tick, side by side, and I'm not sure which is his and which is mine. I squeeze once, hoping he will understand without words what I mean to do. Then I let go, taking a deep breath and one step forward, followed by another and another. I reach for him, the king I cannot see, my arms stretched long in front of me. Varon follows, hovering close.

"Someday, Princess, I was going to tell you everything," the king says, speaking steadily louder and faster. His voice seems to come from everywhere and nowhere at once. "I didn't want it to happen like this. No one was supposed to know—not about me, and not about you. But you were careless; you were *caught*. And I had no choice but to treat you like the other maculae. If I did not, my people would no longer trust me."

I keep stepping, keep reaching. I whisper a voice-throwing spell before speaking so that it sounds to him like I'm still standing in the center of the room. "The forest is burning because of you."

"Tell me, what was I supposed to do? Let the creatures take my kingdom?"

I hear Shay's voice in my head saying, *Whatever it takes.*

The creatures, the maculae, me, the king—maybe we are only trying to keep what is ours. What we *believe* is ours.

Who does the world truly belong to?

Not him.

"We just want to live freely," I say, yelling over the slosh of the waves as Varon and I veer nearer and nearer to the ocean at the northern edge of the tower, skirting behind the thrones. "Not to be killed or enslaved!"

"This land used to be a wild place. No Immaculae, no heartless—just magic, unbridled and everywhere. Do you know how frightening a place like that can be to those who have no magic at all?"

"Magic isn't dangerous, and neither are the maculae."

"Some are, though, and that is the problem. It is that way with all people, with all creatures, magical or otherwise. Everyone is capable of the deepest violence and the highest kindness. Our natures are simply a constant battle between those extremes."

Keep going, I think, forcing myself to concentrate. *Keep reaching.*

"Now that you know what I am, you will learn from me and share my crown," the king says. "But if you will not, *I will have your heart, Rhea Ravenna.* Either way, we will rule together."

Suddenly a hand flies out of the darkness and grasps my upper arm. The scream in my chest makes it as far as the roof of my mouth, clots against the inside of my cheeks, and leaks between the sieve of my teeth as a high, wispy screech.

"Shhh. It's just me." Varon's fingers loosen. "Why did you return for me?"

We don't have time for this. I start to shiver, and I can't stop. "Come o-on. We—"

Varon holds on to me as if I am the only sure, solid thing left in existence. Ocean mist wafts up, and I can feel it around our ankles, and I realize just *how* close we are to the very edge, nothing but open air behind us. "Rhea, *please*. Why did you come for me?"

I force myself to stand still just a moment more in order to give this boy holding on to me an honest answer.

"Because my name is cradled in your bones. Because your heart sounds the same as mine. Because a sky is just unremarkable darkness without the stars. It's empty."

And for a too-short second, I feel his grin, feel the cut and color of it, the clarity: ravenous and red and all, all for me.

"You can have my heart," Varon says, and I return his grin despite everything, despite where we are and the predicament we're in. But then he adds, "Take mine instead."

"Don't—" I begin to protest, but Varon squeezes my hand as if to let me know it's all right and he knows what he's doing. I'm not so sure. "You can't—"

"Swim to safety," he says quickly, quietly. "Get away from here."

He puts his hands on my shoulders and *shoves*.

"*No!*" I fall over the side of the tower, and for a second I'm suspended in midair, the startled sea cringing back in anticipation of the impact of my body. I wait to slam into the waves, my eyes shut, my lungs full of air, not sure when I'll be able to catch my next breath.

But.

Before my toes touch the water, an invisible rope winds around my waist and I know it's the king, jerking me back. I crash not into the sea as Varon intended but onto the floor. *Hard.* My spine flattens on the ground, my neck snaps back, and my head smashes against the tile.

Everything does not go black, because everything already is black.

No—it goes *blank*.

A minute passes, or maybe an hour or a lifetime. The next thing I know, I'm gasping awake. Varon peers down at me, inches away, with his hands on either side of my face, his palms almost unbearably hot as he revives me. A dull throbbing knocks at the back of my skull as he eases back on his heels.

"Rhea, are you all right? Can you hear me?"

I nod, sitting up slowly. My back is sore, and there's an ache in my temples already fading, but otherwise I'm unhurt. Varon helps me to my feet, catching me as I wobble, as I nearly topple to the floor again. Through his touch I feel his magic, warm and flowing freely beneath his skin. The king must have removed Varon's chains to allow him to revive me.

"You might be a bit blurry, but not for long." His fingers brush the outside corner of my eyebrow. I think he meant to touch my cheek. "My sky, I tried to save you. I thought—"

At once the king speaks. "Boy, your chains—put them back on."

"No!" I cry, stepping in front of Varon, as if I could shield him from something that is everywhere, all around us. "You will not use him anymore."

"Would you like to put them on him, then?"

Before I can respond, there comes a creak and a long, agonized moan followed by another moan and another. Bones cracking, tendons snapping, skin ripping. Beside me, Varon raises his hands as he lifts the bodies from their thrones, their stiff knees popping as, slowly, they stand.

Animated but not alive, no hearts to pump the blood through their desiccated veins. I press closer to Varon's side, feeling the warm flare of his magic as the bodies shuffle forward, slowly at first, heels scraping as they drag against the stone, but then faster and faster, inexorably.

A *distraction*. I peel away from Varon and, tightening my queasy stomach, I push myself between the bodies, using them as a shield as they crowd closer and closer to the king. I'm not sure we're even moving in the right direction, but it's worth a try. I reach out blindly in front of me, ready with the curse for stopping hearts, on the tip of my tongue.

There's a clap like thunder on a clear night, sudden and deafening and rattling my teeth. At once the bodies drop to the floor, pile at the king's feet. Seizing my chance, I press forward, stumbling over limp limbs, my arms outstretched.

A powerful rush of wind knocks me backward, and I fall, land hard on my left shoulder, and slide along the floor for several feet before the wind suddenly ceases. I scramble to standing, rolling my shoulder, the sting refusing to fade.

"What do you want from me?" I cry. Varon comes up beside me and slides his hand into mine, and magic crackles between our palms. It hurts, just a little, but I don't mind. "I refuse to take your crown, and I won't let you have my heart. I won't continue what you've started. Why do you think I cast the curse in the first place? To get away from *this*."

"You will not take my crown, and you will not give your heart," the king repeats slowly, and dread rises like a moon inside me, full and sickly bright. "The boy, though—he would give his heart in place of yours. But I do not want a heart with so much death in it. And so I do not care what happens now to the boy." There is a terrible pause, and I wish I could shrink the darkness to the size of my thumbnail and swallow it like a pill, gone. "Do you?"

There is a sudden slopping sound, of waves being parted, water crashing into water, and then smooth, slinking footsteps, growing louder.

That's not the sea, I realize. That's not the sound of sloshing water—it's *singing*. Someone in the darkness is singing, and they are coming closer.

"Varon, oh, Varon, where are you? Come here, my light, my love, and let me have a taste of you."

"Renata?" I whisper, even though I know, I *know* it is not her.

Varon's fingers untangle from mine as he pulls away from me, compelled to approach the nymph we cannot see.

"It's not real. It's just a trick!" I warn, fumbling blindly for Varon's hand, his arm, his hair, any piece of him I can reach. "Varon, *please*—"

"That's right, that's right," the nymph sings, beckoning

him toward her. She may be nothing but a voice created by the king, but once he has Varon in the sea, surely his magic will hold Varon under until he can no longer breathe. "Step farther, step faster, into the open arms of the night."

I can't stop her from singing if she's not even really there to stop. I'll simply have to be louder, to drown her out before she drowns him.

I smile a little to myself, knowing exactly what to do. Easy, easy, easy. And I don't even need magic to do it.

I open my mouth, and scream.

And scream.

And scream.

It feels so, so good. Like waking up from a poisonous dream, sweating and blank with terror and grasping for my own name, my identity forgotten, but awake all the same.

But for once this is no dream, and I do not wake up.

"*Enough*," the king says finally, and I hear it in my head instead of in my ears. At once I go silent, my voice severed. "I will have your cooperation, Princess, or I will have that boy dead. Now, how do you answer?"

"No and no and *no* again."

The ground shakes violently, as if a giant has stamped his foot. I tumble forward, and Varon catches my wrist, righting me, and I'm relieved that he is still near, still alive.

But for how long?

The king *roars*, a trumpet screech blasting through the room, higher and hungrier than any human sound I have ever heard. I cover my ears with my hands, but it doesn't help, the cry cleaving through my mind, a corroded echo trapped inside.

No, it's not the king, I realize, recognizing the noise as it goes on and on—a sphinx. He has conjured a brass-throated beast. Manticores eat men, but sphinxes have no such preferences—they will eat anyone, boy or girl, young or old, human or macula. But only if you fail to correctly solve a puzzle.

Finally the roar fades, followed by a furious flap of wings. Varon grunts, his warmth leaves my side, and I picture him swept up and pinned beneath the creature's forepaws, which keep him in place.

"Say you'll do what I ask of you, Rhea, and the boy will walk free," says the king. "Or else unravel the riddle to save his life."

"The riddle," I say at once. The king forgets that I am a beast of the forest too. How many riddles have I answered? Thousands and thousands. I'm standing here now, obviously uneaten, simply because I know how to think like a sphinx. In the forest you learn quickly how to survive, how to prevent being gobbled alive. I smile, waiting for the creature to speak.

"How is a girl like a sky?" it asks in a rusted rumble. I wait for it to go on, certain there must be more to the riddle, but the sphinx is silent, waiting.

And waiting.

Usually sphinxes' riddles are logical, like *What has a spine but no bones?* and *What walks on four legs at dawn, two legs at noon, and three legs at dusk?*

A book, a man, simple but clever answers. Some riddles are harder than others, and some have multiple parts to them, but always they have one clear solution.

But this? This is something else entirely.

How is a girl like a sky?

I think of what Varon told me when I was the Witch, that he would always find me because all worlds saw the same sky, even in dreams. And how, in the darkness of the attic, he said that if he is a single star burning, then I am an entire sky full of them.

My confident smile shrivels as I clench my jaw.

The king is mocking me.

"This isn't fair!" I shout, and the sphinx grumbles, low. "You said I had to answer a riddle, but this is more like a cruel joke!"

"Is that your answer?"

"No!"

"You are running out of time."

I clutch the sides of my head as if that will help me think harder, faster, but my mind is completely blank, and panic is washing through me. "I don't know, *I don't know*!"

"Then you lose," says the king, and the sphinx grumbles again, but in hunger this time. "Eat."

"Varon, close your eyes!" I cry as I bring my hands up, acting almost without thinking. *"Alita alor!"*

A starburst of searing light explodes from between my hands as I clap them together, so bright that for a split second the whole room is illuminated. I squint through the brilliance but still catch the barest glimpse: of the towering sphinx with his paws holding Varon in place, the half-moon of decaying tooth thrones, the shriveled body of my grandfather, the glint of his crown. The sphinx shrieks, reels back, and disappears, the king's concentration disrupted in the sudden flash.

Varon gasps as the pressure on him is released. I stagger forward, reaching for him.

"Thanks for not letting me get eaten," he says as I find his arm and help him to his feet.

"Who s-says you're not going to be eaten?" I grin up at him even though he can't see me. Even though I'm shaking so hard that I can barely speak. "I was only s-saving you for myself."

He starts to laugh, a true laugh, something I've never heard from him before. Quick and deep, slightly hoarse. But the sound is cut short.

"I see," the king says, and I press myself closer to Varon's side. "You will not let anyone kill the boy. Not me, not a nymph, not a sphinx. Perhaps that honor should be yours alone?"

I grip Varon's arm, my nails sinking into his skin, deeper and deeper. He doesn't cry out, but his muscles go taut. I try to release him, but I can't.

I can't.

"I'm sorry, I'm sorry," I say as a prickling pain snakes down the back of my neck and through my chest, and claws all the way to my fingertips, like a long, curving splinter thrust under my skin and into my nervous system.

"I know it's not your fault, whatever happens," Varon says quickly. "But, Rhea, I—"

"*Stielle,*" the king says, cutting him off.

At once I raise my hands, and lunge.

Varon only barely evades me, twisting and darting away. But as long as I feel him there, the prickle of his magic, then I can still find him. And the king can too.

"Shoot him," the king says, and I close my eyes, concentrating on pushing the king's magic out of my mind. I picture it as a stake driven into my heart, but when I reach to yank it out, my hands won't obey me, even in my own imagination. *"Forla."*

A hard, glimmering crystal sphere of magic forms in my palms, its light cutting through the dark as I hurl it. I try to aim to the side, avoiding Varon as much as I can, wrangling against the king's command, the itching, consuming *urge* to direct it at Varon's chest. I can barely see. I can barely breathe, and I *definitely* can't think straight, but there is no cry of pain or crunch of bone, and I know I've missed him. I haven't killed him.

Yet.

Again the king tells me to shoot, and again I let loose another crystal knot, and again I miss and again Varon jumps aside. But somehow his dodging seems only reflexive. He is not determined—he's resigned.

"Go after him!" I gasp, fighting against the king's control for use of my voice, at least. At another word from the king, I stalk forward, another crystal blooming in my palms, ready to fire just as soon as I locate him. "Don't let me do this!"

"Not on my own." Varon's voice comes from a spot very close, too close, just a little to the left. "I can't match him on my own."

"Shoot!" the king bellows. The crystal arcs out of my palm as the king's will digs ever deeper into me, barbed and poisonous. Varon swears, and I know I've grazed him. I can only pray it's nowhere vital. We circle each other, squinting in the dim.

Briefly I wonder why the king doesn't simply command Varon to stay still so that I can hit him, but then I realize that the entirety of his energy is focused on me. If his attention were divided, he could not control me so easily.

"Let's play a game," the king says then. "A guessing game. Guess my name, and I'll let the boy go free."

I ignore him. I know there will be no end until his heart or mine has stopped beating. Another crystalline shot of magic rips from my hands, but at the last second before it strikes Varon, I shout *"Fifalda!"* and the bullet turns into a butterfly, harmless.

"Then fight *me*," I beg Varon. "Don't make me do this! Varon, *come on.*"

"I will not hurt you," he says, and I spring toward his voice, this time clawing at the air with my fingers, reaching for him. If I touch him, I will destroy him.

I must not touch him.

I try to wrench the king's dark magic from my mind, but it is jammed in too deeply. I attempt a spell, but the words won't come out right. "Release—I mean, *liesig*—I mean"— fumbling, foggy, I mutter *"licsen"* by accident. Snow swirls down from the sky, cold and thick and stinging my skin, the wind whipping my hair into my eyes.

"C-*crawvone,*" I say, a new plan forming, and the snow congeals like blood, clumping together in the shape of a thousand icy crows just over our heads. With a peal of chilling caws and the fluttering of slushy wings, the murder of wraith-birds flies up and out of the ballroom, their frozen feathers glinting faintly in the starlight.

The starlight.

With the snow gone, I can see it: the sky.

The king—he's weakening. His darkness wavers.

As soon as I think it, he tightens his clutch on my mind. At his urging I jump forward, and Varon is right there; we collide, crash to the ground. I land on top of him and hold him there, pinned on his back with my knees on either side of his hips, even though we both know that he is physically stronger than I am, bigger and broader, and that he could easily push me off him. He could push me off him and run. Escape.

But he doesn't do either of those things. *Stupid, stupid!* I want to shriek. But instead I whisper, words meant only for him.

"Tell me a story." I place my palms on his chest and lean down closer to him. "A fairy story."

He does not hesitate.

"We live in a house with no attic," he says, so softly that I could curl up inside his voice and sleep forever. "Every morning, I kiss you awake."

My fingers crawl up, up toward his neck, as I fight the darkness inside me. I can barely breathe around the scream stuck in my throat, joy and despair all mixed up together. He is a wish I want to come true again and again and again.

"It's not too late to save him," the king says quietly, almost soothingly, as if he understands my situation and truly wants to help. "All you have to do is say my name."

I shake my head, crying thick, fast tears. "You don't know yourself, do you? That's why you want me to guess. You're tricking me into giving you your name back, because there's power in a name, and without one, you are nothing." Varon struggles to sit up, but I'm still on top of him and he can't move much. Propped on his elbow, he reaches up with his other hand to wipe my cheeks dry. His fingers are warm, and the gesture only makes me cry harder.

"You don't *have* a name," I tell the king. "Maybe you did once, but not anymore. You're just a pit of blackness, where all the crushed things live. Where all the gutted things go when they are not beautiful anymore, and will never be beautiful again. The things that can't be redeemed." I take a ragged breath and keep going. "And even though you talk of glory and deathlessness, I think you are afraid of your darkness. I think you are afraid of what you will become. You don't want my heart—you just want your name back. You offer me your crown only because you want someone else to bear your burden while you walk free; you want to feel the sun on your skin again, unwrinkled and whole. Sometimes, though, there's no getting back what we've lost. Speaking your name will not be enough."

There is a long, hard silence.

"Squeeze his throat."

I push Varon back down, roughly, so that his skull slams into the floor. My hands crawl to his throat. I sob, and for once I'm glad that I can't see his face.

"Asmorihin."

My fingertips jab into Varon's warm, soft flesh, press on his windpipe.

The wind leaves his chest, and I try to pull back, but I can't. I strangle him.

I strangle him.

I am strangling him.

I tip my head back and look up.

"Help me," I say to the stars. "I am so small. But you—you are vast and bright."

And they say, *Silly girl.*

They say, *Don't you know how expansive you are, how endless?*

They say, *All you have to do is ask.*

A question, not a command. Not like the king, who forced the stars down to scorch the forest.

"Will you come?"

They do not answer.

Instead they fall.

Well, not quite. They don't fall, exactly; it's more deliberate than that.

The stars—they slash, they slice, they *scythe,* flushed and flashing, coming to set the night on fire.

I watch them, and I think the king sees them too.

"What is my name?" demands the king as they get closer and closer. Desperate, pleading: "What is it, what is it, what is my name?"

I laugh, shaky and relieved. Glitter-mist puffs like frozen breath from my mouth, bright in the air around my head. The stars dart down, and I peel the king's magic off me like a scab, revealing the shiny pink skin underneath.

I let go of Varon as the first streak of snickering starlight strikes the floor near us, burning a ragged hole in the stone. The stars streak like rain, sizzling where they land. All around us, the old wing of the castle is melting.

For a second Varon is still, and I am reduced to this, just cold lips and sleeplessness, a girl with a heart hung upside down to dry out, shriveled and preserved at the very moment it stopped.

I wait.

I wait.

I wait.

He inhales, and my heart starts again. I roll away from him, letting him catch his breath. He puts his arm around my shoulders, and I support him as we stand.

The star-spray is everywhere, lacing the room with light, touching down all around but never touching us, avoiding our vulnerable skin and the souls within.

"Can you run?" I ask, a golden glow illuminating his eyes, his cheeks, his lips.

He nods. "Let's go."

We run, never stopping or slowing, evenly and steadily across the room as the darkness churns and strains against the dazzling starshine filling up the space. The Star Fire catches on the castle, and even its steel skeleton bubbles and burns.

The king groans.

I let go of Varon as we reach the door, so that I can lay both my hands against it, and spirals of silver scissor through its wooden surface. The doors crack open, and I turn back to the room one last time. More stars plummet, and patches of spreading flame smolder across the floor like a trail of fiery crumbs, twisting from the spot where we just were. Marking the way to the darkest place in the castle.

But we will not need to find our way back. Never ever.

"Imagine this," I say to the king as tiny specks of stars stick to him and eat away at his skin. "A child. Lying in bed at night, trembling in the dark, picturing the monster beneath her bed. And that monster? It may have green scaly skin, or blood-dipped claws, or a thousand dilated eyes, but that monster is always, *always* you."

A faint, brittle voice: "Only if the child is always *you*."

"You're forgetting: the child can exist without the monster. But the monster is nothing, nowhere, *no one,* without the child who dreams it into being."

There is no reply, only this: a brief, urgent, echoing scream.

Chapter 24

IN THE KINGDOM

Varon and I stumble-spill out of the burning palace doors, tripping and holding each other up as we scramble out of the darkness and into—well, more darkness. The sun is just beginning to peek over the horizon, as if checking that the coast is well and truly clear before rising for the second time in the same day.

My family and Gabrielle and Shay and hundreds of others are waiting for us, so many more than were here before we went inside. Their cracked chains are heaped to one side, as those who are unfettered help liberate the ones in cuffs. While my parents berate me for a solid ten minutes for leaving them and running off into the darkness on my own, I take in the free maculae reuniting with their enchained kin, and the humans helping slick-skinned nymphs to hand out cups of water and rolls of bread. Sylphs susurrate spells to redirect the wind to nudge the sun back up, while sphinxes—the kind ones—tell riddles to the frightened children of all species to make them smile. It seems that most of the soldiers loyal to the king have fled, but the children of the Forest Forgotten circle around us with their weapons, ready to defend against any unwelcome attacks.

But there shouldn't be any more of those—no battles, no war. The stars are back in the sky, leaving only their flames behind on the ground, spreading from the stone wing to the rest of the crystal part of the castle. Nothing else is on fire—only the palace, burning to the ground, and the darkness with it.

Dad gives me another hug, and I know he's done scolding me.

"It was like you *vanished*," Dad says, shaking his head. "I tried going back into the castle, and I thought maybe we were going to disappear one by one again."

"You couldn't have found me without magic," I explain.

"Well, never do anything like that again," he says, but his eyes glisten and his voice wavers. "I am proud of you, though, Rhea. We all are."

Mom sweeps me into a tight embrace, judging that I've been reprimanded enough for one day. "Rhea," she says, "you saved me. My darling girl, you saved me."

"It wasn't me," I say, squeezing her back. "I mean, it *was* me, but only a little. Rose is the one who gave you her magic."

"Yes, she told me." Mom pulls back, and we both turn to look at Rose. She stands separated from the rest of us, talking to Varon with her eyes on the ground. Finally she looks up, and when he offers his arms to her, she steps into him. "I don't know if I'll ever be able to make it up to her. That's her brother, isn't it? Her biological brother? I'm still a little confused about everything and keep thinking I just need a good night's sleep—but then I remember that I've had enough sleep for half a lifetime." She laughs, and when her gaze lands back on me, she stops. Her smile softens but does not slip away completely. "Look at all these people you've freed. *You* did that, Ree. Your father and your friends helped, yes. But none of it would have been possible without you."

I can't look at her. "I shouldn't have run away in the first place."

"Honestly, Rhea, I don't want to think what would have happened if you hadn't." I still can't meet her eyes, so she reaches over and wraps an arm around my shoulders, tugging me to her and kissing my head, right above my ear. She doesn't let go. "If you had stayed here, your wrists in iron, you might eventually have found a way to undermine him. But all of this—this *chaos* still would have happened in the meantime."

"Maybe," I concede, tilting my head against hers. Together we watch as Dad circles the group, pausing to shake hands and speak with each and every person, even crouching down to give the children hugs or an extra roll, humble but confident in his role. I can't help smiling a little; he truly looks like a prince.

We stay like that for a while, Mom and I, just watching, not moving, and eventually my quasi-adopted sisters wander over. Varon has disappeared. I scan the crowd, but I can't find him. Rose sees me and sidles close.

"He went to look for our parents," she says. "Our birth parents, I mean. But I—I don't think he'll find them."

"Rose, I'm *so* sorry. I—" I stop. What more can I say? There is nothing, nothing that will make this okay.

"At least I have all of you," she says. "But Varon . . ."

"He has us too."

She nods but says nothing, only rubs her fists into her eyes, reminding me of how tired I am too. I want to sleep for a thousand years—but at the same time, I never want to sleep again.

"How are you feeling?" I ask, pressing my hand to her forehead, expecting her usual coldness beneath my palm. But instead there is *heat,* her skin sweaty and strange. "Rose, are you all right?"

"Yes. No. I don't know." She stiffens and turns away from me, my hand falling from her face. "I just—I think you were right. It wasn't the magic itself that made me feel so sick. For so long, magic was the reason I had to stay hidden, the reason I could barely leave my house, the reason my parents had their second hearts removed and my brother was taken away. I thought magic was the enemy." She pauses, pressing her palms into her eyes, trying to hide the tears now twisting down her cheeks. "But it wasn't the magic's fault at all. It was just the way I perceived it. The way the *king* perceived it, and the way I began to see it too. I believed I was cursed because of it."

"The anxiety may never go away, but you'll learn how to manage it." I put my arm around her shoulders, startled again by her unfamiliar warmth. "And it's not too late, you know."

She drops her hands away from her eyes. "What do you mean?"

"I could give you my magic. I mean, not all of it, not right away. I'll give you a little bit every day, and that way it'll have time to regenerate and I'll never really lose any. My magic is different from yours, but wouldn't it be fun to design your own dreams? The only thing is, you have to promise to always wake up."

"I promise," she says, smiling a little. "But are you sure? It might hurt."

I smile. "I don't mind if you don't."

"I'll think about it." She hugs me tight. "Thank you, Rhea."

Raisa comes over to us then, wearing her mask, with Renata and Gabrielle at her side. Dad reappears, followed by a slew of guards and advisors, a mix of humans and maculae and chimeras.

"Well, what do we do now?" Raisa says as we watch the fizzling embers melt what's left of the crystal castle. "That palace was super ugly anyway."

The crowd has quieted, glancing around eagerly, anxiously. They look to my family gathered on the palace steps, to Dad standing, straight and proud, next to Mom. The silver tattoo on Dad's arm glows as he steps seamlessly into the role he was destined for his whole life.

Looking out, I spot Varon walking back toward us, skirting around the edges of the gathering, the tops of the tall, straight buildings glinting in the fresh sunlight. His hair hangs limply in his lowered eyes, and there is a ring around each of his pale wrists, red and oddly shiny. There's one around his neck too, and I would do anything to make it disappear, to take it back.

At least we are both alive.

We are both awake.

Look up, look up at me, I think, but he keeps his gaze on the ground, winding carefully through the crowd.

"Wait," I say, grabbing Dad's arm as he turns to the assembly to speak. "Let me."

Immediately he nods and puts a gentle hand on my back, pushing me a few steps forward, as though all along, he's been waiting for me to take hold of this moment.

The air is over-warm and everything is bright—the towers, the sky, the eyes blinking back at me. Shay lingers nearby, and I smell wood, trees, rich and loamy. Raising my voice, my chin, my drooping, tired heart, I speak loudly and surely.

"Listen," I say. "I have an idea."

Varon looks up, right at me. He grins.

I smile. "We can dream a new dream, together."

Chapter 25

IN THE WOODS

The castle, the throne, the altar, the glade where the Witch danced and where the Fox Who Is No Fox told her a most peculiar fairy story—it's all still there, though cracked and gutted. The children too still come at night and wander the crumbled corridors with unwound walls of branches; they stare at the fractured altar and the decaying throne, every one of them wondering where their Witch has gone. They fall into nightmare despair now that it seems their wishes will never ever be granted. They are there, watching and waiting for the Witch to come home.

The children are looking in the wrong place. That world is in ruins, and the Witch has no plans ever to return there. But that does not mean they will never see her again. They just have to look a little harder.

From the other side of a dream, she calls out to them. The lost children turn their eyes to the blank white sky, their hollow moon-rock hearts beating very, very fast.

She says, *I'm here.*

She says, *I'm waiting.*

She says, *Come find me.*

*   *   *

"Stop fidgeting, please, or you'll have clown lips," Raisa snaps, leaning over me with a tube of lipstick as I sit in front of her. "Do you want clown lips, or witch lips?"

"'Itch 'ips," I say, trying to speak without moving my lips.

"Hurry up, or she's going to be late," Rose says, sitting on the end of my bed across the room, her ballet-slippered feet tapping against the wood floor.

"It's not like she hasn't done this a thousand times already." Raisa carefully traces the center dip in my upper lip, her eyes shielded behind the veil she wears so that she doesn't accidentally turn us into shadows; the veil is a thick gauze that she can see out of but that we can't see through. I offer to keep my eyes closed while she works so that she can remove the veil, but she refuses.

"One accidental peek, and you're a goner!" she reminds me. "Remember how long it took to un-shadow Gabby after my veil blew off in the wind during what was supposed to be a romantic moonlit walk? Who would un-shadow you if that happened?"

I can think of one other person who knows that kind of magic, but Raisa is still painting my lips, and I don't dare to speak.

"Mom could do it," Renata chimes, skipping suddenly

288

into the room, her wet hair dripping onto the floor. "She's been practicing."

"Practicing?" Raisa snorts. "More like showing off. She uses magic for every stupid little thing when Dad's around."

"Well, and can you blame her?" Rose says. "She spent her whole life up until now having to hide it. As long as Dad keeps being impressed by it, she'll probably keep doing it."

"Whatever," Raisa says, and rolls her eyes. I mean, I'm only assuming she rolls them, since I can't actually see her eyes, but there's a fairly good chance I'm right.

Ren and Rose continue to gossip about Mom and Dad, about how yesterday Renata caught them kissing behind a tree like some giggling teenagers, and how Dad, when he's not seeing to his kingly duties, keeps trying to out-riddle the sphinxes, making them laugh with weird dad jokes that they, for some reason, find hilarious.

When Raisa's done with me a few minutes later, I take a look in the mirror. I smack my lips, rubbing them together over and over. Black orchid, a deep amaranthine gloss that makes my hair and eyes appear brighter. Just the way I like them.

"You look like a dream," Rose says, smiling at me. It's weird, weird and wonderful, that my magic now flows through her veins too. Some nights, we sneak away in our sleeping minds and design all kinds of fantastical dreamscapes where everything is beautiful just by being.

With a sweep of her arm, Raisa presents me to the room. "Her Royal Highness, Princess Rhea the Dreamer, Who

Messed Everything Up but Then Made Things Pretty Okay Again."

"Wow, such high praise," I say, pinching her arm. "Thank you."

"Um, *ow*."

"Okay, that did *not* hurt."

"I'm going to tell on you!" She bolts across the room toward the door, her veil sliding to one side of her head. "This'll give Mom a chance to practice her punishment magic!"

"Don't you dare!" I chase after her, my red tulle skirt swishing around my knees. My other sisters follow, all of us laughing and tumbling down the hall, past a dozen empty bedrooms that once were full. All of the orphans of the Forest Forgotten have found homes, and though I know I once promised they could live in the castle with me, I think they're happiest right where they are now. Past the last bedroom, we descend the spiral stairs to the first floor, careful to keep our clothes from snagging on the twig walls.

We go down the steps and through the corridors, passing the ballroom with an open ceiling showing the freckly sky and the round warts of the seven moons. Then out the doors, through the crossed-bone portcullis and across the moat, where Renata can often be found during the day, lounging in the sun. Into the trees and down the path that leads to the glade, where there are many other paths that will lead to many more homes, custom-designed by the ones who live there.

I sprint and skip and laugh with my sisters down the path through Graiae Forest, the air warm and windy, and call hello to a startled group of sylphs as we flash by. Around another curve in the path, we reach the glade where Mom and Dad and Shay and most everyone in the forest has gathered, sitting on the soft grass in front of my carved molar throne. Raisa walks straight to Gabrielle, who is near the front of the endless assembly and is visible tonight in her human skin instead of her bright orange fox form. Renata smiles at a group of young men shrugging together like maybe it's a little uncool to be here but they want to stay anyway. Rose shakes her head and pulls Renata away, but not before my youngest sister blows the boys a kiss, stunning them into silence. After midnight there will be dancing, dancing until the sun rises in the east, led by Rose, who has been giving lessons during the day to anyone who wants them.

But first, this: it is time for me to be the Witch.

Interspersed with the forest folk are the ones who have come from other worlds, from every world that has ever existed, in space, in time, in someone's mind. They look at the pointed turrets poking above the treetops in the distance, gaping at the revelry of shadows leaping over the faces of the strange and marvelous creatures surrounding them.

I give them time to stare, to take it all in, while I search the swarm for the one familiar face I haven't spotted yet, the one who is always, always there, even on the bad days. Especially on the bad days.

As much as I wish I could, I can't erase the things Varon has had to go through up to this point: the year of servitude, losing his parents, being lost in Darkness. I can't magic away the erratic quaking of his hands that occasionally overcomes him now that it's all over; I can't cast a curse to banish his fevered nightmares, or the unpredictable anger that spurts to the surface, or the disengaged dullness that steals over his features for hours at a time. I can only hold his hand as he shivers so violently that I fear he might shatter, or kiss his closed eyes as he struggles to sleep again after a bad dream, or sit quietly beside him in the darkest part of the woods until he comes back around to himself. Sometimes we stay there all day, deep in the forest; we're a little bit afraid of it, the dark, but we go there anyway. Again and again and again.

Lately, though, he's been spending every morning working on a secret surprise project in an undisclosed location somewhere nearby. I have a hunch it might be this: a house with no attic, just big enough for two.

Actually, it's more than a hunch; I have fox eyes all over these woods.

With relief I finally see him, hovering at the very back of the gathering, leaning against a tree. He watches me, his arms crossed over his chest, his black hair blown into his face by the breeze. When our eyes meet, he speaks.

And I hear him, I do, even all the way over here. Across the glade he shouts, "The sky is stunning tonight!"

"Do you think I can catch a star later?" I say, but only so he can hear, a voice-throwing spell. "Do you think he'll ask me to dance?"

His voice comes back, softly, as he uses my same spell. I see his lips move, and then, right in my ear: "I do."

I blush. I don't know much, but I do know this: I am an inhale. And he—he is an exhale. And we will always be together, each of us right behind the other, linked, until the very last breath.

Blushing still, I look out at the children, and the adults too—because adults and almost-adults, I've decided, need wishes just as much as children do. They'll all get their wishes, soon enough. But before they eat of the rose in my heart, I have something else I've begun to do. Something to tell them.

I am the Witch of Wishes, but I am also the Witch of Words. Of stories.

Well—one story in particular.

I say, "Would you like to hear a fairy story?"

I use my narrator voice, which is a little deeper, a little wiser-sounding than my regular voice. It's my Witch voice, my moon voice, a voice to entice even the stars clear across the universe to twitch, to itch, to tiptoe close. So close that suddenly the night looks almost identical to the day, overbright.

I say, "All right. I'll tell you. But be warned: *fairy story* is a misnomer. There aren't any fairies in it, you see. But there is a princess, and a curse, and a king, and a prince, and a future queen, and a gray gorgon, and a nymph, and a bright girl with bright magic. There are foxes and sphinxes and manticores. There is darkness and sleeping and magic and light, lots of light. There's an attic and a castle and screams that put together what has been torn apart. There's foolishness and laughter and love. Speaking of love—there's also a boy, a great necromancer. He has many names, some of which are long forgotten, and others that no one will ever dare to forget. Oh—and there's a witch. Still want to hear my tale, a fairy story that is no fairy story at all?"

I smile: at the eager children, at the boy across the way, at the listening stars, at my sisters and my parents and my friends gathering around the glade to hear my tale, a tale about all of them. And about me too.

I say, "Let's start with the Witch in the Woods."

Acknowledgments

If a book is a wish, it takes more than one witch to make it come true! My deepest gratitude to all who had a part in granting it.

In particular, I want to thank my agent, Penelope Burns, for championing me and my work from the beginning and guiding me through the writing and publishing processes. I would be truly lost without you! My editor, Monica Jean, for taking my vision for this book and making it the best it could possibly be. I'm forever grateful for the chance you've given me to put Rhea and her strange dreams out into the world. And everyone at Delacorte Press and Random House, for all the hard work behind the magic that made this book a reality, including but not limited to Barbara Marcus, Beverly Horowitz, Felicia Frazier, Becky Green, Kimberly Langus, Richard Vallejo, Tim Mooney, Carol Monteiro, Ray Shappell, Leo Nickolls, Jaclyn Whalen, Colleen Fellingham, Alison Kolani, Tamar Schwartz, Tracy Heydweiller, Elena Meuse, Dominique Cimina, John Adamo, Elizabeth Ward, Lisa Nadel, Adrienne Waintraub, and Shaughnessy Miller.

Thank you to the many teachers and professors who have inspired and encouraged me over the years. And especially to my Columbia College cohort, for sharing your stories and pushing me to be a better writer. I'm so fortunate to be part of such an awesome, talented group.

To my coworkers and friends at the Barrington Area Library, for your endless enthusiasm for books in general and this book in particular, and for making every day at work so much fun.

To my best friends: Jessica, for book meetings and being the coolest witch I know. Erika, for telling it like it is. Amanda, for always being there for me. Kirsten, for a Magical Place Where It Never Rains. Vanessa, for our many weird and wonderful adventures that could fill an entire book.

To Granny and Papa, for opening so many doors for me. To Gram, for never letting me go hungry (I miss you). To Connie and Jerry, for welcoming me into your family. All my aunts, uncles, cousins, nephews, niece, sisters- and brothers-in-law—you're the best. Also the loudest (Cullottas, you know who you are). I'm truly blessed to have such a kind and supportive family.

To J.D., my favorite brother and the funniest person I know, for always eating ice cream with me. To my sister and best friend, Kara, for laughing at the same things I do, for Disney movie marathons and sing-alongs in the car. I'm so grateful to have you both in my life.

Thank you to Dad, for all those eight-hour drives back and forth to college and letting me listen to "thumpa bumpa" music on the radio, and for being someone I can always count